D.A. CAIRNS

The Devil Wears a Dressing Gown

The Devil Wears a Dressing Gown collection is dedicated to my children, James and Alana, in the hope that one day, through my stories, if by no other means, they will understand me, and that they will maintain a good relationship with God.

Contents

Acknowledgement

I would like to thank all the editors of the numerous magazines and web zines who have liked my stories and published them. Most of the stories were rejected numerous times by other publications before they connected and found homes. All writers know about rejection, and I am no different, but I would like to take this opportunity to say thank you for all those rejections which came with personalized feedback and encouragement. Nothing puffs up the chest of a writer like words of encouragement- except maybe awards and astonishing sales.

I also need to thank those people who have inspired these stories. Some strangers, some brief acquaintances, some friends and some family. With gratitude, I acknowledge the contribution made to my life by every person I've ever met. We are all the product of our experiences and most of our experiences involve other people. I am who I am, to some extent at least, because of you.

One

The Devil drinks Jack Daniel's

*T*he wind whistled around his ears as he instinctively drove his hands into the pockets of his loose-fitting jeans and walked stiffly along the uneven footpath. Darkness had just crushed the daylight, and the rain which had been falling since morning had finally stopped. Stephen Daniels cursed the footpath as he stubbed his foot and stumbled forward. He cursed the wind as it battered him around the head, and he cursed the cold which penetrated his crumpled suit. Most of all he cursed Mrs. Daniels- his wife, for forcing him back out onto the streets in miserable weather just after he had arrived home from another arduous day in the office.

Thinking of the office made him curse that damned job as well. Hour after hour sitting at his desk, staring at the computer screen, receiving, checking and sending mind-numbingly dull reports. A torturous daily commute, crammed inside hot and stuffy train carriages, with nameless other miserable and exhausted drones who bounced along the train tracks dreaming of home, a hearty meal, a comfortable chair and fresh air.

So many people existing, not living just existing, running on a treadmill, wearing themselves out while getting nowhere. How had he become one of them? Working for the glory and the ever-increasing wealth of society's handful of queen bees. Working because they had to and laboring so hard that when the precious commodity of leisure time became available they were too tired to savor it. Working ridiculously long hours to provide for their families while sacrificing quality time with them. What happened to his dreams? How had the big picture innovator fallen into the rut of mediocrity?

Stephen approached the welcoming light which shone out through the foggy windows of the Gymea Hotel with gratitude for this nearby refuge, but still cursing under his breath. Damn the milk he'd been sent out to buy. Damn the world. Its devices and deceits. A system which forced so many people to spend most of their adult lives engaged in occupations which put food on the table and a roof over their heads, while stealthily destroying their souls in the process.

Pushing open the heavy doors, he stepped into warmth and security, sighing with satisfaction and relief as he began to defrost. Stephen had often entered this haven after an argument with his wife Jane, or straight from work after a particularly unpleasant day in the toilet cubicle otherwise known as an office. It was a safe place, comfortably full of familiar and usually happy faces. A round of drinks or two with your mates. Non-threatening conversation about football and motor cars, and merciless criticism of politicians. A place where you could always find a sympathetic listener even if he was standing behind the bar, pouring your drinks. Ten tables with just enough room around each one to fit a few straight backed wooden chairs. A solitary pool table stood unused at the far end of the room to the left of which were the toilets. Sparsely decorated with the odd football and cricket poster on the walls, and polished wooden floor. A man's place. It smelled of beer and stale tobacco, and was filled with baritone voices and raucous laughter.

The bar was only a few steps inside the door, and as he lifted a glass of cold Victoria Bitter to his lips he smiled, finding great pleasure in the fact that although he had not ordered the beer, he definitely wanted it. He raised his glass toward the barman and nodded his appreciation. No questions. No disapproving looks.

Draining half the glass at the first draught, Stephen's thoughts returned to his home and Jane. She would still be fuming, still ranting and carrying on in her melodramatic fashion despite the fact he had left her a good twenty minutes ago. Probably still throwing the odd thing around the place, making a mess which she would clean up as soon as her rage subsided. When she got like that there was no stopping her, no turning off the tap, no way to reason with her or to pacify her. Jane's short temper had been amusing and even slightly appealing during their courtship and early in the marriage, but now it was like a recurring nightmare. Neither funny nor cute. Just occasionally frightening. The milk of romantic tolerance had well and truly curdled.

A tap on the shoulder arrested his thoughts and he turned to see his mate John standing beside him.

'Why didn't ya come and say gidday ya bum?' he asked, waving his hand toward a table by the wall.

'Didn't see you there,' replied Stephen truthfully as he looked over to the table where two other men were sitting.

'Who are those blokes?'

'Kev on the left's from work and I dunno the other one. Just some bloke we were talking to. He seems okay. Swears more than any man I ever heard, but he's friendly enough.'

Stephen looked again at Kev then the other bloke and felt a pang of familiarity. Probably just had one of those faces, he said to himself, dismissing the thought. The conversation seemed oddly intense too.

'Gotta go mate,' said Kev. 'You want another?' he asked, pointing at the empty glass.

Stephen shook his head, wished Kev well then turned to stare into the row of bottles opposite him behind the bar. He decided to go home after this second beer and see if Jane had cooled off. An hour would have passed since he left: usually enough time for her to have completely exhausted her anger.

Apparently, Jane was very unhappy about something although she never referred to any specific grievance. She would take some little issue - tonight for example he had forgotten to buy some milk on the way home - and turn it into a war. A one-sided fight always ensued and ended when Stephen fled the scene.

So frequent was this kind of disturbance that Stephen began to dread going home. He knew, as he suffered like a sardine in a tin can on the peak hour train, he would find a hearty meal and a comfortable chair and fresh air when he arrived home. What he would not find very often anymore was what he wanted most of all; peace and a welcoming smile. It was no longer just hell at work and hell on the train, but hell at home as well. Stephen changed his mind and ordered a third beer.

The barman who knew Stephen usually went home after two schooners, poured a third and asked casually, 'You going for the record tonight mate?'

He opened his mouth to reply but was drowned out by a burst of laughter and back slapping from a nearby table. A good joke most likely. Probably something to do with sex and certainly unfit for family consumption. The kind of joke a man could only enjoy among his friends. Stephen smiled and turned back to the barman, but he had gone to serve another thirsty soul. Watching as he fired a nip of Jack Daniel's into a shot glass, Stephen became aware of the burgeoning effect of alcohol in his bloodstream.

A fuzzy warm feeling permeated his body. He felt he was moving slowly as he raised the glass to his lips and took another mouthful, but his dulled senses were lying to him. Laughing quietly at himself for being a cheap drunk, he swiveled on his chair and searched the room for similar life-forms.

Fixing his gaze as best he could on Kev and the other bloke John had been sitting with, he was amazed they were still engrossed in conversation. He didn't realize that two men who had just met could talk for so long. What could they be discussing? It was such a female thing to do, to sit like that facing each other, and so close. Weird. As he continued watching, he noticed the swearing bloke would touch Kev on the arm or shoulder every now and then. Fascinated, and thus unaware he was staring at them, it was not long before he inadvertently attracted their attention. When Kev looked his way, Stephen turned his head quickly, cursing his lack of discretion. There was something about the other man and the way he held Kev spellbound that sent a shiver down Stephen's spine, but he told himself it was the booze screwing with his head, making him act strangely. He hadn't eaten either, so that was strengthening the power of the alcohol.

'Another VB thanks bartender,' ordered Stephen after downing the last of third.

He felt really hot now, not comfortably warm but hot, so he took his jacket off and lay it on the bar. In an effort to get his mind off Kev and the magician, Stephen forced his thoughts back to Jane.

He loved her more than when they had finally started seeing each other as boyfriend and girlfriend. They had been friends since childhood and he had always loved her. As a boy it was a crush, an exciting feeling of adoration, a kinship which was more like sibling love. While their bodies developed and their emotions matured they experienced it together. They grew up together, though Jane was always a little taller than Stephen and a lot smarter. His love for her remained although she rejected any chance of them being more than just friends on several occasions during their high school years. He dated other girls because that's what boys did, and Jane did not want him. Jane dated other boys and unintentionally caused a jealousy in Stephen which raged for a number of years, driving him towards trouble. Shoplifting, break and enter, car theft, heavy drinking and drug taking. Aged seventeen, Stephen was an accomplished hoodlum and not the kind of boy with whom Jane would ever get involved.

The bartender snapped his fingers in front of Stephen's face to get his attention. An experienced barman, he knew the signs to watch for in his patrons. Signs indicating their drinking was something more sinister than social and therapeutic. He was probably concerned about Stephen who he knew was not a heavy drinker and was disinclined to drink alone.

'Is that bottle half empty or half full?' asked the bartender as he leant on the bar and tried to make eye contact with Stephen.

Reacting slowly, as the intoxicated do, he tilted his head and scratched lightly at his clammy forehead, massaging loose skin over bone, testing its elasticity.

'Half empty my friend,' said Stephen, 'and I reckon I should do something about making it fully empty.' He laughed and added to his joke: 'Fully empty. That's funny.'

The barman smiled the same smile he always gave drunks and said, 'Do you think you might have had enough for tonight?'

'I haven't had any yet. I've been drinking beer since I got here.'

'I meant alcohol in general, boofhead. I reckon you should call it quits.'

Stephen suddenly sat bolt upright and pointed his finger at the barman who had stepped back in surprise. 'I reckon you should mind your own business and give me a shot of JD right now!' he said a little too loudly before adding, 'Please.'

'You're a bit off your face, Steve. You've had enough,' the barman insisted.

Stephen was caught off guard by the use of his name and he was for a moment able to focus on the bartender's face and calm down a little: chagrined if not exactly contrite.

'I'm sorry mate. You're probably right…'

The bartender nodded wisely. 'I am right.'

'You're probably right but you know me. I'm no trouble. You ever seen me in trouble?'

'No. But I never seen you drink so much before either.'

'Look…' Stephen was running out of things to say, his head was starting to spin again, but he really wanted one more drink. He looked around for an ally and noticed that Kev and his mate had gone.

Turning back to the barman he said, 'Gotta a spare smoke?'

'You don't smoke.'

A hand on his shoulder startled Stephen, causing him to spin around so fast he almost fell off his seat. When he had resettled himself, he saw that eerily familiar face with which he had developed a moderate obsession.

'Shit you scared me!' he said.

'The name's Luke,' he said extending his hand and deliberately overlooking the apology Stephen expected.

With some difficulty Stephen found Luke's hand with his own and shook it vigorously. 'Steve. How ya goin'?'

Addled by the beer, all sorts of thoughts skipped about in his mind. Would this guy try and have a long and intense conversation with him? Would he touch him and charm him? What did he want? What breed of psycho might he be? Why hadn't he left with Kev?

Luke released Stephen's hand and said to the bartender. 'I'll take care of this bloke. Give him a JD and I'll have one too.'

The barman looked from Luke to Stephen and back again, apparently thinking for a moment about refusing but deciding against it. 'He's your responsibility now then?'

'Yeah he'll be okay,' replied Luke confidently.

All this back and forth between the barman and Luke made Stephen feel like a schoolboy sitting in the principal's office at high school with his parents after he had been busted smoking on school grounds. He was just an object of discussion, an errant child who needed other, wiser heads to make his decisions for him and to mete out whatever punishment they felt necessary. Annoyed at being treated that way he decided to speak up and said, 'I'll be responsible for my fucking self.'

Again Luke's hand was on his shoulder and once more he jumped. 'Knock it off will ya!' Stephen protested.

Luke moved back a pace and held his hands out in front of him, opened palms in a gesture of retreat, then he winked at the barman who nodded and left them alone with the bottle of Jack Daniel's.

'What happened to Kev?'

'I sent him home,' replied Luke flatly.

8

That amused Stephen. 'What, are you his mum?'

Luke smiled, watching Stephen laugh.

'Donny seems to think you're hitting the turps hard tonight, what's up?'

Taking a sip of his drink, Stephen avoiding answering immediately because he was still irritated by this character, Luke. Doesn't know me from a bar of soap but comes over and says he'll look after me and asks me why I am so drunk. Who does he think he is? Gently he put his glass down. Noticing how heavy it had become, he wondered if it was a heavy glass or if something was wrong with his hand. There was definitely something wrong with his head because when he tried to speak he found his tongue uncooperative.

'Who's Donny?' mumbled Stephen.

'The fucking barman, Dopey. I thought you were a fucking regular here.'

Now he was being a smart arse and Stephen didn't like that either. He found himself being rubbed completely the wrong way by this man and had a very strong urge to ask him to leave in less than polite terms. He restrained himself. 'Well... yes I am but...you're not. How come you know him?'

'I fucking asked him, and I've got a good fucking memory.'

Stephen decided to fight fire with fire. 'You like that word, don't ya? Don't you know any other adjectives?' Feeling pleased with himself, Stephen took another mouthful of bourbon from his glass and looked to Luke for his response. Being by far the more sober of the two, Luke was more articulate than him and Stephen had the feeling that even without the booze, Luke would be too clever for him: his tongue sharper than a sword. Disappointed that Luke did not answer him, Stephen felt that in the simple act of silence Luke was again trying to impose his superiority on him. The ball was now back in Stephen's court.

When he went to have another drink, Stephen found that he was looking into three bourbon glasses, so he put them down. He didn't feel like talking anymore so he began to inspect his hands, all the time aware that Luke was waiting for him to speak.

Rubbing his hands together, Stephen was disgusted by their smoothness; the result of two years pushing a pen. Where had all his beautiful calluses gone? Before the career change forced on him by Jane's constant nagging, he had worked outdoors. Under the sun, sweaty and dirty, his hands were rough and worn from the handling of bricks and the use of shovels and the carting of wheelbarrows. He loved working as a laborer because it kept him on the move as he traveled around the city from job to job, and it kept him fit and it wore out his strength so that at the end of each day he was tired and ready to sleep in peace with the satisfaction of having done a hard day's work.

He looked at his hands. Pen pusher. Paper shuffler. Screen starer. Suddenly he felt like smoking a joint and stealing a car. That would show the manipulative Mrs Daniels what for. He imagined blowing a plume of cannabis smoke into her face and watching her cough. For five years he had wanted her unconditional love and for five years he had been frustrated into despair.

Stephen turned to look at his new friend and marveled at how he seemed content to sit there beside Stephen and not say anything. He was certainly an unusual man and Stephen began to warm to him. Maybe it was the alcohol, maybe it was hopelessness. What harm could it do to talk to Luke? He was a stranger to Jane and Stephen so he could perhaps be of some use. A mediator? A shoulder to cry on? Why not? If he didn't like Luke's advice or his opinions he could tell him where to stick them.

It seemed absurd, but Stephen asked him anyway, 'You didn't answer my question. Don't you know any adjectives besides the f-word?'

Luke grinned. 'The f-word? That's very quaint but I think *fucking* sounds better. It just happens to be my favorite at the moment. I like swearing and I like blaspheming as well. Especially around religious folk.'

'You like swearing,' repeated Stephen slowly, 'and you like blaspheming especially around religious people...folk was the word you used, wasn't it? Religious folk? That's also very quaint.' He shook his head and took another hit of JD.

'Swearing is a relatively new thing,' continued Luke. 'I'm talking about general swearing. Men have always sworn. Even Adam swore.'

'Adam who?'

Luke ignored the question. 'What they called swearing in the old days, you know before *fuck* and *shit* and those kind of words, was actually blaspheming. *Goddammit* for example. It was blaspheming. Taking the name of the Lord in vain and breaking the third commandment. So men who wanted to swear, but did not want to offend anybody, especially not God by breaking one of his fucking commandments, started being a little tricky and using substitutes like *gee* and *golly* and *gosh*. Bloody stupid if you ask me.'

Enthralled now, Stephen wondered if this was the same spiel Luke threw on Kev or if he had more of this kind of interesting and irreverent editorial.

'So you really like swearing, eh?'

'Fuck yeah. I invented it. I love it.'

If Stephen wasn't so drunk he would have challenged Luke's

claim to being the inventor of swearing because it was obviously rubbish, but the sad fact was he didn't even hear it. It was becoming increasingly difficult to distinguish sounds and decode words.

'So how about you Steve? What's your story? What do you love?'

Sluggish of thought, Stephen had to think about that one. What did turn him on? Before he could figure it out and answer, Luke started again.

'What about drinking? Alcohol I mean. I love it and I'm not talking about the occasional social drink or a glass of wine with your meal. I'm talking about getting shit-faced; fall-down, make a complete goose of yourself, wreak havoc, get arrested kind of drinking. That's what I call fun.'

Then as if to prove his point, he poured himself another glass of bourbon and downed it in one go before slamming the glass down on the bar and yelling, 'Bring us more Jack Daniel's!'

A minute ago Luke had been talking and acting controlled and sober, but now he was suddenly acting like a barfly. Stephen was still trying to come to terms with this sudden change when Luke's hand crashed down on his shoulder for a third time.

'I told you not to do that,' said Stephen, shrugging off Luke's big hand.

'Come and sit down at a table with me. It's more comfortable. This barstool is killing my back,' said Luke, returning to his calm alter ego.

Stephen nodded his agreement and gestured for Luke to lead the way. When he stood Stephen noticed he was very tall, had to be close to two meters, and built like a rugby player with broad shoulders and a thick neck. His closely cropped hair was dark brown. He swaggered instead of walking. Collapsing into a chair at the closest table to the bar, Luke motioned for Stephen to join him which he did, albeit reluctantly because of a random idea which just occurred to him: this guy was unstable and probably dangerous.

After waiting for Stephen to take his seat, Luke spoke.

'As I was saying. I love to get really drunk but I am so used to alcohol now that I can't get fucking drunk anymore. Just can't. Fuck it but I can't have enough to affect me at all. You would not believe how much whiskey I've got to fucking drink before it fucks me up.'

Stephen gave Luke a puzzled look as he had visions of Tony Montana spraying as many expletives as bullets while he dealt with his enemies. He was about to ask the obvious question, but Luke answered first.

'That was just pretending. Fuck, I have to pretend to be drunk. What a joke, eh?'

'Yeah,' said Stephen, trying to figure out how he could get away from this bloke. 'What a joke. You fooled me.'

'I'm good at it. I've had lots of fucking practice. Pretending, lying, deceiving. It's good shit.' Luke shook his head violently from side to side as if he was being attacked by a swarm of bees and said, 'That's enough about me. How about you? Talk to me. I'm a good listener.'

To say that Stephen was disinclined to confide in Luke after all he had seen and heard from the man would be to grossly understate his feelings. He had to find a way to leave without offending Luke because he sensed that he was now expected to stay until he was given permission to leave.

'What did you mean before, when you said that you sent Kev home?'

'Nothing. I just suggested he should be getting home to his

fucking wife and children because it was getting late.'

Stephen looked at his watch for the first time and was shocked to see that nearly two hours had passed since he left home. Jane would be okay by now for sure, but how was he going to get away? Unfortunately, he stared at his watch for a fraction too long.

'What's wrong? Have you got to be somewhere? I see you slowing up a little in the drinking department. Can't you handle the fucking pace?'

'My wife and I had an argument,' said Stephen, instantly regretting it. 'So I took off to give her time to cool down. That was a couple of hours ago. She'll be okay now. I probably should get going.'

'Fuck that idea. Giving you a hard time, was she? Nagging you about something? They're good at that. You probably forgot to buy milk on the way home or some fucking stupid thing like that.'

The look on Stephen's face betrayed him and elicited a knowing nod from Luke. How did he know that? Just a lucky guess? He emptied his lungs quickly through pursed lips, finished his drink and rose from his chair.

'Fuck me,' said Luke. 'I was right. Listen hang around for one more drink. Another ten or fifteen minutes won't make any fucking difference will it?'

Stephen wanted to say that it would make a difference and insist he really needed to get home, but something in the way Luke looked at him helped him decide to stay and attempt a graceful exit again after the next drink. Maybe he could give Luke some yarn about his life and make out like he was revealing intimate secrets. Maybe that would satisfy him. Stephen was not a man who enjoyed confrontation and he did want to a make a scene so finally he consented to one more glass of Jack Daniel's, before excusing himself and going to the toilet.

On his return, he was dismayed to find that Luke had not only bought them both another drink but had brought a whole new bottle of JD over to the table. He was amazed that Luke remained so lucid and articulate as he reckoned he was drinking two glasses to every one of Stephen's who, himself was unable to walk straight let alone think straight. His earlier claim about being impervious to the effects of alcohol were evidently true.

Stephen settled himself down on the chair and studied Luke's face. He had a model's features; square jaw, generous almost feminine lips, straight nose and large well-spaced eyes with longish lashes. Annoyingly, Stephen had to concede that Luke was a handsome man.

'Drink up my friend,' said Luke with a boyish grin. 'Drink up and tell me your problems.'

Stephen sipped his drink without noticing the subtle change in taste. He sat forward in his seat. Luke mimicked his action.

He had decided whilst in the toilet that he would not attempt to lie to Luke because he was a hopeless storyteller. Never being any good at bending the truth he had seldom got away with it as a boy and had consequently adopted the adage; honesty is the best policy. The way he figured it, life created enough trouble for a man without him going to look for it by being dishonest. Ironically, he was about to open up to a confessed and unrepentant liar.

'Well,' began Stephen slowly. 'My wife is a very unhappy person and apparently I am the cause of this unhappiness. She's never come out and said it straight like that but after many years of problems and of me wanting her to accept me the way I am and her trying her hardest to change me...I reckon it's me she's

15

mad at.'

'Fuck me…mate, do you know how many times I've heard this same story?'

So now Luke was a wise counselor who had years of experience dealing with marital and relationship problems. His tone of voice was so close to being condescending that Stephen again felt compelled to leave and leave quickly before he lost his temper. Getting into a blue with this strange man might not be a good idea.

'Yeah I know it's a common problem,' answered Stephen evenly. 'What's the answer though? I love her and in her way she loves me, but things are not going well. We just have different expectations and that is always bringing us into conflict.'

Realizing he was out of breath, Stephen picked up the three glasses in front of him and tried to lift them to his mouth. The glasses dropped to the table and spilled their contents onto Stephen's lap and then to the floor. As the cold liquid penetrated his pants and into his privates, Stephen jumped up with a yelp knocking the table towards Luke, and sending his own chair crashing into an adjoining table.

'Fuck!' exclaimed a wide-eyed Luke who had managed to prevent their table being overturned. 'What the fuck are you doing man?' Then he started to laugh.

All eyes were on Stephen as he stood there paralyzed with embarrassment. He heard the laughter building and surrounding him as he watched Donny come over with a rag to clean the spill.

'Sit down ya fucking goose!' ordered Luke.

Stephen began to laugh as well as he resumed his seat. Initially it was embarrassment, but before long he was able to see the funny side and share the amusement of the other patrons.

Donny had mopped the floor, wiped the table and replaced the offending glass before Stephen had moved. As the joking at his expense abated, he realized he was completely relaxed and gratefully accepted another glass of Jack Daniel's from Luke who was still smiling. The alcoholic haze lifted slightly, and his head spun more slowly now as he downed the contents of the glass and slaked a powerful thirst which cried out for more.

'That's better, eh?'

'Better than what?'

'I don't fucking know,' replied Luke and the two men laughed some more, cementing their new friendship.

'Now listen Steve. About this fucking bitch of a wife of yours…'

'Yeah fucking bitch,' agreed Stephen pouring himself yet another drink. What? Did I just call my wife a fucking bitch? He was not aware that Luke had stopped drinking and had moved his chair around the table closer to Stephen.

'I'll tell you what the answer is. I tell all the blokes the same fucking thing. I told Kev this before I sent him home to the miserable cow that he's married to. I'll tell you the answer. I'll give you the solution and you'll fucking do what I say and you'll be a happy fucking man again. Understand?' He touched Stephen lightly on the forearm as he spoke and then on his shoulder while he waited for him to respond.

Stephen forgot all about the suspicions and ill feeling he felt as he watched Luke and Kev talking earlier in the night. He forgot the irritating arrogance and condescension in Luke's voice. He forgot that he considered this man unstable and dangerous. Now he was all ears as Luke's charisma and the bottle of JD enchanted and overwhelmed him. Greedily he lusted for the salvation Luke was about to offer him. A fawning disciple hungering for guidance.

'Piss Jane off. Get rid of her. You think she loves you, but she loves herself. If she can't fucking accept you the way you are then you are better off without her. You dread going home. What kind of bullshit is that? Why make yourself miserable by bowing to all her demands? You hate your fucking job? It's not you mate. You're only doing it for her and it's about time you did some stuff for you. Fuck her. She's dragging you down. You got any kids?'

'No. Jane doesn't want any.'

'See? She's fucking selfish. Anyway, that's not your problem. Kids are a pain in the arse so she's right there, but she's got nothing for you. She loves her fucking self and that's it. Are you with me Steve?'

Stephen nodded and poured himself another glass of whiskey. When he finished, he grabbed the bottle and held it over Luke's empty glass.

'Not now. You lay off it too. That's enough for the time being.'

The bar was filling up again as a second wave of drinkers came in from the cold. With dinner over and their children safely in bed, the boys were coming out to play despite the complaints from their long-suffering wives. Only vaguely aware of this activity, Stephen wondered why he could hardly feel the effect of the alcohol in his system. Bizarrely, each drink seemed to be sobering him up now: getting undrunk. Still a nagging thirst persisted.

'So you told Kev to go home and break up with his wife?'

'Yeah. It was the best thing for him,' said Luke flatly.

'What about what's best for his wife and their children?'

Luke suddenly squeezed Stephen's forearm with his big hand and held on tight as he said. 'Fuck them! I thought you were listening to me. I don't give a shit about them and neither should Kev. He's better off without them. Like you'll be better off when you leave Jane. Pay attention for fuck's sake. I'm trying to fucking help you.'

Although clearly angry, Luke's voice remained calm and when he finished speaking he released Stephen's arm and patted him on the shoulder. This time Stephen did not say anything. Looking down at the table he replied, 'Sorry Luke. You're right.'

'Don't fucking apologize. I never fucking say I'm sorry. Mainly cos' I never am.'

Stephen stared at him, trying to ascertain if he was serious, then they laughed again.

'So should I get on home and give Jane the bad news?'

'Not yet. First, I want to convince you it's the right thing for you to do. Remember, think about yourself now. People can like you or they can go fuck themselves. That's their business. Why should you give a shit what other people think about you or whether or not they like you? Fuck 'em. Think of yourself. We are going out my friend. You can leave the whore to fester in her narcissism for the rest of the night.'

'I need a drink,' said Stephen who was becoming hoarse. As the pub filled with merrymakers the volume increased and they had to talk louder to be heard over the top of the din.

'I said to lay off it for a while.'

'Just water mate. I'm thirsty.' Then he stood up and quickly walked over to the bar. Donny had seen him coming out of the corner of his eye and was there waiting for him.

'No more for you blokes.'

'Just some water thanks Donny. We're leaving soon.'

'About bloody time,' said Donny as he handed him a glass of water. 'You right to get home? You're not driving, are you?'

19

'Not driving and not going home,' stated Stephen before turning and walking back to his table from where Luke had maintained an unblinking vigilance.

'All right, so how you gonna convince me?' asked Stephen.

'I know a few good places in town that are open all fucking night. We're gonna get ourselves some fucking women and more fucking booze and we're gonna party hard 'til the fucking sun comes up and then you are going to go home, wake your wife up and tell her to get fucked.'

Stephen would never have even listened to all this rubbish let alone spent hours in a hotel drinking and then agree to go out and party with a bloke he barely knew. He would never have believed the lies Luke told him and never have behaved so selfishly and irresponsibly. In his right mind, he would have laughed at it, but he was out of his mind: so far off his perch, thanks to the booze and Luke's overpowering confidence, he couldn't remember what the damn thing looked or felt like.

Luke grinned at Stephen who dumbly grinned back.

'Let's go!'

They stood in unison and Stephen waved to catch Donny's attention, then pointed to the door. Donny held up his hand to wave. Before quickly dropping it on the top of his head, drawing it roughly through his hair.

As Stephen and Luke headed for the door pushing their way through the crowd they failed to notice a newcomer entering the stuffy and foul-smelling atmosphere of the pub. He was an average looking man, average height and average build. There was nothing remarkable about his appearance so nobody paid him any attention. Slipping easily through the jostling noisy drinkers he headed directly for Luke and Stephen.

Suddenly Luke stopped as he collided with a patron, causing

him to spill his drink. Stephen looked up too late to avoid walking into Luke's back who stumbled forward again. Stephen had a clear view of the new arrival, but ignored him. He helped Luke regain his balance. Stiffening at the sight of the man who was only a meter from them, Luke grabbed the guy he had bumped into by the shirt and punched him in the face. There was confusion as tempers flared. Stephen tried to pull Luke away, but was grabbed from behind and spun around. Despite all the yelling and the abusive threats flying back and forth, calm descended and Stephen was released. The violence was like a sudden gust of wind. The noise quieted and he could hear the word *sorry* being repeated by different voices. When he turned back to where Luke had been grappling with the man he punched, he had vanished. Luke was gone.

Bewildered, Stephen began to ask where he had gone. He asked one man, then another, then another, but received the same reply. 'Don't know. Don't care.' Finally, he asked the ordinary looking guy who had moved quietly to Stephen's side.

'Did you see where my mate went? The big guy who...' he trailed off, rendered mute by something undefinable in the man's eyes. It was he who spoke next.

'The man was not your mate, Stephen.'

Stephen wanted to argue the point but could not. It was as though he was peering out through a fogged up windscreen waiting for the cold air-conditioned air to clear it so he could see where he was going. Unexpectedly the fog clears and the road is visible. Stephen saw and thought with clarity now and he remembered. In stunned silence, he allowed the man to lead him out of the pub. Men stepped aside but said nothing as they walked towards the door.

'It's time for you to go home,' said the benevolent stranger.

'Jane is worried about you. She loves you and has begun to understand the reason for your marriage problems.'

Outside the pub, a taxi was waiting. The man opened the back door for Stephen and said, 'Go home and forget that man who called himself Luke.'

Stephen stopped. 'How did you...? He did not know the question, but the man had an answer.

'I had a quiet word to Jane. Go home and talk to her and things will improve for you. Trust me.'

He gently pushed Stephen towards the waiting taxi, but Stephen resisted out of curiosity. 'Who are you?'

'I am your friend,' he replied with heavy emphasis on the word am, as Stephen finally broke free of his overwhelming gaze, and climbed into the cab. Pulling the door closed, Stephen turned to wave good-bye, but his mysterious saviour had disappeared.

Two

Alice in Badland

(first published in the anthology, Paper Boats -Dreamhouse Publications, July 2015)

'*H*eated confrontations caused by rash words based upon judgementalism, which is itself precariously balanced on a pedestal of intolerance and ignorance, may make for compelling television drama, but does the theatre of fiction truly reflect the dynamic of life?'

Shannon scratched his head.

'Do you know what I mean?' pressed Alice as she stared into the side of her friend's head.

'You lost me at precariously.'

Alice had known Shannon since they were at a school. He was a true eccentric. Always slightly out of place and out of step, but remarkably perceptive on occasions. He had struggled at school. Battled to connect with the realities of formal education and the requirements of convivial society. He didn't like the rules, and consequently wouldn't play the game. Certainly lacking book smarts, he nonetheless had a rare authenticity, and despite

23

his capacity for seeing through people and their deceptive and manipulative ways, he was never condescending. Never rode the proverbial moral high horse. Alice had never had a better friend. He was rare and special. Gifted in fact. Many people didn't understand him but that didn't bother him either. Unperturbed as ever, the epitome of laconic, Shannon stared at the road ahead and drove at exactly five kilometers per hour under the speed limit.

'The stuff you see on TV,' said Alice. 'Friends who say horrible, thoughtless things to each other during angry arguments, and then they make up and quickly move on. That's entertainment.'

'Uh-huh.'

'We've been friends for a long time.'

'Twenty odd years now,' he agreed.

'I don't recall you ever doing anything to make me angry. I can't remember you ever yelling at me or swearing or abusing me.'

'Why would I have done that?'

'Exactly.'

Shannon turned his head briefly to look at her. 'Are you all right, Alice?'

'In fact, I have a lot of friends with whom I've been friends for many, many years and the only time I can remember anything bad was when I used to drink. You remember that time, I was going out with Adam's mate, Andy, and Andy tried to push me to go all the way with him one night after we got smashed together?'

'You slapped him several times and kicked him in the nuts, but he was still trying it on, like he was possessed by some demon of lust or something...'

Shannon often talked about demons and angels and ghosts and

other supernatural phenomena. By his tone, he might as well have been talking about breakfast cereals. He said he had seen stuff and he knew stuff. It was almost impossible not to believe though she reckoned herself a skeptic and had no firsthand experience of such paranormal shenanigans. A demon of lust? More like a horny teenager with no self-control. Alice refocused and joined the retelling of this well-known story.

'Adam heard the fuss and came in on us. He totally exploded with a rage I had never seen before, and the violence which followed made me sick. I was frantic, hysterical, screaming at him, but I couldn't stop him. I think he only stopped beating on Andy because he was exhausted.'

Although Andy recovered fully from the merciless beating he received from Adam, the two of them never spoke again. Alice smiled macabrely to herself. There was an example, in her life, of TV like drama. She could hear Shannon talking in the background, but she tuned him out, eager to find another such incident in the annals of her existence. She wracked her brain to no avail. Her life was dull. If she wrote her story, it wouldn't amount to more than a lengthy Facebook status update. Everything was so nice and calm, like a relaxing picnic on a perfect day by the sea.

'You should be glad,' said Shannon, breaking through the fog of Alice's private musings, 'That you have had a peaceful and happy life.'

'I'm not happy Shannon. And there's no peace without happiness.'

'Actually...'

Alice cut him off. 'Save it Shannon. I'm not happy. I'm bored. I need some excitement, some drama. Wouldn't it be awesome to have a life like the lead characters on ER? No monotony there. There's sex and violence, rage, life and death decision making, fatal errors. Not just existence. Not just passing time, like me. I don't know who I am, or what I'm doing. I'm a piece of driftwood floating down a river. Human detritus.'

'Steady on,' said Shannon. 'What are you talking like that for? You've got friends and family, and a boyfriend now. You've got a good job and you're good at it. Your health is good. Have a look at yourself. Forty two years old but you look more like late twenties. You're beautiful and intelligent.'

'Shut up!'

'I was just trying to give you some perspective.'

'I don't want perspective. I want some heart pounding thrills and gut wrenching tension, and I want you to shut up, okay?'

Remorse whipped her like a cat 'o' nine tails and she flinched. She had gone too far. She wasn't mad at Shannon and he didn't deserve to be spoken to like that. An apology was crystallizing on her tongue when another thought poured cold water on it. Will he forgive me if I don't apologize? If I start acting like a bitch all the time, alternating nasty sarcasm with icy indifference, how long will he put up with it? Where the hell did that come from? Now I'm going to turn nasty and feral? Why? To see what happens? Her pulse quickened. The very idea of such an experiment excited her. Her keenness suffocated her conscience which was protesting as strongly as it could given the circumstances. Alice remained stubbornly silent for the rest of the journey even though she could feel Shannon's confusion and hurt. Well Shannon could take his trite perspective lessons and shove them. Sure, she had a boyfriend now, but she was past forty and deadened by the disappointment of not having found the man of her dreams and carried his children in her womb. By now she should have been a soccer mom, a member of the

P.T.A., a housewife with philanthropic pursuits to occupy her spare time. Her children should have been her favourite topic of conversation, and she should have mastered the line about how she loved them to death, even though they drove her batty. She should have had an affair, and hypocritically hated her husband for having one as well, but then forgiven him because she was too afraid to live alone again. And what about the children? She should have had to make that impossible decision between her own happiness and the emotional welfare of her children. Our marriage is a smoldering train wreck but let's stay together for the sake of the children.

Was this guy she was with now, Chris, going to marry her, or was he just passing the time with her until hot little Miss Right came along with her gym toned body, dazzling smile and factory enhanced breasts? He was overseas on business. Probably found someone else already. Alice looked down at her breasts and felt the urge to grab them and validate their genuineness. She should have had a cancer scare. Breast cancer was so common, why had she missed out? Why had nothing happened to her?

'Alice?'

'What?'

'We're here.'

Without a single word of thanks or even a simple good-bye, Alice climbed out of Shannon's car and, after slamming the door behind her, walked briskly across her front lawn and up to the front door. She didn't look back, though she felt sure he was sitting there staring after her.

The house was quiet. A silent and damning testimony to her aloneness. Her parent's only child, she had inherited the house, which they owned, when they died. Now there was a love story. Mum and dad. Married for forty-nine years, three hundred and sixty four days when Al, her father, had died of a sudden and massive stroke. Her mother, Pat, had wilted a little more with every hour that passed following her lover's death, so it was no surprise when she passed into the afterlife just two months later. If she wrote her parent's story it would make a tremendous book. A definite bestseller. The phone rang, interrupting her thoughts.

'Are you all right, Alice? What happened back there?'

The plaintive compassionate tone in Shannon's voice almost made Alice cry. Her experiment wasn't going to work. Shannon was too much of treasure to her, and she was way too soft.

'I'm sorry Shannon. I really am. I don't know what possessed me to act like that.'

'Do you want me to come around and perform an exorcism?'

Alice laughed, soothed by her friend's ready forgiveness. 'No, I did it myself already. I'm fine. I'm so sorry.'

'Okay, see you later.'

Everyone she knew was so nice, and there was nothing wrong with nice, was there? Nice is good. Nobody goes searching for terrible people to hang out with. Miserable, cynical, nasty, bitter people didn't make good friends. Did that mean that all the world's bastards and cows were friendless, and living in putrid isolation? How did that work?

Alice fell onto her soft lounge and gratefully accepted its embrace. These musings were pushing her close to insanity. The very concept of utilizing her valuable time to contemplate these dark questions was disgusting. Twisted. Was she twisted? She wriggled on the smooth cool leather, contorting herself like a worm exposed to sunlight. Is that what lunatics do? Maybe she should get up and start banging her head against the wall in order to pulverize her demented ponderings. When she stopped thrashing, Alice noticed the quiet and she shivered. Dense and ominous. She forced herself to rise from the lounge and go for a drink: a very strong drink.

The gurgle of Coke landing on a liquid bed of overproof rum was suddenly drowned out by the sound of the telephone. Alice finished pouring her drink, then turned to stare at the phone which was flashing as it lay on the kitchen counter.

'Hello?'

'Miss Bradshaw?'

'Yep.'

She filled her mouth with the rum and Coke while waiting for the invisible interlocutor to speak.

'Patrick from CSB media surveys. Would you have time to participate in a short survey on home media use?'

'Would you have time to come over and have a drink with me?'

Alice took another draught, and closed her eyes. Waiting again.

'Ah, I'm working,' said Patrick, clearly thrown off his spiel. 'Miss Bradshaw, would you be willing to...'

'Is that a no Patrick? That sounds like a no to me.'

Alice emptied her glass and sighed. 'Last chance buddy.'

After a pause long enough to allow Alice to refill her glass with a stronger combination of hard and soft drinks, Patrick spoke. His tone altered. Softer. Conspiratorial. 'I don't finish until 9. Would ten, ten thirty be too late?'

'Nope,' she answered quickly before drinking again from her glass.

'Can I confirm your address, Miss Bradshaw?'

'See you tonight, Patrick.'

Laying the receiver slowly down on the counter she stared at it as though expecting it to ring again. Did Patrick know where she lived? He had her phone number, but did that automatically mean he had her address?

Shannon sounded surprised to hear from Alice again so soon, and also by her indistinct speech as she breathed each word down the line to him.

'Are you drunk?'

'Just a quick question. Telemarketers.'

'Mmm?'

'If they call you, does that mean they know where you live?'

'Yeah, I think so. Maybe. Why?'

'Nothing. Sorry, I have to go. I'm meeting a friend. Bye.'

She hung up as Shannon pressed her for more information. Alice knew she had to leave the house. Her head was spinning but her thoughts were strangely lucid as she hurriedly went to the toilet and changed her clothes. Patrick would have to be disappointed. What? He's not going to show up. That's crazy. I'm crazy.

Half an hour later, she parked her Mazda 2 in a dark lane off George Street and walked a block to the entrance of the worst named club in Sydney. Flash. Apparently, it was meant to be some sort of oblique reference to the paparazzi, and the pretentious claim of the club's owners that Sydney's A-listers, and the cream of visiting foreign celebrities danced and drank there. Tonight she would be drinking there, and her plans for the rest of the night were at best, loose, and at worst non-existent. The neon lights adorning Flash, welcomed her, together with the leering eyes of a couple of young male clubbers who were hanging around the front under the watchful gaze of a bouncer. The club's guardian smiled at Alice, but she ignored him as she marched in.

Alice made her way to the bar and ordered a glass of water

and a schooner of Tooheys New to chase it down. The barmaid had a nose ring and it glinted as the reflection of the club's lights danced on it. She grunted something about a price, causing Alice to tell her to speak English, or if that was English, then to open her mouth wider when she spoke.

'Ten dollars, smartarse.'

Alice pulled a twenty dollar note from her purse and said, 'That's very expensive, but I guess as long as you didn't add any mucus to my beer, I'll have to pay.'

'Are you going to sit somewhere else?'

With her pulse racing, Alice stared into the dark almond eyes of the other woman. 'I could move around to that side of the bar and pour the drinks to prevent customers getting snot in them.'

The barmaid's eyes widened then narrowed, before she walked away to serve another customer.

Alice followed the woman with her eyes, hoping that her glare would burn a hole in the lycra singlet she was wearing. No such luck. The ring in her snout obviously did not make her a sow, nor did it affect her self-control. Admirable indeed. Alice sensed a body behind her, feeling the heat emanating from it along with the pungent odour of masculinity, and some other unknown scent. She turned to face him.

'G'day, my name's Mark. Can I buy you a drink?

'I might not be able to taste it though, Mark.'

'Why's that?'

'Your aftershave is more powerful than a speeding locomotive.'

'Yes, but sadly it can't leap tall buildings in a single bound.'

Alice returned his smile in spite of herself. She swallowed a mouthful of beer then sipped her water.

'I'm glad you like my aftershave. It's new.'

'What's it called? Superman Returns?'

Mark laughed very naturally, seemingly unperturbed by Alice's acerbic quips. 'Just Superman actually.'

This guy was nice, dammit. Another nice guy. She looked down at her blouse to see if it was emblazoned with the words, 'nice guys apply here.' I'm going to have to try harder to blow him off. I do have a boyfriend after all, Alice reminded herself.

'Well Superman,' said Alice casually, 'I think it's time for you to find a phone booth, rip that cheap shirt off, miraculously lose your pants and zoom off to save the world. We're all good here.' She raised her glass to Mark and winked at him. She was satisfied that she couldn't have been any stronger in her rebuttal of his advances. Except of course if she gave it to him straight, and simply told him where to go. Alice watched him pondering his next move. Surprisingly it was not away from her. What's he thinking? Seeking a clever retort or a polite surrender? Damn, he's good looking. If he keeps standing there I might just have to lead him off to a dark corner and ravish him.

'Ravishing charm Miss...?'

'Mrs Bradshaw.'

Would that reference to her marital status send his eyes to her ring finger, or had he already glanced and seen it bare?

'Mrs Bradshaw,' said Mark with something like distant fire flickering in his eyes, 'Would you like to accompany me to a dark corner of the room, for a drink and more in-depth conversation?'

Alice had misjudged this confident and sexual man. He was bad. He had tried nice, but his smooth-talking charm had rolled off Alice like water, so he had switched his attack to wicked and forceful. There was no denying the salacious intent of his invitation. Alice suddenly felt very hot. She sculled the rest of her beer, but that afforded no relief for the parched tightness of her throat. Before she could find the necessary witticism to repel Mark, he was all over her. So close she could taste Superman on her lips and it nauseated her.

'And don't even think about telling me to leave you alone. I know this is what you want, so let's stop wasting time, Mrs Bradshaw.'

Pushing hard against Mark's chest, Alice stood and swayed for a moment as blood rushed to her head. Mark stepped back to maintain his balance, thus giving Alice the opportunity to leave which she took without a second thought. Was he following her out? Should she tell the bouncer to stop him and let her get away? She had blown him off when she entered but his job was to protect patrons. Fighting to control her breathing and feeling as though she had a volcano erupting in her stomach, she walked right into the back of the bouncer.

'Watch it love,' he said without animosity.

'There's guy who might follow me out. He's tall and wearing a pale blue shirt and he stinks of Superman. I don't want him to follow me, okay?'

The bouncer looked confused but nodded. Alice gave him her best smile which was hideous given her state of mind: scared to death and sick to the stomach. She pushed past him and would have broken into a run had she been able to control her legs. There was an urgent voice inside her head saying run, hurry up, but her legs were in rebellion. She couldn't feel her feet. Were they frozen? Was she running in the snow barefoot? Was this a massive overreaction? She had toyed with Mark. Maybe she did want him. She thought of Chris, her boyfriend: lifeless, joyless Chris. Sensible, safe Chris. Alice stopped dead in her tracks. Breathless, she stood and stared at the ground.

'Are you all right?' a faceless voice asked.

There was a gentle hand on her shoulder. She shrugged it off as though it were repugnant, like a cockroach. I do want Mark. He might hurt me. He won't hurt me. He might hurt me. Alice took a deep breath and walked back to Flash. Very slowly. The bouncer smiled a crooked smile and welcomed her as though for the first time. Her question about Mark following her out evaporated in the heat of the bouncer's forgetfulness. What would she say to him? Apologize? Yeah, apologize and tell him she would be his Lois Lane. Alice saw Mark straight away, standing where she had left him at the bar. He was chatting with another woman, flirting, no doubt offering her the same lines as Alice had gagged and nearly choked on. Never mind, the other woman was no match for her. She would simply grab Mark and drag him away.

* * *

Alice couldn't move when she opened her eyes. Through a blurry haze she saw a vaguely familiar face and heard a comforting voice, but pain intruded, piercing her flesh, and she cried in pain. She started to hyperventilate. Then Superman assaulted her nostrils and she screamed.

'Calm down. I'll call a nurse. You're all right, Alice.'

Frightening thoughts rampaged through her mind. She was hurt. How did she get hurt? Had Mark beaten her? Raped her? Alice squeezed her eyes tightly shut. She couldn't remember. She recalled meeting Mark and the exact words they had exchanged during their intense verbal foreplay. She had left, she knew that. Fled in fact way from him and the club, propelled by fear then inexplicably drawn back to him. To danger. Why? Why had she returned. What happened next?

'Alice?'

Alice opened her eyes and realized her blurred vision was the result of only being able to see out of one eye. Focusing was difficult. Her breathing was amplified in her ears.

'Alice? You're in hospital. You had a fall and your friend brought you in.'

'Friend?' Alice shifted her one-eyed gaze from the unknown face, to the man standing quietly to her left. 'Shannon? What happened?'

After receiving assurances from the nurse that Alice was going to be all right, Shannon pulled over a chair and sat down beside her. She listened without taking her eye off him as he recounted the events that led to her being here. She had called him from her car; crying, hysterical. She'd told him where she was and that she was badly hurt and that she had done something really stupid. As her friend gently reminded her of his arrival at the lane where she had parked in the city, and how he had helped her to his car, and driven her to the hospital, the memories drifted back. Hazy and unclear at first, like her sight, but gradually crystallizing into vivid images. She wanted Shannon to stop speaking.

'Do you want to talk about what happened?'

'I went back to him, Shannon. Why did I do that? I suspected. No. I knew he was trouble, but I went back to him. Why?'

'Who'd you go back to?'

'His name was Mark.'

'Mark who?'

'I don't know. I just met him at Flash.' Alice turned away from Shannon. Her face burned.

'So you met some random at Flash and then what?'

The silence slapped her face as she argued with herself, asked

35

hard questions then warned herself to back off, to say nothing more. It grew heavier as she delayed, uncertain what she should say or how to say it. Shannon deserved the truth and maybe it would assist her somehow if she verbalized her thoughts. Was there a suggestion of anger in his voice just then?

'Tell me what happened Alice.'

Alice related all the details of the initial encounter, her resistance, her flight, her foolish and mysterious return. The walk to the car which she had suggested was a better option because it was closer. Mark's firm hold on her arm as though he feared she would run again. His lascivious whisperings in her ear, his free hand on her breast; squeezing. Rough. The arrival at her car. His impatience as dark as the alley where they stood beside her car. His mouth upon hers, his hands pulling at her clothing. Oh God, she had wanted it, wanted him. She liked the dread, the foreboding ignition of some primal passion. He was causing her pain, gripping tightly, pinching her and pulling her hair. Out of control, she submitted to his animal lust freely. It was bad. He was bad. She was bad. Then she heard a loud crack. Something snapped and she noticed the limpness of her arm. The pain was terrifying like an electric shock which violently tore her from the swamp of lust. When she fell she hit her head on the side of the car and everything started to spin wildly.

'Stop Alice', said Shannon. 'Stop it. That's enough. It's over now and you're going to be all right.'

Alice finally looked at her dear friend and saw his tears.

'We'll find the bastard who did this, and sort him out in time, but for now you just need to concentrate on your recovery.'

Swallowing hard before she spoke to clear the knot of emotion which Shannon's tears had triggered in her, Alice said, 'We won't find him. We won't look.'

'I already informed the police. They'll be in to talk to you before the day's out.'

'I'll forget everything, Shannon.'

'What? Why?'

'Trauma induced amnesia. It was my fault anyway.'

'You don't believe that.'

Alice attempted a smile. 'If I want to deceive myself then I will. It's not that hard to accept lies about yourself especially when they come from within.'

Apparently lacking the will to continue to persuade her, Shannon was lost for words and merely reached out his hand to lightly squeeze her good arm. 'You should get some sleep,' he said. 'I'll come back later.'

Watching him go, stung. He was obviously bewildered. She had infected him with fatalistic despair, but she could not summon any regret. She was alive and her body, though broken, would heal. Alice felt strong and a sense of freedom and peace blanketed her as she drifted off to sleep. Why did she feel this way? It didn't make sense, but she liked it.

* * *

With her arm still adorned in a cast, Alice approached Flash calmly, and with settled intent. Two long weeks had passed, and her eye socket had healed to the point where her vision was normal and all that remained was a halo of sickly yellow around her eye. She had expertly buried that under make-up and donned her slinkiest dress. The cast was hardly fashionable, but she reasoned it would elicit sympathy and function brilliantly as an ice breaker. Her three-inch heels clicked on the concrete as her leather handbag flapped happily against her hip. Alice didn't expect to find Mark at Flash. Even though he had no doubt not intended to hurt her, he might be worried about the possible ramifications of his consensual and frantic dalliance with Alice. Things had just gotten a little out of hand. No, Mark, her Superman was gone, but she was very hopeful of locating and latching onto another hero to make her feel alive.

She breezed past the bouncer, ignoring his smiling welcome, and into Flash. The pig snouted barmaid saw Alice approaching, and after rolling her eyes, hastened away to the other end of the bar. Alice grinned, and licked the sugary sweetness of heightened anticipation from her lips.

Three

Black Sparrow

(first published in Aphelion, December 2015)

*T*urning his Triumph off the highway and onto the emergency lane, he rolled to a stop, killed the engine and kicked down the stand before dismounting. Darkness caved in around him as his headlights went out, but almost immediately the moon took up the mantle and bathed the scene in soft luminescence. In the still of the night he surveyed his surroundings.

'Lovely night for it,' he said as though someone were listening. 'Perfect.'

He had left the road where it straightened out after a sharp bend and before it proceeded across a narrow bridge. The gurgle of a creek below was joined by an owls haunting call. Looking down over the bridge he noted the drop was probably only five metres, but the water was shallow and permeated with jagged rocks. On the side where he had parked, a stout gum tree stood like a sentinel halfway between the edge of the emergency lane and the creek. Lifting the visor of his helmet, he looked once more from the bend to the tree, to the creek and back again, before nodding and returning to the Triumph.

Sitting sideways on the seat, he stared back up the road. A cloud swallowed the moon and rain began to fall. Large drops beaded, then caressed the well-worn leather of his jacket as they ran down and off him to crash on the steaming bitumen. A car approached at speed and zoomed past, followed by another. The biker glanced at his watch.

'I'm ready when you are, my friends.'

The rain increased its intensity and the temperature dropped ten degrees, but he sat as still as a rock, watching, waiting.

A new set of headlights poked through the driving rain as a car rounded the bend. He recognized their shape and size, but geometry and a knowledge of cars were only needed as confirmation. The hair on the back of his neck bristled and he tensed as he stood and walked out onto the road into the path of the oncoming Falcon.

'Show time!' he yelled as the lights temporarily blinded him before suddenly being wrenched in an alternate direction. He dived clear as the car spun and slid off the highway. Rolling to his feet, he turned to see the Falcon bounce and bump its way through the low shrubs at the side of the road, eventually holding a steady sideways trajectory towards the tree. The beating rain barely drowned out the snapping and cracking of breaking branches and glass smashing. He heard screaming and smiled. The Falcon clipped the gumtree and flipped, rolling down the incline. Once, twice, three times over then splashed silently into the shallow creek caught by the calloused hands of the rocks.

'Beautiful,' said the biker. he quickly looked around before strolling over to the side of the road and making his way down the slope. 'Nice work.'

As he neared, he could see the slumped, motionless figures in the front seat. The driver's head forward, the passenger's back, the Falcon a pathetic twisted wreck. The rain eased a little allowing a duet with the bubbling creek to be heard. He went to the driver's side first and crouched to peer in through the smashed window. The man's face was covered in blood from countless lacerations, but the biker noticed little bubbles forming, and foaming at the corner of his mouth. He reached out a black gloved hand and felt for a pulse in the man's neck. Very faint.

He leaned in close and whispered in the driver's ear. 'It's time to go.'

The driver gasped, gagged then breathed his last.

Turning his attention to the passenger, a thin brunette with long wildly tossed hair, he reached for her, but stopped when she suddenly opened her eyes. Wide, shocked, whites blindingly bright in the darkness. They closed again as her head, momentarily strong on her neck, slumped back against the headrest. Had she seen him? Could she see at all? It did not matter. The last movement had taken her head out of the biker's reach, so he withdrew his hand and walked around the back of the Falcon to the passenger side.

As he squatted by the door, he paused and turned his head quickly, looking back up towards the highway. Without further movement or noise, he stared into the murky shroud of the gumtree, squinting as though that action might magnify and brighten the object of his attention. Was it his imagination?

He stood and studied the ever-sharpening contours of the gumtree's branches and leaves. There was someone watching him, and he knew for certain who it was.

41

* * *

In the gumtree, Daniel wiped the hot tears from his eyes and extended his right hand out into the rain. He cupped it to gather some water, then splashed it on his face. He felt gut-wrenching misery, helplessness, and anguish as he watched. All the awesome power of the entire Heavenly Host rendered impotent by the Lord's edict. *Leave them to their work.* There was never any question of his obedience, but Daniel still burned with impatient zeal, still wanted not to be hamstrung, still yearned for the unbridled freedom to save the lost wherever he found them, whatever the cost.

He knew he had been seen but it did not matter. Both of them had a job to do and neither would interfere with the other's business. This too angered Daniel, as did the knowledge that the other would enjoy Daniel's rage, would feed off it ravenously and joyfully. It was evil beyond measure. Why did the Lord have to tolerate it? Daniel sat still, and waited, never taking his eyes off the biker as he went about his devilish duty.

* * *

Satisfied with the knowledge he would not be interrupted, the biker refocused on the skinny woman in the front seat, staring for a second at her bulging stomach.

'Disgusting creature,' he said as he spat in her face.

In a flash of clarity, she revived for an instant and turned to look directly at him. He saw the confusion and horror on her face and relished it. The moment passed, and she lapsed once more into blissful unconsciousness. She would probably survive if he called an ambulance immediately, but that was not part of the plan. Her time was over. There was no way of knowing how long it would take for her to die, but he reasoned he had sufficient time to watch. He wanted to. He stared at her, studying her, touching her and poking her. Laughing at her as her breathing grew shallower and blood boiled from her open mouth, he was entranced.

Sirens wailed in the distance. Getting louder. Closer. The biker took a last look at the woman as she died finally. He cursed himself for being careless and unprofessional then glanced up at the road and saw red and blue lights dancing in the trees. At ground level, hard white light stabbed into the flesh of the night. The biker placed his hand over the dead woman's perfectly rounded stomach and nodded before standing to greet the emergency service workers as they picked their way down the incline.

Someone else must have witnessed the crash, but where were they? The angel in the tree would not have interfered. The nearest town was a good hour away. How long had he been here? He checked his watch. Seventy one minutes. Who had called the police? He had a few questions, but the police would no doubt have many more.

The approaching officer directed the paramedics to the car as if they needed help finding it, then asked the biker if he had called the accident in.

'Yes.'

'You witnessed the accident?'

The repeated use of the word accident amused him. Ignoring him for a second, the officer called to the paramedics.

'Both dead,' came the reply. 'But we got an unborn child here. We gotta act fast.'

'What's your name?' said the officer to the biker.

'Joseph Smith.'

'You got I.D.?'

'Yes,' he said as he reached into his back pocket for his wallet. He tried hard to cover the smirk. The choice of Joseph Smith as his alias was inspired and he was very proud of himself. What a wonderful servant of darkness that man was, he thought. Before he could remove his license and show it the officer, the latter was called away by the paramedics.

'Hang around all right. We're not done yet,' he said as he left. Joseph nodded. 'I'll wait up by my bike.'

The officer did not seem to hear him. As he walked back up the slope, he noticed another man coming down, striding purposefully towards the wreckage, seemingly untroubled by the uneven and slippery ground. Joseph would have admired his confidence and balance if he had not recognized him first. He was dressed simply in jeans and a brown overcoat. A red baseball cap covered his head while a large black umbrella protected him from the rain: the angel in the tree.

As they passed each other, they stopped and stared. Two tall strangers. No words were shared. They weren't necessary. Joseph noted the look in the other's eyes and as always found it disturbing. Like all of his kind, his eyes were large and brilliantly green in colour. Joseph knew both what he was doing there and that he knew the reason for Joseph's presence, and consequently expected to see something different in his expression. Anger? Hatred? Contempt? But the windows to his soul were pure like his mind, holy and focused. They showed Joseph the worst, the most vile and destructive of all the emotions the Creator had ever implanted in his beloved beings: love. Joseph turned away.

* * *

Daniel was praying because he needed to quell, or at least

44

conceal, the torrent of rage inside and because he felt compelled to by the encounter with Ishmael, or whatever he called himself these days. It was not easy for a saint to ignore evil. They had met once before, and would no doubt meet again. He had heard that Ishmael was now a Black Sparrow and that fact would certainly lead to their paths crossing many more times henceforth. Daniel watched him walk away and studied the patch on the back of his jacket. It was sick. He felt sick.

Although he prayed, it was not for Ishmael, but for himself and especially for the unborn child. He was the last of his family and would be called Michael by his adoptive parents. His road would be hard and long, and he would face seemingly insurmountable challenges. His enemies would be numerous and callous, his friends difficult to find and impossible to protect, but he would succeed. He must succeed. Before his destiny could unfurl, Michael must first fight to enter the world of men. His was to be a violent birth followed by a violent life, but one which justice demanded.

At the side of the car, Daniel asked the paramedics permission to stay and pray for the child.

'What? Are you some kind of minister?' asked one of them over his shoulder.

'Something like that,' conceded Daniel as he watched them work.

The passenger door needed to be cut, as did the A frame, so they could attempt to remove the woman. The roar of the grinder and the shriek of metal being torn by it was an unholy symphony which made Daniel wince. Four men now gathered by the car where a stretcher had been prepared and together they carefully lifted and dragged her out. An argument erupted.

'She's already dead,' said one. 'The child's life is all that matters now.'

'We don't have the equipment,' protested another.

'Just cut her abdomen and remove the baby.'

'We don't even know how old it is. Whether it will survive.'

'It will die anyway. Stop wasting time. Let's do it!'

Finally, action. Daniel watched, impressed as ever by the bravery and compassion of humans, as a careful twenty centimetre incision was made, the skin and fat retracted, the baby removed, the umbilical cord severed and tied off, and the newborn, its fate still uncertain, wrapped in a blanket and hurriedly carried up the incline to the ambulance. Daniel took one last look at the two victims. Timothy Gray, twenty years old. An only child whose parents had died in a car crash three weeks ago. A bright young man who had fallen in love with a beautiful sweet girl. Vanessa. They had married two months earlier despite the protests of Timothy's parents. She was just eighteen years old, a high school drop-out, abandoned first by her good-for-nothing father when she was five, and later by her alcoholic mother when she was sixteen. A broken soul who had found some love and healing in Timothy's arms. The child she carried was not an accident and would have been loved and cared for, the way all children should be, if only given the chance.

The tears surged in his eyes once more as Daniel turned away and trudged up the slope back to the road. The merciless rain continued its drenching assault. With every step his anger grew, seething and snarling. He saw Ishmael's face in his mind and imagined it disintegrating to dust as he crushed it. A voice came from somewhere, a voice he recognized speaking words of comfort and peace, pouring ice cold water on his fiery rage. Daniel unclenched his fists, his jaw relaxing as he walked on.

* * *

'So,' said the officer to Joseph continuing with his questions. 'You said your name was Joseph Smith?' He paused for the nod of assent then proceeded to ask Joseph about the exact circumstances surrounding his presence at the crash site. The latter dutifully answered his questions including the risky assertion that he had telephoned for help.

'Could I see your cell phone please?'

Smart cop, thought Joseph, as he pretended to search his body for it, patting and feeling his pockets.

'I can't find it. It must have fallen out when I was down by the car.'

The officer seemed quite willing to accept that. 'Were both occupants of the car alive when you reached them?'

Joseph said that he could tell they were still breathing, but as he did not have any first aid training, and because they looked so bad, he did not know what else to do for them other than call for help.

'Did you realize the woman was pregnant?'

'No,' lied Joseph.

He raised his eyebrows before shaking his head and saying, 'Damn shame. If the kid makes it, he'll never know his parents. Another poor orphan comes into the world. Born in tragedy.'

Joseph was appalled by the officer's sentimentality. He knew some expression of sympathy was required and would have been appropriate, but he simply said, 'Can I go now?'

The officer stared at him again, but Joseph remained impassive, so he changed the subject and asked some questions about the Triumph which Joseph answered impatiently. He put his hand on Josephs' shoulder and pushed it forward gently, glancing at the patch on the back of his jacket while asking, 'Who do you run with?'

Joseph allowed the officer to view it. It was made up of two concentric circles. The inside circle colored red, the smaller outside one was black. On the red one was a black sparrow pecking at a cross lying on the ground. One claw was placed on the cross, the other held aloft a small dagger. Above the picture, inside the black colored circle was written the word Black, while below it, also in white cotton, was the word Sparrows.

'Never heard of them,' said the officer.

Joseph smiled, hoping it appeared sincere, and asked again if he was free to leave. The officer waved him away with a troubled look on his face, so Joseph turned and walked to his Triumph.

* * *

Daniel had been watching calmly from the shadows, but with Ishmael's back turned he saw an opportunity. He leaped forward and broke into a sprint which carried him across the thirty meters that separated him from Ishmael in the blink of an eye. Ishmael spun around, suddenly aware of Daniel's presence but too late to prevent the first blow to his head. He tumbled off the bike and was immediately beset by the wrathful saint again. More punches to the head, striking harder and harder, as hard as he could until his energy was spent and he stopped, exhausted.

Ishmael lay still beneath him as Daniel removed a small gold knife from his pocket and clicked the blade open. It gleamed in his hand as he lifted it high and drove it down deep into the heart of his adversary. As Daniel tried to calm his breathing, shame began to seep into his spirit and he wilted physically, suddenly overwhelmed by grief. A tide of nausea washed over him. He heard a voice and turned to see the police running towards him.

Ishmael was already fading out of existence and Daniel realized he would have to leave immediately. Summoning what last reserves of strength he could find, he sprung off Ishmael's body and raced into sanctuary of the forest.

* * *

The baby, Michael, survived and Daniel was present at the hospital when the doctor took him off the critical list. He prayed for Michael and also asked forgiveness for his own disobedience and healing for his wounded heart. Would do it again though? At the very thought of the Black Sparrows, Daniel gnashed his teeth and clenched his fist.

Four

Jack and Jill

'*H*urry up honey,' said Jill as she climbed the gentle slope of the grassy hill. 'I brought you along for your muscles you know but if you don't get a wriggle on, we're going to run out of time.'

Jack knew it was his fault. If they were late, if they were early. It was always his fault. Even when he couldn't for the life of him figure out what he had done. Why resist the irresistible? If Jill wanted to blame him, to pour out her frustration with herself, all over him like tomato sauce over a meat pie then he just had to wear it. That's what you did when you loved someone, wasn't it? And Jack loved Jill more than his own life, more than anything, more than anyone. He was thinking about a response but was discouraged by the idea of the effort. The physical exertion was almost more than he could handle as it was.

'Did you bring the second bucket like I asked you to?' said Jill.

He stopped. Disabled not by her question, or the tone of voice with which she delivered it, but by the terrible realization that he had actually not remembered the second bucket.

'Jack?' Jill called out, as this time she stopped her impressive march, and turned to look at him.

It was at that moment, Jack decided to keep walking. After all, with Jill temporarily frozen half way up the hill, he could use the chance to try to catch up to her. Had he given it deeper consideration, he might have realized that a tongue lashing from Jill at close range was probably on the cards, and as her acerbic barbs had been known to strip paint off walls, he would be in danger. He automatically slowed his pace.

What the hell was he doing carting a ten litre tin bucket up a lonely knoll to collect water from a disused well? Being a good husband, that's what he was doing. Jill was doing a project as part of her studies in Creative Arts. She was training to be a primary school teacher and was focused to the point of twisted obsession. Anyone or anything which impeded or even threatened to block her progress was liable to be streamrolled by her bloody-minded determination. Force of nature was a term which barely scratched the surface of her violent stubbornness.

She had decided to do a photographic representation of the nursery rhyme *Jack and Jill*. Although she was given a choice of nursery rhymes, selecting Jack and Jill was a fait accompli given their names. Her concept was based around an adult contemporary version, and despite Jack's protests that she should be designing material for children, she had enlisted him as both her sidekick and co-star. Jack had other queries in relation to the practicalities like who would take the shots of both of them, and why Jill wanted to risk shooting in fading light, but she had dismissed his queries as nuisances, and insisted he simply do what he was told.

Jack's 'yes mam' had oozed unwilling servitude, but Jill had carelessly overlooked that as well. It was, as he said, his job to carry out her wishes, if he wanted to maintain the peace, and he certainly did.

Each step sounded like a dull bell chime in his mind, echoing the mocking words of his mates at the local. Doormat. They were all such big heroes treating their wives like dogs one day and sex toys the next. Abusing their generosity, exploiting their insecurities, making themselves kings over their cowering serfs. One of the bastards even hit his wife when she, according to him, deserved it, and then boasted of it. Recalling all this, made him wonder why he hung out with them. Why he bothered with a bunch of selfish Neanderthals. Why they reminded him of Jill. How they somehow resembled masculine versions of his own wife.

Finally, Jack reached her, and he met her barely suppressed rage with an insipid smile. 'Sorry baby.'

'Wait here while I set the camera up on a tripod at the top of the hill.'

'Sure.'

Jack watched her leave, and drag a few more pieces of his heart out of his chest and along the ground in her wake. He needed the rest. Working in an office for three years had left his cardio fitness wallowing around the level of an obese pensioner. A few deep breaths shuddered through his respiratory system. He thought about the mistreated wives of those former friends of his at the pub, and felt empathy. Their pain was his pain, and he knew why they stayed and allowed themselves to be abused. He wondered if they had ever thought about leaving their spouses, escaping their tyranny. Jack had never had such a notion until now.

'Don't move, Jack,' called Jill from the top of the hill, beside the well, and behind the camera which was now stationed on a tripod.

Jack raised his hand to acknowledge her and hoped he hadn't overstepped with such a gesture. She had told him to stay still.

When apparently satisfied with the position of the camera, Jill made her way down to him and explained what they were going to do. Jack nodded as he listened, Jill repeated herself more times than were necessary even for a three year old to understand. Jill looked at her watch and counted down from ten before saying 'action', and leading Jack up the hill.

'Smile honey,' said Jill. 'It's lovely day. Great to be alive and roaming the picturesque countryside with the love of your life.'

Bemused, Jack played along, keeping cool on the outside even as his stomach churned. He could only hope there were no outward signs of his inner rage. Jill seemed oblivious anyway. Deliriously playing the role of nursery rhyme Jill and expecting him to play Jack with equivalent amounts of exuberance.

At the top of the hill, Jill skipped ahead to fiddle with the camera. She said nothing to Jack and appeared to have lost interest in him, or even to have forgotten he was there.

'Okay honey,' she said, rounding on him with an ambivalent smile. 'Let's set you up for the well shot.'

'Jack and Jill went up a hill,' said Jack through gritted teeth, 'to fetch a pail of water.'

'That's the spirit,' replied Jill.

Suddenly Jack remembered the next bit of the rhyme and he gulped. A wicked thought pounced on this perceived threat to his personal safety, and Jack morbidly welcomed it. Savoured it. Courage suffused his bones: roared through his blood as he summoned the intestinal fortitude which had been lacking for so long. Ironically, Jill had provided Jack with an opportunity which he could not pass up.

'Jack! Pay attention honey!' said Jill. 'Over here. Come on.'

With those words, Jack's newly discovered bravery deserted him, and he jumped to attention at the sound of his master's voice. What had he been thinking? Madness. Stress induced insanity. He would never hurt Jill. Could never hurt her. He loved her.

'For this set of shots,' said Jill, 'I need you to move towards the well, then lean over and attach the hook at the end of that rope to the handle of the bucket. Okay?'

'Too easy baby.'

Jack walked over to the edge of the well as instructed, lifted the bucket over the edge, leaned across and reached out for the hook. It was quite a stretch and he felt a tingle of fear as he extended himself beyond what he considered comfortable. Sadly, he did not have very much time to consider the matter. The unmistakable stab of an open palm caused him to lose balance and fall into the well. He screamed all the way to the bottom where he was abruptly silenced by the dry rock floor.

Jill peered over the edge of the well into the darkness, and said, 'Jack and Jill went up the hill to fetch a pail of water, Jack fell down and broke his crown and Jill called the police to report a tragic accident.'

Five

The Devil You Know

R obert Keating awoke to face the new day, blinking furiously as if trying to force the sun back down again, and with it all the troubles and pressures awaiting him. Had he known what was to take place that day he might have stayed in bed. But Keating was an habitual early riser, who slept as little as possible.

He looked around at the hard, sterile lines of his modern apartment and thought that although it looked like a hospital, it was fashionable and functional.

'Activate Remote Home Systems,' ordered Keating as he sat up in bed and ruffled his thick brown hair. 'Shades open half. Television on.'

The TV came on immediately, but the shades stayed closed. Keating groaned at the inefficiencies of RHS, forgetting that a service call had been arranged for that morning.

He yawned as the early news came on.

'*March 15, 2034. It's six a.m. I'm Abigail Stanton. Good morning. Association of Southeast Asian Nations President, Li Kwon Yo, announced last night at the conclusion to the seventh ASEAN forum that the powerful Asian economic bloc would leave the Asia Pacific Economic Cooperation group officially on June 22, 2034.*

Australian President Robert Keating who has been involved in intense negotiations over the past several months mediating between Yo and United States President Cain McMurtry, is expected to issue a statement this morning.'

'Dammit!' cursed Keating, springing out of bed and storming to the kitchenette.

'Coffee black. Videophone on. Calling Damien Chen in KL.'

After a brief pause Damien's face appeared on the screen. He did not seem surprised.

'Yes Robert?' said Damien flatly.

'I just saw the news. What the hell is going on, Damien? Did you know that Yo was going to make that announcement?'

Damien did not answer immediately which was unlike him.

'Damien?'

'Are you running jammers?'

'Of course. AIC approved Series 6. What's wrong?' asked Robert.

Damien hesitated again and when he finally spoke it was in a hushed tone. 'Robert I'm in trouble. I head an anti Yo group called Group 9. We're all in serious trouble. Yo has surrounded himself with yes men; Asian ultra-nationalists. They agree to whatever he says and encourage him in his stupidity. Anyway, we were barred from last night's meeting. I had my suspicions, but I didn't know for sure.'

Robert stared hard at his friend's face. They had first met on assignment for their respective governments at a trade and industry conference in Bangkok in 2014. He had never seen the slightest hint of fear or doubt on Damien's face until now.

'Damien how can I help?' asked Robert urgently.

'It's too late, my friend. I don't know what will happen. I'm sorry. It's been a pleasure working with you but, I'm going to lose my job at best and at worst-'

'Your connection has been terminated at KL,' said the videophone. 'Attempts to reconnect have been unsuccessful.'

Robert raced off to the shower, frantically searching his mind for logical explanations for the sudden end to their conversation. He called his secretary Denise and told her to cancel all the day's appointments and try to contact Damien Chen or anyone at the office of ASEAN's Chief Secretary. Denise dutifully objected, restated his literary and insisted that he fulfill his obligations. Robert thanked her for the reminder but told her she should do as she was told.

'By the way, I need my driver downstairs in five minutes.'

'Yes sir,' she said before disconnecting.

Robert dried off hurriedly and dressed himself. What had happened to Damien? The obvious answer was too painful to contemplate. The announcement by Yo had really come as a surprise. What could he do?

Fiddling with his tie in the mirror, the Australian President purposefully calmed himself then looked with some satisfaction at his reflection. Older than he looked, he was pleased to be often described as youthful, handsome and confident. Confident? He was expected to give a statement about Yo's shock declaration, but what could he say? He didn't know anything yet. Nonetheless, the public were well acquainted with politicians feeding them platefuls of empty rhetoric, so he would think of something.

'Door open,' he said to the RHS and walked out into the hallway. 'Door close. Deactivate Remote Home Systems. Activate security.'

He stepped into the lift and was on the ground floor in ten seconds. The driver, waiting for him as requested, opened the door for Robert.

'To the office sir?'

'Yes,' replied Robert as he climbed into the spacious interior of his 2010 Cadillac limousine. 'Videophone on. Calling Cain McMurtry in Washington.'

McMurtry's face appeared. He looked every day of his ninety years, but his eyes were focused and serious; his mind as sharp as ever. An intelligent and determined man.

'Hey Rob you've got some trouble down there,' said McMurtry with typical directness.

'Trouble every bloody where Cain.'

'Did you know?'

'No I didn't,' answered Robert abruptly.

The US president looked suspicious and with good reason thought Robert. He had placed an enormous amount of faith in Robert to convince Yo that ASEAN should remain in APEC. Both men knew how important the huge Asian markets were to the continued buoyancy of their respective economies. Both also suspected that more than just plain economics was at stake.

'What are you going to do?'

'I'm seeking an urgent face to face meeting with Yo.'

'Will he go for that?' asked McMurtry doubtfully, knowing Yo's distaste for personal meetings.

'He bloody well better. I'll get back to you later Cain.'

Robert felt a bump and the Cadillac shook slightly as the driver deactivated autodrive and left the freeway. He heard the RMA announcement interrupt the radio news warning that any vehicle exceeding the non-freeway speed limit of 50 kilometres per hour would be turned off and the driver fined. Aware he was running out of time, Robert wished he had never approved the amendments to non-freeway traffic laws. In 2034 you could not speed, and road accidents had been eradicated.

Leaving the Cadillac and striding up the stairs, Robert wished he could also eradicate Li Kwon Yo. The man was a pain in the arse with no respect for the protocols of 21st century diplomacy. He was aggressive and a proud racist. Yo was a relic who had risen to the presidency of the world's largest and most powerful trading bloc.

Inside his sparsely furnished office, Denise was waiting for him. She looked fantastic as always. Tall and curvaceous, she was wrapped in a red body stocking with her long auburn hair flowing over bare shoulders. Denise not only looked like she had just stepped out of Playboy, but she performed her duties consistently and faultlessly around the clock. She was perfect and so she should be. Robert had paid over a quarter of a million dollars for her and that was without the optional sexual functions programming.

Denise smiled warmly and asked Robert if he wanted a coffee.

'Yes. Did you get through to Damien?'

'There was no answer at that number. I called the Vice President's office and was told that the Chief Secretary's department was no longer functional. When I asked what that meant, the line was disconnected.'

'I have to go to KL. ASAP.'

'Sir,' said Denise reverting to reminder mode, 'You have a meeting with a Council of Religious Experiences representative at eight thirty and an appointment with the Prime Minister at eleven.'

'He's a pain in the arse too,' barked Robert, speaking his thoughts out loud.

'Sir?' asked Denise with a look something like puzzlement on her face.

'Cancel the bloody meetings. Tell CORE that I have bigger fish to fry and ask the Prime Minister to stop bothering me.'

'Sir, may I remind you of the proper constitutional relationship between the President and the Prime-?'

'No Denise, replied Robert. 'You may not. Cancel reminder mode and get me- actually get us both on a plane to KL.'

'Yes sir,' said Denise cheerfully.

Denise's diplomatic skills would ensure that neither of the two men he was supposed to meet with that morning would be overly upset. She was continually proving her value.

'Call a press conference for eight o'clock.'

Denise left the office as Keating plonked down into his thought chair, an antique red leather recliner.

'Music on. Volume low.'

What could he say to Yo to make him change his mind? It seemed impossible now. Through the months of negotiations, he remained open minded and non-committal. Listening carefully to the US point of view as relayed by Robert and the opinions of other senior diplomats. He appeared to be a rational man who was coming to a rational conclusion about the value of ASEAN maintaining its APEC membership, then suddenly Yo says no, we're leaving. Why?

'Videophone on. Calling Cameron Ford, Intelligence Corp.'

If anyone had more information about Yo than Robert it was the IC. Perhaps Ford could give him some insight, some way to get through to Yo. Maybe some information to use against him.

'Yes Mr. President?' said Ford.

'You've heard the news Cam. What're we going to do?'

Ford stared straight ahead, and said in a cool detached voice,

'If the President is asking for my professional opinion on how best to deal with ASEAN's defection from APEC…then Li Kwon Yo should be removed from the equation, sir.'

Robert had no need to ask what that meant. He felt instantly uncomfortable. A political assassination. A common weapon of terrorists in the twentieth century, but unheard of nowadays. How could such a thing be done? And by who?

Ford interrupted Keating's thoughts. 'Mr. President? Did you hear me?'

'I want you in my office at eight fifteen.'

'Yes sir.'

Robert wanted to go down in history as a President who really made a difference, but sanctioned murder was a highway to infamy: a step too far into darkness. But Yo, in having made the announcement, had apparently made up his mind so maybe there was no other way. What else could be said?

Were there any benefits to ASEAN's exit from APEC? Military and political analysts had been flooding cyberspace with dire warnings about the expansionist nature of Li Kwon Yo's government. Experts claimed that secession from APEC was only the first stage in ASEAN's master plan to invade Australia. Alarmist? Self-justifying? Maybe so, but even with a substantial and well-armed fleet including ten aircraft carriers, and a sophisticated satellite coastal surveillance system, a full-scale invasion from the north would be impossible for Australia's Defense Forces to repel.

The Australian public believed the threat was real. So did all the national leaders of APEC including Cain McMurtry and Keating himself. It was impossible and naïve to not even consider it, and the implications for his legacy. He would go down in history, infamous as the man who presided over the invasion and occupation of Australia. He exhaled, emptying his lungs, gripping the padding arms of his recliner.

Keating blustered through the press conference saying that he believed Yo's announcement was somewhat premature and that he was on his way to KL to talk with the ASEAN President with whom he had a good relationship. He stated emphatic confidence in achieving a satisfactory resolution.

Fifteen minutes later he returned to his office to find Cameron Ford waiting for him. Ford repeatedly insisted Keating had to go and meet with Yo, then asked for, and was given permission to make some programming alterations to Denise who he assumed would be accompanying the President on the trip.

Denise had got them on an eleven thirty flight to KL. Although unable to contact Damien or find out what may have happened to him, she had talked to Yo's cy-sec and arranged a meeting. Keating was silent the whole trip. His stomach churned at the thought of what he had given his consent to. What if he was implicated? What if it failed? It would fail, he told himself. Yo was untouchable. He would be surrounded by bodyguards and would more than likely not even leave his office unless absolutely necessary. This mission was a grave error: a potentially fatal political one.

Yo was a hedonist. Although married, he openly kept several mistresses and often visited KL's gentlemen's clubs to use the services of their first-rate cy-pros. Occasionally, he would even have sex with human prostitutes. He was a heavy drinker, preferring cheap local whiskey, and a chain smoker. Famed for his arrogance, he was a man who denied himself nothing, and granted little to others unless there was a benefit for himself.

As Keating considered all the information about Yo's dark side furnished to him by IC, he began to feel better. It occurred to him that he might be doing ASEAN a favour by disposing of such a detestable and immoral man, perhaps bestowing a great gift on the world.

Walking through customs, surrounded by his team of cyber-minders, Keating focused on his job. The initial meeting would have to be superficial and cordial. Next, as Ford had suggested, Keating would have to invite Yo to dinner at Yo's favourite restaurant, Three Coins. After dinner, where again no business would have been discussed, Keating would express his interest in some cy-pro company and according to the plan, Yo would happily take him to The Golden Lounge. At that point Ford had ceased his briefing. What was it he had said as he left? You just enjoy yourself Mr. President.

A swarm of media representatives buzzed around Keating and his men as they moved briskly through the airport and out into a waiting limousine. From there they went directly to Yo's office. Yo had ignored protocol again by failing to send his deputy to officially receive Keating at the airport. He tried to ignore the breach as he smiled warmly and extended his large hand towards Yo who stood as he approached.

Despite telling himself otherwise, Keating could not relax and was so nervous he felt sick.

Ford had warned him to play it cool. To show no signs there was anything wrong. To make Yo feel as if maybe he had come to congratulate the ASEAN president on his boldness rather than berate him for his arrogance and stupidity.

Keating tried hard to play the game, but the more he thought about it, the sicker he became. Wasn't it wrong? His conscience was ripping his heart out and vexing his mind. Several times during dinner at the Three Coins, Yo asked if Robert was all right.

'You look a little pale my friend?' said Yo with paternal concern in his voice.

Pull yourself together Robert, he told himself. You are going to blow the whole thing. He's already suspicious.

'I'm fine. Just a bit tired that's all. It's been a busy day. I wouldn't mind a nice relaxing massage actually,' replied Keating, still managing to play the game and lead Yo further into the web in which he would, if all went to plan, become trapped and die. Yo's eyes twinkled. He was hooked, but he did not know it. Flushed with the success and the power of self-aggrandizement, he was blind.

At the Golden Lounge Keating, perused the menu and found a cy-pro to his liking. She was identical to Denise and he had no intention of having sex with her either.

He was still married and would be faithful to his estranged wife until he died. That's what he had said in his vows. They called him old fashioned and quaint, but secretly admired a man of such unswerving principles. The same man who was now participating in a murder.

Keating laughed at the irony as they went to separate rooms, and nodded as Yo wished him all the best in his quest for relaxation while laughing like a schoolboy.

As his Denise look-a-like cy-pro began to undress, Keating excused himself and went into the ensuite to have a shower. His mouth was dry, his heart racing. He wanted it done. Over. He suspected that Denise would be substituted for Yo's cy-pro and kill him during sex. His head was pounding with tension. During his very long shower he heard an explosion.

Media reports called it an assassination. The incendiary bomb used, presumably, by the cy-pro had turned both bodies into charcoal in a few minutes. There was no evidence. A long list of suspects, but not a shred of evidence. It was a perfectly executed murder. There were several reports focusing on the coincidental presence of Australian President, Robert Keating, and the fact he was unharmed, but nobody believed the Australian President would do such a thing. It was inconceivable.

Keating slouched in his thought chair unsure of how he felt. He would definitely win re-election for his second and final term, and he had certainly stopped a likely invasion- at least temporarily, but did the end justify the means? He sighed as he realized he had no answer. If he tried hard enough, he would convince himself he did not care. He had done his job and served his country well.

Six

The Voice

(The Devil made me do it.)

(first published in Raven's Light, June 2013)

I
t had been a long day. The rain was relentless, the wind aggressive and the cold, bitterly hostile. It had been a hard day. Leibman's mood mirrored the black weather with its dark skies, as he had mechanically gone about his business.

Now he sits alone in his living room, as he does at the end of every day, staring at the television screen and he hears the voice. He remembers the first time he heard it and how it frightened and confused him, and how it still has the same effect. Nearly a year has passed since that first encounter and in the ensuing months he has been subjected to a battery of probing antipathetic psychologists as they delved for endless hours into the murky depths of his mind, only to reach the conclusion that there was no voice.

'No, Mr. Leibman,' the doctor said in a confident and detached tone, 'I do not believe that you are suffering from multiple personality disorder.'

He paid on the way out, handing over his credit card to a pretty young lady with a vacant smile and glazed eyes.

'Yes, Mr. Leibman,' said another doctor, as he scribbled on a prescription pad, "You are in a state of melancholy, but I cannot in good conscience assert that you are suffering from depression. May I suggest that a lack of sleep is the possible cause. Try these. One each night before you go to bed.'

Leibman accepted the prescription wordlessly and paid the receptionist on the way out.

'No, Mr. Leibman,' began a third doctor, a very thin woman with large spectacles and pale skin, 'You are not becoming demented. Perhaps, if I may propose...your id, your own ego is communicating with you on the subconscious level. Nothing to worry about. It's quite normal.'

His id had told him to snatch that fancy ballpoint pen from her grasp and jam it into her forehead, and he wondered if he should share that with her and ask if that was quite normal. But after standing and staring at her for a moment, during which he imagined that very act of violence as she squirmed in uneasy silence, he left and handed over his credit card to a middle-aged blonde with large breasts and blue nail polish.

Leibman recalls all those words, those professional tones and those forced expressions of compassion which looked more like twisted pleasure than genuine expressions of empathy. The voice had told him those doctors were morons, and he had agreed.

The howling wind distracts him momentarily and he propels his thoughts away from the past to hone in on the present. Now: this microscopic drop in the ocean of timelessness where he exists but cannot really live. He has forgotten how. All the joy has been sucked from his body and he feels shriveled and ugly. Unwanted. Useless. He breathes in deeply and exhales very slowly. Leibman feels time decelerating. This technique is supposed to relax him, he read about it somewhere, but he wonders why because with the passing of time slowed, his agony is prolonged. Yet there is an otherworldly serenity about it which attracts him like a moth to a flame.

He breathes again, concentrating, focusing, and the wind fades as the room darkens. He draws another breath, filling his lungs then expelling the air almost imperceptibly through his open mouth. After repeating this action several times, Leibman begins to feel light headed so he smiles and reclines on the lounge. The voice begins to speak.

Sometime later, he wakes up but he's in his bed. He must assume he has been sleeping, having fallen into slumber on the lounge and then woken at some point and removed himself to bed. Other explanations are too disturbing to contemplate. Looking at the clock, he is surprised to see that two hours have passed because he feels as though he has slept for much longer. He's hungry which is a good sign he tells himself, and he feels encouraged for a second until he remembers that is the way it always happens. The pattern of his existence is fixed in a prison of heartless monotony from which there is no escape. Leibman has neither defense nor recourse, so he simply goes to the kitchen and eats.

Chewing slowly on an egg sandwich, he concentrates in order to overcome the gagging sensation he feels whenever he eats. He tries to draw on a memory of a good taste, something delicious but it's as though he has never had such pleasure. The sandwich, like everything else he eats, tastes like soggy cardboard and he only eats half of it. Somehow despite the discomfort and inconvenience of eating he has been able to sustain his body. He is thin but muscular due to the nature of his work and the fact that physical exercise often provides a refuge from boredom and anxiety. Leibman has also managed to master the nausea which during his waking hours is a constant yet unwelcomed companion. Reflecting on all this, Leibman fails to comprehend how he survives. Or more importantly, why?

It isn't just the drudgery, the isolation, the lack of sleep, or the dissatisfaction with food, it is an indefinable feeling of brokenness, a pain in his soul which tortures him. A heavy sensation that he is dying and although he wants to die, he knows he won't. Then he realizes that it must be the voice which keeps him going. This psychological tormentor who exacerbates Leibman's physical affliction with every whispered curse has handed down a life sentence without the possibility of parole. There is no light at the end of this tunnel. Leibman feels his heart being torn in two and blood erupts from the wound with volcanic force.

Now he feels angry, but he struggles to resist the rampant rage because he knows where it leads and even though he is seldom strong enough to fight, he has at least, a relic of righteous desire which always provides sufficient strength to begin the battle, if not conclude it. Mulling over the situation, he knows this sequence of events is also just a cog in an evil machine.

Later, having belted the punching bag until he was breathless, and his knuckles red and raw, Leibman feels a little better. Suddenly he remembers that it is Saturday, and in a torrid panic he races inside the house to learn the time. It's still early. He has been seeing a girl on the weekends and she is proving to be an oasis so he does not want to miss their date. Although he knows she would forgive him and accept whatever feeble excuse he proffered like she has done on two previous occasions, he really doesn't want to disappoint her again. She is a solution to his troubles, a salve to his wound, and water to slake his thirst.

Ironically, he met her in the waiting room at one of the numerous psychologists he had visited, and even more ironically she was one of those receptionists who typically took his card and processed his payment perfunctorily and professionally. She, however, had been charming and courteous. Leibman doesn't really know why she'd treated him differently, and in fact is not at all sure that she did favour him with any special regard and yet when their eyes met something happened. Undeniable. Irresistible. A truly miraculous burst of confidence produced a bumbling invitation which was received with a heart melting smile and the words, 'Yes, I would love to have coffee with you.'

As they chatted about the weather, she commented, 'You don't seem like there is anything wrong with you.'

Leibman sipped his coffee and decided to avoid the issue. 'Did I tell you I think your boss is a bit cold for a doctor? She has the personality of a refrigerator.'

Alice smiled. 'She's a good doctor. Very professional.'

Leibman made a sound of unconvinced agreement and studied her face briefly so as to not make her suspicious. 'How long have you worked there?'

Alice dutifully and cheerfully answered his questions and the conversation progressed down all the safe major highways of acceptable social interaction until finally, when Leibman felt very comfortable, he steered the talk into a back alley which only residents frequented, and he confided in her. Everything except the voice because it was after all, still only early in their relationship.

Apparently, Alice had not been frightened off and they had

continued to see each other.

Leibman worries continually that something will go wrong. He feels as though he is walking along a precipice and that at any moment the edge will crumble beneath his feet and he will tumble to a merciful death on the jagged rocks below. Although the voice has remained sullenly silent thus far during his interludes with Alice, there is always a chance it may interfere. He foolishly imagines it to be a jealous lover. The voice does not love however, it manipulates and confuses, it hunts weakness in its prey and devours it with wicked relish. Leibman is more afraid of the voice than he has been of anything in his life. Even his childhood fears of heinous monsters under his bed, and later his wild fear of bees after a random stinger nearly brought about his death via anaphylactic shock, pale in the face of the threat that the voice poses to his sanity.

As barbs of anxiety begin striking him, Leibman feels hot and agitated. He wonders if he has time for a nap but worries that if he oversleeps, he will miss Alice. The truth is, he misses her already. His heart longs for her whenever she is absent. Would it work to have Alice with him more often? Could he somehow wear her like a holy talisman to ward off Satan? Was it greedy of him to want so much more of her? Would she give him any more of herself? His head aches with the desperation of these unanswerable questions so Leibman makes himself a cup of tea, hoping the ritual will calm his mind. With the tea made, he sits on the lounge and stares at the blank television screen. He shudders. Once he thought he saw something there, a shadow, a formless, nameless apparition of terror.

At five past five, Leibman starts from sleep and for a foggy disoriented minute or two he doesn't know where he is. Slowly he focuses and familiar shapes assemble before his blurry eyes.

A lamp, a clock, a hard back copy of Bryce Courtney's Sylvia, his favourite jacket on the floor, dusty blinds cover the window, bedclothes crumpled like unwanted refuse. His mouth is dry and his neck is stiff, so he rubs it and rotates his head slowly and it brings a portion of relief. Then he notices the time. He rises, showers and dresses and leaves the house at six, bound for Anzac Parade, Kensington where Alice lives with a friend on the seventh floor of an apartment building in the heart of the retail and commercial strip. To Alice, his friend, his lover, and his saviour.

He feels as if he is floating as he walks from the car park to the foyer and presses the button on the intercom. Hope floods his soul as he thinks of the sweetness of Alice, her voice, her breath and her soft touch which always makes him shiver at first and causes her to giggle. The voice is a distant darkness, far away in another world, like the war between ethnic tribes in Sudan which is real and terrible but no threat to him.

He has decided to ask Alice to move in with him, and now as he waits for her to respond on the intercom, he reckons that if she likes that idea he might even ask her to marry him. An image of marital bliss plays in his mind and it comforts him. He smiles, feeling secure and peaceful, almost normal.

Just then, Leibman hears a familiar voice behind him.

'Hey,' she says casually.

He turns to see, Alice's flatmate, Wushan, standing and smiling at him. He isn't sure whether she likes him or trusts him but he doesn't care.

'Alice isn't answering.'

'You guy have date?' she asks in her occasionally cute but mostly irritating accent.

Leibman nods and forces a smile to hide his annoyance.

Him not replying to the question doesn't faze Wushan, she simply states that Alice is probably in the shower, and he should come up with her. 'No poplem.'

His mood is souring, like milk left too long in the refrigerator as Wushan babbles away during the elevator ride to the seventh floor. Leibman hopes he has made the correct noises and gestures at the appropriate moments in the conversation so that she believes he is participating. Of course, he isn't, he's rehearsing his lines. Wushan's presence is an unaccounted for factor, but it won't hinder him. He realizes he loves Alice; she is light in his darkness and like breath in his lungs he must have her. He needs her. Buoyed, he quickens his pace to the door of her apartment which makes Wushan laugh. He doesn't hear her laugh or the words she says afterward as she fiddles with the key in the lock of the door. Leibman's heart is racing. He can't wait to see her, to hold her.

Rudely, he pushes past Wushan who has stopped in the hall for some reason and is standing still. Is she shaking?

In the living room, Alice is lying face down on the floor covered in blood. Wushan is swaying, terrible emotions rocking her insides with hurricane force. Leibman notices her open mouth and her trembling lip. At first, he thinks it is not his beloved Alice lying on the floor but who else would it be? He crouches to touch her as he feels a creepy numbness spreading through his body like an opiate injected into his vein. Willing himself to breathe, he brushes blood matted hair from her left cheek which bears a gaping wound. He sucks in a deep shuddering breath as he reveals her eye, wide open with indescribable terror. Now he hears the air leaving his lungs and exiting his frozen body through his mouth. There is no other sound. Then, from deep within the horrible silence, comes the voice.

'You shall have no other gods before me.'

Leibman understands instantly, and leaves Alice's apartment. He says nothing to Wushan, who has begun to wail hysterically, because there is nothing left to say. His final, futile hope lays dead on the floor.

Seven

Intersentential Phenomena

(first published in WiFiles in 2012)

*I*t was two in the morning. My ashtray was full, overflowing in fact and I was staring at it, watching the half finished and scrunched up butts transform into hideous looking little monsters whispering to me about my putrid lungs and the violence being done to my arteries.

It was very quiet, so quiet that the silence was a distraction. My desk was covered with coffee stains and dirt and ash, begging to be cleaned for the first time in months. This book was going to be the death of me. I only slept when I could no longer keep my eyes open, and only ate when faint with hunger. Raising a half empty glass to my lips I savoured the bite of cheap whiskey, before returning to the manuscript.

Out of the shadows squeezed a thick fluorescent paste which explored and infiltrated every crack in the wall and every hole in the ground, as it made its way towards the pile of fetid carcasses in the centre of the yard. Alarms were sounding and workers were running from the plant, stumbling and staggering, gagging on the fumes spewing from the leaking reactor.

Duke Porter arrived at the gates of the lower yard as darkness descended on the Blackwater Industrial Complex. Flashing his badge, he walked up the driveway and bellowed at anyone who blocked his path or looked like they weren't doing anything useful, to get the hell out of his way and let him do his damned job. Carefully he reached out to touch the gate.

'Don't touch that! It's burning hot!'
Duke quickly pulled his hand away as though bitten by a snake.

A stabbing sensation in my hand caused me to stop typing, and withdraw from the keyboard slowly, like reluctantly releasing a loved one from an embrace. I felt hot. Drinking again from the dirty glass, I read over the last two paragraphs. In the corner of my eye, I saw something glowing, but when I turned to look at it directly, there was nothing. Rubbing my eyes, I stood and walked to the bathroom. I felt really hot, uncomfortably hot so I ripped my shirt off and tossed it on the floor in the hallway.

As I splashed cold water on my face, I thought about Duke Porter, and how much I loved and admired him. He was everything I wanted to be, and simultaneously everything I knew I would never be. My hero and my best friend.

A lethal stink penetrated my nostrils while I was standing staring at my dripping, haggard face in the mirror, but the alarm I felt at first passed quickly when I realised it was emanating from the pile of sweat laden clothing on the bathroom floor.

No longer feeling unnaturally heated, I returned to the office, listening to the whispering trees as they brushed the windows, gently rocked by a cool breeze. The curtain fluttered over the desk flicking the upper layer of cigarette butts from the ashtray onto the floor. For a moment I thought I saw the glowing again but I relegated it to imagination and determined to return to the book.

Duke Porter apologised in his gruff and insincere way before ordering the plant worker who had saved him from considerable pain to get away from the gates because they were dangerously hot.

Grabbing a stick from the ground, He pushed it against the gate which to his surprise yielded instantly and swung inwards to reveal an apocalyptic scene. Amidst flashing lights and blaring sirens smoke poured from countless infernos and Porter felt bile rising in the back of his throat at the sight of the ragged and disfigured carcasses in the centre of it all. It looked like a ball of twine except this string was limp and rotting body parts. Dogs mainly, but a few cats and as he looked more closely, more than a few pigs. The luminescent paste poured through every gap between the bits and pieces of dead animals and filled all their orifices, lighting them from inside, weirdly like a Halloween pumpkin.

Again I saw the glow, but this time I refused to ignore it. Wait a minute, I thought, I am seeing what I am writing. Despite assuring myself thus, I still walked slowly to the corner of the room where I had seen the light. The room was dark apart from the focused beam which illuminated my desk, and a faint gleam floating wearily through the window from the streetlight out front of my house.

'Pigs,' I said aloud. 'Zombie pigs.' As I examined the wall, I realised I was alone and talking to it as if it were my trusted friend. Had I been talking out loud all night? There was nobody here to tell me whether I had or not, and I could not remember. I peered intently at the wall, pushing my face closer and closer to it. It stunk of dirty laundry too.

'Okay,' I said to the wall. 'I can talk to myself if I want to. What's wrong with that? It's actually a mark of incredible and indisputable genius. But where was I…ah yes, writing a horror masterpiece. Duke Porter and the Zombie Pigs.'

The breeze kicked up into a wind which sent the curtain flapping over the desk again so reluctantly I shut the window, and lit another cigarette. I was getting hot again.

The Duke stood dumbfounded before the open gate, unable to move a muscle. Others gathered behind him to watch the fantastic spectacle of decaying carcasses reanimating. The paste was somehow reviving them. Gradually the twisted ball of flesh began to unravel as one mutilated animal after another disengaged itself from the mass and stood groggily on their paws. Porter and the other onlookers were frozen in horrible disbelief.

After some time I realised I was sitting motionless. Shirtless and sweating. Dry mouthed and confused. I looked at my hand and saw the cigarette had burned right down to the butt as it lay unsmoked between my yellow stained index and middle fingers. A glow from the corner was accompanied by a fresh wave of dank bathroom odours. Or was there something else in here? Yes, a rotting smell. A childhood memory of a rat which my dad had trapped and killed under my bed without knowing it, confirmed it.

I didn't realise immediately that my glass was empty even though I drank from it.

'I'm pretending to drink,' I said to the wall. Then I waited for an answer. When none was forthcoming, I continued, 'I am delirious. I need a drink of water and something to eat.'

An angry gust of wind whistled through the cracks of my house, and the office door slammed shut. I jumped. I could see Duke Porter walking slowly towards the gate of the incinerator yard, but his face kept changing. First himself, the imagined likeness of Brad Pitt, then me, the antithesis of him, then a pig's face. I was moving towards the door, so slowly that I might have needed an hour to cover the five steps needed to reach it. When I finally arrived, it was locked from the outside.

Stupefied by alcohol and sleep deprivation, I had not, up to this point in time, considered seriously what might be happening to me. As I wrenched and ripped at the door handle with both hands fortified by panic, I cried out for help. An over reaction? Couldn't I have easily slipped out the window? Guilty on two counts but as I said, I was freaking out!

I spun around to look at the computer screen and watched the words I had written dance on the screen, fading in and out, and my head began to feel like the only part of my body still functioning. But it was heavy and caused me to lose my balance. I heard glass shattering and felt pain, sharp and cruel in my stomach and my arm before I lost consciousness.

Duke Porter shook off his fear like sand from a beach towel as he steeled himself with the resolve of a superhero. He commanded all the stunned bystanders to leave immediately, assuring them that he, Duke Porter, had everything under control. At that moment he felt invincible. Although he had no plan, his heart swelled with the courage of a pride of lions as he stepped forward towards the mob of four-footed living dead. Picking up an iron bar he had spotted on the ground, Porter began to beat his left palm with the weapon and threaten the zombie animals with death should they attempt to pass him. For a moment neither Duke nor the animals moved so he kept on drumming his palm with the rod of iron, and swearing insults at the evil creatures.

Suddenly I stopped typing and looked at my hands, they hurt, especially the left one and my palms were all cut open. Blood covered the keyboard and the desk, and my glass was empty again. I screamed in pain, fright and frustration as I tried to remember what had happened to me. Wasn't I on the floor a second ago? I could not even recall what I was writing about anymore. The door! The door was locked from the outside. I was trapped. I panicked, then I fell. The window! I cursed myself for not thinking of the window before. Rushing to the window, I told the wall how happy I was to be free, to be alive.

Half way through however, I lost heart. I had totally forgotten that somebody must have locked me in the office, and that somebody was possibly still in my house. I am ashamed to say that at that crucial moment my courage failed, and I retreated back inside the office to consider my position. The mixed stench of body odour, wet towels and rotting flesh was so thick in the air that I gagged on it every time I took a breath. I lit a cigarette, sat on the floor and listened. At first there was only heavy silence which brought me tremendous relief, but then a heard a sound. An unexpected sound coming from just outside the office door. I crawled along the floor to get closer to the door and as I did the unmistakeable sound of snorting filled my ears with a new kind of terror. A flashback again to my childhood where I was surrounded by grunting porkers, covered in mud, slipping and sliding, desperate to escape their stench while in the background I could hear my brothers laughing. I hated pigs!

It was then, in an instant of miraculous clarity that I realised I was writing my own worst nightmare. A light came on, its beam fingering its way under the door, and the animal sounds disappeared. Again I listened. Cowering, rigid with fear. Light began to break into my office cautiously as though not wanting to disturb me, but I was already extremely disturbed.

Magically the increasing light infused me with some courage, and after smoking another cigarette with insane alacrity, I edged closer to the door, and stretched out my trembling hand towards the handle. Still locked. I heard a strangely familiar voice. Mum?

I called out, 'Mum? Mum, is that you?'

Footsteps, the handle turning, her voice clear and concerned. 'Are you all right, dear?'

The best way to describe my answer was incoherent babble. I mentioned the lights, the pigs, the heat, the smell, the blood, and the locked door in a continuous verbal stream which could not have made any sense to her. The look on face said as much.

'Did you say the door was locked?' she asked. 'It wasn't locked. I opened it straight up.'

81

BANG!

I jumped and grabbed for the security of my mother's embrace. 'What was that?'

She pushed me away gently and looked me in the eye. 'Something fell…probably the broom I was using. I stood it against the wall when I heard you calling. What's wrong with you?'

'A broom?' I said incredulous. 'That wasn't a broom, mum.'

She turned and walked away but before I could ask where she was going, she bent down and picked up a broom off the floor. When she turned, I screamed. Her face was a pig's face, framed in her hair. I spun on my heels, skating on the slippery tiles, and flung myself back into the office slamming the door shut behind me. Picking myself up off the floor, I noticed the computer screen was still on, the screen saver apparently not functioning. I read the last words I had written as though they had been written by somebody else.

The rotting mangy animal zombies eased confidently towards Duke as he stood defiantly between them and the gate. They barked and yowled and grunted menacingly as they advanced. Porter swung at the first of the pigs and his rod of iron connected with its head instantly dissolving it in a splash of green paste. Too easy, thought Duke. Even as the animals began to surround him, increasing their numbers, he was confident he could dispatch the whole hellish horde back to the cesspool abyss from which they had sprung. Duke Porter felt no fear.

I suddenly remembered the satanic beast which had impersonated my mother waiting on the other side of the door. Waiting? Why? I had not locked the door. I hesitated. Duke Porter felt

no fear. I created him, I feel no fear, I told myself, but still I sat;
a heartless statue.

The office door opened, I felt the light on my back but I did
not turn around. I was ready to die, and this realisation relaxed
me. Shoulders unhunched, heartbeat slowing, breathing quite
normally, I prepared myself for death.

'What have you done to this room? Mandy's only been gone
for two days and you've turned the house into a pig sty. Boy,
am I glad I decided to come over and see how you were doing.
Badly, apparently. What is that smell? Is that you?'

Mum kept on yabbering as I turned very slowly to face her. I
still expected a pig's face to greet me, but was relieved to discover
nothing but an angry and disappointed scowl on my mother's
face. Sheepishly, I listened as she ranted and raved, criticising
me for this and that, berating me for my lack of self respect,
lambasting my laziness.

She wanted me to wash and help her clean up but I protested
that I needed to finish the chapter I was working on. I yielded
to her undeniably authority when she said I would not write
one more word until I smelled and looked like a human being
instead of a pig.

'Mum,' I said, 'I'll do whatever you say but can you please stop
talking about pigs. I hate pigs!'

Eight

Deceased Estate

⁓⟨∘⟩⁓

'*D*oesn't it creep you out?'

John glanced at his young offsider, deliberating whether to answer or tell him to shut up again. Too many questions. Too much inane banter. If he'd had the strength of two or three men he would have worked alone. He kept quiet, knowing that Yang would speak again, if only to fill the distasteful silence.

'I mean going in to a house where someone died and touching their stuff. Does it smell? Man, just the thought of it, gives me the willies, you know?'

The older man sighed, loosened his grip on the steering wheel then tightened it. 'It's just furniture, okay. We pick it up and carry it out to the truck. That's what we do. Move furniture. Every house is just a house. People live. People die. We move furniture.' Although he knew that wouldn't satisfy Yang or stop his blabbering, he rested; comforting himself with the thought that he had given it his best shot. John had done countless deceased estates, and despite what he said to Yang, some of them had disturbed him a little as well. Not that he could ever

84

put his finger on what exactly bothered him, but there were occasions when something felt weird. He recalled one job in particular which had so troubled him that he had not been able to sleep that night. A deceased estate. An old man who passed into the afterlife alone in a big house filled with the detritus of a long life. It did smell too. Stunk of death and decay. Reeked of yesterday's odours. John shook off the memory like sand off a beach towel. He was used to this stuff now. Even liked it a little.

'Furniture has history,' said Yang. 'It tells stories.'

''Bloody hell mate. What are you? A philosopher?'

Yang stared straight ahead, unaffected by John's ill humour for he was accustomed to it. It was a temporary gig which paid pretty good money and he enjoyed the physicality of the work as well as the more than decent pay. He could endure the sour old timer for a few months until he had the money he needed to make his big break. John took him for a fool and treated him with undisguised contempt, but Yang's skin was thick. Being an immigrant had forged a certain resilience, as it did with most. Australia had at first seemed full of excitement and wonder, then drudgery and disappointment took over. Frustration after frustration had sorely tested his faith, squeezing the hopeful exuberance from his bones. Until he met Suzie, and then the game changed. John was typical of many narrow minded, crusty farts he had met during his time in Wollongong.

'Take a lounge for example,' continued Yang. 'A couple buys a lounge, maybe the first lounge. Let's suppose it's new. They take the plastic off, and they sit on it. Then they move it. She wants to try it here, and there, and what about like this. He says yes to everything, playing his role, until she settles on a position and they sit again. She kisses him. The lounge is important to her. It's a symbol. Maybe it's the first piece of furniture they've bought together. She kisses him again. He kisses her back, and then they christen the new couch which is marked for the first time with humanity, stained with sweat and a little semen."

The truck rumbled to a halt out front of a dilapidated bungalow which hid behind overgrown shrubbery on a large, and mostly neglected block of land. Having managed to filter out most of Yang's rambling yarn about sex on sofas, John swung the truck out from the kerb in a wide arc to line up its rear end with the driveway. He then reversed in. It seemed unlikely that the truck would fit, but John persisted until it had nested comfortably beside the house with enough room between it and the garage to allow the back doors to swing open.

Yang reached for the door handle.

'I reckon you'll have better luck this way mate.'

After trying to open the door anyway, he found the aforementioned shrubbery stubbornly resistant to the idea, so he clambered over on to the recently vacated river's seat, and slid down on to the ground as gracefully as he could. He's noticed how smoothly John always got in and out of the truck. Striking Yang as neither flexible nor fluid in his motions, John nevertheless possessed impressive agility.

'Back door,' called John from the rear of the truck.

Yang noticed the silence. It was a hot morning, steamy and still, stifling life. He wiped his forehead, feeling the sheen of perspiration which had assembled almost as soon as the truck's engine was turned off and the bliss of air-conditioned crispness stolen.

'Are you coming?' roared John. 'Or are you waiting for a bloody invitation?'

A whisper in the bougainvillea caught Yang's attention. He froze, listening carefully to hear the words.

Meanwhile, John had retrieved the spare key, opened the door and was already walking through the house assessing once more the volume of furniture. He'd completed the process when he quoted for the job, but now he was imagining everything in here, packed inside the truck. Packing a truck with furniture and belongings was like doing a jigsaw puzzle. People thought moving furniture was all about muscle, but brains were required to do it efficiently. When he reached the living room which was towards the front of the house, he looked at the lounge and smiled. Sweat and a little semen.

The fabric three seater looked to be in relatively good condition, as though it had not been used much compared with its companion recliner which showed signs of having housed a man rather than merely providing him with a seat. It looked comfortable, inviting. John sat down and nested in the luxurious softness.

Yang strained his ears, but heard nothing more. He could smell jasmine as well as the bougainvillea and other sweet garden fragrances: an aromatic tour de force stewing in the humidity. The heat was oppressive. His shirt stuck to his skin. He had grown used to it over the years, learning to endure, if not enjoy it. He walked to the back of the house, noticing the rotting garage which leaned to one side as though about to faint from exhaustion.

The rear porch was small and crowded with overgrown potted plants. He smelled the roses before he saw them, majestically crowning long, thin, thorny stems. They reminded him of Suzie, who loved flowers and had infected him with her love of nature. A spiritual woman, she had allowed him to reconnect to a side of himself he had neglected during his quest for meaning in adventure. He loved her, not only for the beautiful person she was, but also for the way she made the whole world seem brighter and more wonderful.

'John, where are you?' said Yang as he opened the back door and entered the house.

'Living room.'

Inside the house, it was cool and malodorous. The exact opposite of the outside world. Yang felt uneasy as the ancient mustiness assaulted his senses.

'This chair,' said John, as Yang entered the room, 'is incredibly comfortable. Seriously, it's no wonder the old bloke spent most of his time on it.' He closed his eyes and sighed. 'Hell of a spot to kick back and croak it, don't you think?'

Yang saw a shadow pass over John's face, and thought he saw otherworldly sparkles glittering on his eyelids. His discomfiture ballooned. 'Shouldn't we be getting on with it?'

'Damn straight,' said John, startling Yang with a speedy exit from the recliner. He gestured to the lounge. 'I didn't notice any sweat or semen on it. Maybe you should check, eh?' Then he chuckled wickedly. 'Master bedroom first. Let's get that mattress.'

As he followed John down the hall, Yang studied the walls and fancied they had never been cleaned. They may have once been splashed with brilliant white or whatever fashionable shade was popular at the time, but time and neglect had facilitated the accumulation of grime. He looked more closely and saw a fine mist escaping from invisible pores. Running his hand along the wall, produced balls of slime on his fingertips. He walked on, slowly becoming aware of the sponginess of the floor.

'The carpet's wet,' he said.

'Just smells wet.'

'No, it's wet. Look!'

John ignored him. 'It's pretty ripe in here, isn't it?'

Yang reciprocated John's avoidance and crouched to feel the floor with his hand. It was dry. To take his mind off the disconcerting sensations he was experiencing, Yang said, 'It smells very bad in here.'

'That's what I said.' John grabbed a hold of one side of the mattress. 'Give me a hand with this, will ya?'

While searching for the handles at the side of the mattress, Yang observed it slowly changing colour, darkening. Just as he slipped his hand inside one of the handles, the mattress seemed saturated with blood, and the handle snapped from its weight. 'Blood.'

'Don't be so bloody squeamish,' said John. It's just a little stain.'

'The whole mattress is soaking with blood. I'm not touching it!'

'What's wrong with you?'

When he looked again, the mattress had returned to its normal shade of grey and Yang could see the golf ball sized blood stain near the edge. 'Nothing,' muttered Yang. 'All good. Let's get on with it.'

As they shuffled down the hall, Yang did his best to overlook the stench and the slimy wetness: the combined effect of which was that he felt as though he was walking through a sewer instead of a house. He mustn't let his imagination run away. He had to keep his fevered and worsening delirium at bay. Work hard. Work fast. In the midst of his private pep talk, John suddenly dropped the mattress and went into the living room.

'What are you doing?' asked Yang.

John snuggled into the recliner and closed his eyes.

Yang repeated his question.

'Just resting,' said John. 'I feel really sleepy all of a sudden. I just need a nap. Do what you can and I'll help you later.'

'Are you out of your mind?'

'Or you can take a break too. No hurry is there. Lay down on the lounge. It looks comfortable.' Then he chuckled unpleasantly again, quietly this time as though he didn't want anyone else to hear.

'John? John!'

Noticing the steady rise and fall of the other man's chest, Yang realized he was actually asleep. He had no idea how anybody could fall asleep so fast. Yang stood there staring, wondering what to do. The last thing he wanted to do was lie down on that sofa. He gazed at it and saw that it was blood red, but he couldn't remember what colour it had been before. Maybe it was red. Nausea brought on by the acrid atmosphere mingled with confusion, and disgust and something new: fear.

'John! Wake up! We have to get out of here.'

Yang tried to pull him up by the arms, then by reaching around his back under his arms, then he slapped him. John was dead to the world, and too heavy for Yang to carry. With adequate effort, he might be able to pull him onto the floor, and that might be enough to rouse him. He tried, but John now seemed so attached to the recliner, he couldn't even move him forward. Was it sweat which glued his back to the chair? Yang attempted to pull him by one arm – both of his hands clasping John's forearm, he yanked and pulled, cursing all the while, but it was all to no avail. Yang slumped on the floor, exhausted by the effort of trying to move John or at least wake him, but he recoiled instantly at the wet touch of the carpet. It felt as though it was sucking at his clothes. He sprung to his feet, heart racing in a state of panic now. What to do? What to do? What should I do?

He scrambled out of the living room and into the hall where

he slipped and crashed into the wall. The plaster gave way, cracking beneath his weight. Yang winced, then regained his feet, heading for the back door. The room seemed darker now, the air even heavier. He could hardly breathe. His head was swimming, and pain was screaming from different parts of his body. His hand. He looked and saw no wounds. His back, but then it was gone. His chest: sharp pain. Then none. He could hear his heart beating loudly inside his ears, his body seemed to have been separated from his mind. He could not do anything. Could not move anything. Could not feel anything. The smell and the heat were overwhelming. If only he could get to the door and escape. It could not have been that far. Just a few more steps. Surely. He vomited then, and for a moment, was reconnected to his body: momentarily, but long enough to feel the fall, and the slushy welcome of the putrid carpet. He struggled to his feet again, fighting the debilitating fear with everything he had. Then everything went black.

'Yang! Yang? Are you alright? Talk to me. Say something.'

Cold water was splashed on his face, reviving him. It was still dark, but there was a luminescence to it, like a light shining behind a thick curtain. More water. Cold. So refreshing. He opened his eyes slowly.

'Talk to me.'

'What happened?' croaked Yang.

'I dunno. You flipped out. Had some sort of panic attack or something.'

Yang eased himself to a sitting position and accepted the bottle of water which John offered to him. 'A panic attack? Really?'

'I told you there was nothing to worry about, but you got yourself all worked up about this being a deceased estate. I tried to calm you down, but you were talking all crazy like bloody mattresses and wet carpet, and strange whispers.'

Yang sipped from the bottle, savouring the healing coolness. 'But you were asleep on the recliner, and I couldn't get you off.'

'Me sleeping on the job. Fat chance,' said John. 'Like I said you just had a panic attack or something I reckon. We have to get back to work. We've lost a bit of time with these shenanigans of yours.'

After drinking some more water, then emptying the remaining contents of the bottle over his head, Yang said,' I imagined it all?'

'All in your head mate,' John said. Then he chuckled wickedly, but quietly as though he didn't want anyone else to hear. As the laughter died on John's cracked lips, Yang thought he heard whispering in the bougainvillea.

Nine

Shaking Hands

֎֎֎

'Why are your hands trembling?'
Lek did not even hear the question as he focused all his energy into placing the smoking aromatic joss stick in the sand filled bowl resting on the shelf. His eyes narrowed, his flesh crawled, his hands were shaking with fear as he knelt before the family shrine.

'Mother of Mercy, what are you afraid of?'

Finally, Lek managed to press the joss stick into the sand. Carefully he pulled away allowing his arms to drop by his sides, but he remained kneeling. He studied the black and white picture of his grandfather next to the bowl; dull and faded. Lifeless like the man it portrayed. A man Lek had never met, yet one he knew so much about, and feared more than any living thing. Beside the photograph, stood an empty can of Coke, and next to it an emerald Buddha, just six centimetres high.

Lek's mother, hauled him to his feet and squeezed his shoulder hard. 'What's wrong with you? Tell me why you're acting like a baby!'

Her voice sounded to Lek as though she would not be pleased by whatever answer he gave, so he stayed silent. Eventually his mother released her pincer like grip of his shoulder and left the room. The light faded as day gave way to night and Lek stood staring at the photo of his grandfather. Soon only the faint glow of a candle illuminated the shrine, leaving the rest of the small room buried in darkness. Turning his gaze slightly upward to look directly at the flame, Lek gasped as it flickered wildly like something or someone was trying to extinguish it. Dancing in a liquid wax filled crater, the orange flame enchanted Lek, and caused him to feel light headed. He swayed in the darkness which held him in a soft, suffocating embrace. Invisible hands pushed and pulled his thin body.

Out. Out went the candlelight taking Lek with it into nothingness. He awoke on the floor with his sister shaking him gently.

'Lek! Lek! What are you doing on the floor? Are you all right? Mum's calling you for dinner.'

She left before Lek had time to understand the questions let alone formulate answers. He didn't know why he was on the floor. Looking up, he was blinded by the naked electric bulb hanging from the ceiling and this reminded him of the candle. He rose from the floor slowly, in case he was injured, and went to investigate. He found that the candle was no longer burning but the wick still felt hot to the touch. Lek understood he must have fallen asleep for only a few minutes. He looked at the photo of his grandfather and shivered involuntarily.

Never before had Lek travelled down the stairs and into the kitchen with such alacrity. His breathless arrival startled his mother, but she recovered quickly. Hands on hips, she scowled. 'Where have you been? Didn't you hear me calling?'

'I…,'

'Have you washed your hands?   Well, hurry up then.
Grandma's waiting for you.'

'Grandma?'

His mother left before he finished his question or answered
any of hers, but that was not unusual. She never seemed to have
enough time, always rushing around, making Lek hurry, making
him feel uncomfortable and hassled and resentful. Grandma, on
the other hand, had plenty of time. Some, who disapproved of
her ranting homespun philosophy, felt she had too much time
on her hands, especially since the death of her husband but Lek
thought she was wise and patient and he enjoyed listening to
her speak about the past and about the other side, even though
the latter subject frightened him.

He crept out of the kitchen and across the polished wood of
the living room floor to where his family were sitting around
the cane mat that served as their dinner table. He noted his
two sisters kneeling side by side, receiving empty plates and
returning them loaded with steaming jasmine rice. His father
sat cross legged at one end of the mat sipping straight scotch on
ice from a short glass. Grandma sat with her legs folded under
her to the right while she leaned on her left hand. She alone
acknowledged his arrival with a smile after Lek greeted her
formally by bowing low and pressing his open hands together
with fingers pointing up.

'You look pale, Little One. Are you ill?'

'Just lazy,' said his mother.

Lek was trying to decide whether he should describe what
had happened to him upstairs or not, when the lights dimmed
momentarily.

'Ah!' cried Lek, squeezing his eyes shut.

Feeling a soft patting on his head, he slowly opened his eyes to see Grandma, still smiling at him. 'It's all right,' she said. 'He wouldn't be so rude as to interrupt our meal.'

Lek quickly looked around to see if anyone else had heard her, but they were engrossed now in their food, conversation reduced to a small supporting role. He turned back to Grandma and would have asked her who she was talking about except for the fact that she too seemed more interested in the ball of sticky rice and papaya salad headed for her mouth than in further discussion, and the truth was Lek already knew exactly to whom she referred.

'Why aren't you eating, boy?' said his father. It was a command not a question.

Lek looked at this hard man who hardly spoke to him, wondering why he had chosen to be like his dead father; a severe and distant caregiver to his children. What about love? Maybe he didn't have a choice. Maybe he did not understand love.

'Eat your food, Lek,' insisted his mother. 'Mother of Mercy, can't you spend even five minutes in the same world as the rest of us?'

That being yet another question not requiring an answer, Lek received a plate of rice from his sister, and joined the meal in silence. All the while he wondered about grandma, and the matter-of-fact way she seemed to say that grandfather was still around. He shivered again and dropped his spoon. Crash, onto the plate. 'Sorry,' he said softly.

Lek loaded the spoon with rice and lifted it to his mouth but as he did he became aware of a foul smell invading his nostrils. When he lowered the spoon to look at it, the rice it was rancid and riddled with yellow maggots.

'Ahhh!' cried Lek as he flung the spoon down onto the plate.

Grains of rice bounced and spun across the spread and the spoon landed on his mother's plate. He could faintly hear her familiar cry of Mother of Mercy as he sprang to his feet and dashed out into the yard. Lek stood there on the warm grass as though rooted to the spot, his chest heaved and his eyes darted from one threatening shadow to another.

Sometime later when he had calmed down, his grandmother approached him. 'I guess I was wrong,' she said.

'Huh?'

'I guess I was wrong about him disturbing our dinner.'

Sensing safety in a sympathetic ear, Lek found his reason and eventually his voice. 'What's wrong with me Ya?'

The old woman led him off the grass, back under the awning where she gestured at a broad teak bench. 'Sit down, Little One.'

Lek watched the darkness as it lurched menacingly towards them and he saw the creatures of the night, floating in the blackness, their green eyes unblinking and unfocused.

'Can you see them too, Ya?'

She turned slowly in response to the question as though she was thinking about her answer. 'Yes,' she whispered conspiratorially, 'I can see them.'

'Are they dangerous?'

'Do they look dangerous?'

'I feel terrified.'

'That's not what I asked you.'

Lek finally tore his eyes away from the many creatures, shapes and shadows which seemed closer now, and looked at his grandmother. Her eyes were clear and warm. Lek felt peace flooding in, washing away the fear as if he were somehow receiving it from her like a live giving injection.

The wise woman observed the change and patiently waited

for her grandson to speak.

'They look dangerous but...' said Lek as he stood and gazed again into the supernatural gathering.

A scream from inside was followed quickly by the sound of glass shattering. Lek moved to the back door to investigate.

'Wait! Little One. He's going to play with everyone else now.'

All the lights went out in the house as Lek stepped in through the door. The temperature dropped as though he had suddenly walked into a refrigerator. He could hear voices, unfamiliar voices whispering and snickering.

'Mum! Dad!'

More faint, sinister laughter wafted through the cold dark air, swirling around Lek and each word he spoke was answered by an echo; a mocking voice, teasing and cruel, fading in and out in the frosty atmosphere.

A candle flared to life from a corner of the room and he turned quickly to see a shadow glide from the corner to the safety of nearby gloom. Suddenly Lek was reminded of his grandmother's question, and it fueled him with courage, a feeling stronger than he had ever known.

'I'm not afraid of you Bu,' he said. When only silence replied he said it again but louder this time. 'I'm not afraid anymore.'

A little girl's voice said, 'You should be Little One. You should be.'

'Who are you?'

'Who are you?' demanded another voice, this one of an old woman.

Then a multitude of voices began speaking at once, all around him so he could not tell where they were coming from. Stretching out his arms in the darkness he swung around in circles but felt nothing and eventually tumbled to the floor, dizzy and tired. 'I'm not afraid,' he mumbled. 'I'm not afraid. Not afraid.'

* * *

When he opened his eyes, he was lying in his own bed, under a light blanket. The whole family was gathered there in his room, studying him with anxious expressions.

'We've called the doctor for you Little One,' said his mother.

Lek smiled at her. It had been a long time since she had called him that, and it made him feel as though he had just awoken from a nightmare. 'What happened?' he asked.

'When you ran outside you banged into the door jam and knocked yourself out. There was a lot of blood, but we stopped it now, and thank the Lord Buddha you woke up. We were so worried. Why did you run off like that?'

Lek's grandmother answered for him. 'The boy needs rest now. I'll sit with him until the doctor arrives.'

After they left, grandmother moved closer to his side and gently dabbed his forehead with a wet cloth. 'It's not over yet, Little One,' she said cryptically.

'Huh?'

Noting the confusion in her grandson's eyes, she sighed and smiled at him. 'They saw you run into the door jam, but that's not what happened.'

'It's not?'

'First you saw something in your rice and then you saw the creatures of the night in the backyard. We were talking and then there was a scream from inside the house. You went inside to check it out and the lights went out.'

Realization dawned on Lek's face. 'The house was full of people.' He looked at his grandmother for confirmation and she half nodded so Lek continued. 'Dead people?'

She nodded more definitely this time.

'Creatures of the night?'

'No,' she said, 'they don't like the indoors. They don't like being boxed in. It reminds them of death.'

'What are they?'

'Animals, demons, a mixture of both, some ghosts even choose to be with them. I don't know why. Maybe it has to do with the circumstances of their deaths.'

There was a knock at the door, followed by the entry of the doctor who formally greeted Lek's grandmother then smiled at him. Lek froze when he saw the doctor's face, and if he could have looked away, he would have seen the same reaction from his grandmother.

'You both look like you've seen a ghost,' joked the doctor as he moved closer to Lek. In his mind, images of the family shrine were flashing before his eyes. The empty Coke can, the sand bowl, the incense, the Emerald Buddha, the photograph. Then the mental slide show jammed. The doctor so much resembled his dead grandfather that Lek decided it was in fact the same man; death wearing living flesh. It had to be.

The doctor, totally unaware of all that was rampaging through Lek's mind, sat on the edge of the bed and asked him a series of questions which Lek answered honestly yet mechanically. Next, he examined the cut and the golf ball sized bump underneath it. 'Ran into a door jam eh?' he said.

Lek saw a sparkling green iridescence in the doctor's eyes.

'What on earth were you running from?'

Before he could answer, the lights went out and he was plunged once more into solitary darkness.

'Ya?' cried Lek frantically. 'Ya? Are you still here? Ya?

The lights came back on and all was quiet. Lek's grandmother sat beside him mopping the sweat off his forehead. She was singing.

'What happened? Where's the doctor?'

The old woman stopped singing and looked at Lek, smiling sweetly. 'The doctor hasn't arrived yet. Did you see someone else?"

'I thought I did but…what's going on? I don't know what's real and what's not any more. I can't stand it, Ya. Help me.'

A knock on the door. A bang on the door. A continuous thumping on the door.

'Come in!' yelled Lek. 'Come in.'

With a crash the door was unhinged and smashed on the floor, wood splinters flew, and a cloud of dust plumed to fill the room. Through the cloud appeared a frighteningly familiar face, attached to a thin skeletal body clothed in grimy rags and carrying a black briefcase.

'Doctor's here, Little One,' breathed the wraith. 'Here to heal…or maybe peel.' The hacking laugh that followed exploded from its mouth in a rush of putrid gas. Lek was paralyzed as his dead grandfather, the ghost doctor, slowly approached his bed.

'Stop laughing, you old fool.'

'Is that you Ya?' said Lek.

'Hush, Little One. I'm talking to your grandfather.'

The hideous apparition froze, turned its head and extended a bony finger in her direction. 'You always spoil my fun. Even in death, I can't have my fun.'

Lek thought he sounded like a child being roused on by a parent.

'You're scaring him. It's not funny.'

Slowly, before Lek's disbelieving eyes, the ghastly ghost

transformed into his grandfather. With his shoulders slumped and his head bowed, he looked suitably chastened as he stood in silence and waited respectfully for his wife to speak. Her words were stern. 'Why Dear?'

For a moment, it seemed to Lek that his grandfather was afraid to answer for fear that whatever he said would be unlikely to mollify his angry wife. Patiently, she waited, glaring at him.

'I'm bored,' he mumbled.

'Bored? Is that it?' she demanded. 'You're telling me you've been scaring your grandson half to death because you're bored?'

'The others...'

'Others? What others? Even in the grave you're a sheep. You've never been able to stand up for yourself. Never had the courage to lead. Never...' and on and on she went.

Lek watched the old ghost wilt and wither under the verbal attack and he began to feel sorry for him. Maybe it was incredibly dull being dead. All the magical powers and trickery he had used to bedevil Lek counted for nothing now as he cringed and cowered under the assault of his former earthly master. He glanced at Lek. There were tears in his eyes and his hands were shaking.

Disappearing from the room suddenly, the apologetic apparition left his words floating in the room. 'I'm sorry,' he said. 'I am, really I am. It was just supposed to be a little bit of fun.

Looking down at his hands, Lek remembered how they trembled every time he had to pray at the shrine in front of the picture of his grandfather. How he feared him and his ethereal presence. How he feared stinging criticism or stinging rebuke. How he felt fragile, vulnerable and worthless. He turned his hands over a few times, palms up, palms down, and noted with great satisfaction how steady they were, and how strong he felt.

Knowing he must thank his grandmother for saving him, he then turned to where he thought she was sitting beside his bed. The wise old lady had also disappeared, or perhaps, wondered Lek, perhaps she had never been there at all.

Ten

By Way of Explanation

⁂

I have kept this journal going for nineteen years now but this will be my final entry. I briefly entertained the idea of giving this last installation of the serial of my life a fancy title like, *By Way of Explanation: The circumstances surrounding, and the reasons for my suicide*, but it sounded too pretentious and frankly, I couldn't be bothered. Never during the course of this written chronicle of the highs and lows of my life have I wasted words, so why begin now?

This journal of mine will be easily found, after my body is, because I will make no effort to conceal it. While I lived I would rather have died than allow anyone to read my intimate thoughts and deeds, but now on the eve of my death…well, I'm sure the irony does not escape you.

No doubt the person who finds me, and my journal, will go straight to the last entry in a search of answers. So, it is answers I will attempt to provide. Whether they will prove satisfactory to whomever reads or hears them, I cannot know. I will be dead, and despite the adult fairy tale, which we use to comfort ourselves, about our loved ones looking down from heaven,

I will be gone and no longer interested in or in touch with this world. Dead is dead, I reckon. When I leave this thing called time, I'll be somewhere else-that's assuming there is any existence after death-out of time.

Apart from fantastic Hollywood images of Heaven and Hell, and a knowledge instilled in me during my childhood about the rules for who goes where, I really have no idea what awaits me on the other side.

I'll tell you one thing though, I am not afraid. I fear neither the process of death nor the uncertainty of what lies beyond the act itself. I have given it a lot of thought, maybe too much thought. That, I think, has been one of my more serious problems, too much thinking. No matter how I have reasoned it out, I cannot convince myself that death is something to be avoided. I have never feared death, and now I have, or should I say, now I will, prove it.

To the inevitable question which arises; why? Why did I kill myself? It strikes me as amusing to talk of myself in the past tense, so I will continue that way. Why did I kill myself? People say things like, he hated himself, he hated life, he was depressed, unhappy, lonely, he couldn't find a reason to live. All reasonable points and possibly true in many instances, but not at all applicable to me.

My life was not marked by undue suffering. My upbringing was normal. Mum loved me, so did Dad in his own way. He was away from home often on business trips and was consequently a distant father in both senses of the word, but he provided well for his family. Nothing went wrong. I had no disabilities or tragedies with which to contend or overcome.

Admittedly, I was very shy which caused me to come to prefer my own company, and therefore be perceived as a loner.

However, I had a few good friends whom I trusted and liked, so I wasn't lonely. I had a secure, well-paying job with an international financial institution, and married an impossibly sweet and beautiful woman with whom I had three bright and healthy children.

It all sounds great, doesn't it? So far, all I've done is give good reason to live, not to die. No grounds in any of that for dissatisfaction with the world. No cause for complaint about life and how she treated me. What then was my problem?

I remember one day, a zealous young Christian approached me on the street, his face alight with joy and bannered with a wide smile. After introducing himself he told me how Jesus had posed the question, what does it profit a man to gain the whole world yet forfeit his own soul? I told him to get fucked.

I always felt there was something missing in my life, something not quite right. Although I could not identify it exactly, I knew there was something wrong with my life and by logical extension, something wrong with me. When I say always, I really mean particularly from about the age of fifteen. More specifically, the first time I got drunk on a bottle of cheap wine in the grounds of my old school. I remember well the delicious euphoria of intoxication and the thrill of doing something so 'naughty', and how quickly that glorious feeling disappeared when I unloaded the contents of my stomach on the grass a few hours later.

If I need to apologize for all this wandering down memory lane, then I do. I recognize how self-indulgent it is, but it's my journal and, just in case you weren't able to work it out while I was with you, this is who I am.

Any suggestion that I ended my life because I hated myself is wrong. The truth is, I loved myself too much to allow me to suffer that existence any longer. It should be called a mercy killing, not a suicide.

If there was one event which pushed me over the edge and helped me to finally decide upon this course of action, then it was the disintegration of my marriage. My wife left me, and although we were both at fault for the break-up, I didn't love her enough to accept my share of the blame. I didn't love her enough to say I was wrong and to ask her forgiveness. I was the only victim and damn it all if I would not hold onto that pain.

I know I pushed her away from me and into the strong embrace of a better man than me, but it was her choice to be unfaithful. Wronged, I loved myself too much to forgive her even though I too was guilty of breaking our marital vows. No, I didn't have an affair, but I gutlessly abrogated my responsibilities as a husband and a father. I was unfaithful to her and after a while I stopped trying or even pretending to care.

The separation and subsequent divorce caused me more suffering than I showed to anyone, so I tried to comfort myself by saying that I deserved to be treated better than that. It doesn't matter anymore, anyway. My marriage is history and so am I. Me, the man who loved his children and his wife and everyone else in his life, only when they pleased him. No person could please me all the time and I just grew tired of expecting so much from people but being continually let down. No hate though, I never hated. Not even toward my job did I bear any ill feeling. It simply bored me.

Lack of stimulation in my life caused me no end of frustration. I dreamed of much yet achieved nothing and my failures were always someone else's fault. I couldn't stand it anymore.

To all my friends and family who loved me despite my selfishness, I want to say thank you for trying to make my life bearable. Some of you may also be hoping for an apology from me, expressing my sorrow for the pain I have caused you, but I think rather that I should be congratulated for relieving you of the burden of having to tolerate me. If I'm sorry, it is only in this, that you may fail to be grateful for the favor I have done you.

My final request, if I may be so bold, is that you not sentimentalize my life as I've always felt disappointed by the lack of honesty at funerals. The bottom line is that I'm gone, I'm dead, and some of you are glad about that which is okay because I'm glad I'm dead too.

Eleven

The Devil's Been Delayed

'Strange how the memory works isn't it?'

'What?' Felix looked puzzled. 'What are you on about Religious Man?'

I had spoken out loud unintentionally. Hence my co-worker's bemusement. The flow of boxes down the conveyor belt had eased to a trickle, the two major lines of product, Listerine and Mylanta having already ceased production for the day. One of the smaller lines, Ponstan had a technical fault and was on temporary shut-down.

'I said it's strange how the memory works.'

'Yeah right,' said Felix without interest. 'I'm going to the toilet, so you can stay and figure out how your memory works.'

'Where's Houdini?' I called to the back of his head as he walked away. He didn't respond.

Houdini was so nicknamed because of his propensity to disappear when the workload became heavy and then magically reappear when it had eased off. Like now. He did his job though and was known to be very interested in the leading hand position should it ever became vacant. We were all amused by his objective as it seemed that Charlie would never leave unless he was carried out on stretcher. However, we had lost one of our comrades recently and were expecting a replacement sooner rather than later.

There was nothing coming down the line, so I sat down on a half-packed pallet and watched Felix disappear through the large double doors in the near corner of the finishing section of the factory. I tried to recall what I was thinking about before but could not. Nor could I remember why I had spoken those words out loud. Then I realized that illustrated the truth of my comment about the enigmatic workings of the mind. I wondered again whether such thoughts made me weird. Everybody had idiosyncrasies.

'Charlie says there's a new bloke starting today,' said Houdini who had materialized from somewhere behind me.

'Yeah,' said I. 'He's late on his first day. That's getting off to a bad start, eh?'

Houdini grunted and made himself look busy with nothing at all. We never talked much, Houdini and I. I don't think he talked much to anyone. Not that I noticed anyway.

'He's here now, said Houdini after an unnecessary pause. 'Getting his uniform and a bit of orientation, paperwork and stuff.' His eyes roamed around the factory floor as he spoke, and I found myself following his gaze although I knew he was simply avoiding looking at me. It was nothing personal.

'Paperwork and stuff, eh?' I said to fill the gap in conversation. Boxes began to travel down the line again, providing me with a good excuse to shut up and avoid further forced conversation. It was a pleasing thought; there was going to be a new boy. A new boy meant that I would no longer wear that title. I would be teaching another bloke the nuances of the job. It was a pseudo promotion. That was the positive side. The other side of the coin was potentially not so good. What would this new bloke be like? Would we get on? Would he be a good worker? A quick learner? I had become accustomed to everyone and everything now. It had only taken a few weeks to get into the swing of things. A few weeks of working daily together had enabled me to find my place in the group. My niche. I belonged now. But what about the new boy? Would he fit in? Only time would tell.

Suddenly he appeared, rounding the corner to the left of the frontline, walking beside our leading hand Charlie.

Charlie was riding a pallet truck as he usually did. Having two dickie knees, he walked as little as possible. Walking was somewhat painful and awkward for him. Football injuries had done that. Despite his slight incapacitation, no one questioned his value to the finishing floor team.

The frontline was the next port of call on the new boy's tour.

'Where's Felix?' roared Charlie, who never waited until he was close enough to a person to actually speak to them in a normal tone of voice. 'Where the fuck is he?'

I thought it odd him being so upset about Felix' absence in light of the fact there were only three lines of product running, and Houdini and myself were there to handle it. But that was Charlie; angry, bellowing, swearing; getting the job done. He was really a decent sort of a bloke. On a couple of occasions, we had gotten together for a few drinks at the pub after work and during those social moments, there was none of his belligerency to be seen. Perhaps he left it all at work. Maybe he required alcohol to underpin good humour.

'It's all right Charlie. We've got it under control,' I said confidently while stealing a glance at the new boy.

'What? Where is he? Who's floating? Dammit. Fuck!'

I wondered whether all this was just Charlie being himself or a deliberate display of his authority designed to impress and intimidate the new recruit, who walked silently beside him with a faint smile on his face.

The latest member of our team was of average height, around the one seventy five, one eighty mark, and of average build. With thick, dark brown hair and an unremarkable face except for a pair of Gene Wilder type bulging eyes. He wore the ill-fitting white shirt and trousers uniform, with a shower cap sitting uncomfortably on his head, the way it did for all of us when we started. It took some time to work out how to wear the thing to comply with safety regulations and not feel like a complete idiot.

The only thing about him or his appearance that was unusual was something I didn't really notice at first. The guy was smiling continuously. It was really weird. Like he thought everything and everyone was funny. Was he happy at having secured this new job? Was he amused by Charlie's melodramatic vehemence? Or was he embarrassed at having to parade himself around the finishing floor in a shower cap? Whatever the reason for his permanently cheesey grin, it was disturbingly odd.

'This is Geoff' began Charlie.

'Geoffrey,' interrupted the new boy, emphasizing the last syllable of his name.

For an instant I thought Charlie was going to get stuck into him for interjecting and tell him where to stick his second syllable, but all he said was. 'Show him what to do, and for fuck's sake take care of the lines. Float! Don't just hang around here right?' And with that lofty injunction, he was off, leaving the rest of the introductions to us. Geoffrey shook my extended hand and asked how I was after I told him my name. He looked me square in the eyes when he asked me. Houdini followed my lead and repeated the process, carefully avoiding Geoffrey's glare.

'I'll stay here.' said Houdini, pulling rank and delegating himself the easier task. 'You take him around and service the lines.'

I likewise directed Geoffrey to do the more menial, heavy lifting tasks as I gave him a more in-depth look at his new work environment. Conversation was confined to questions and answers relating to work. It wasn't that I was not curious about Geoffrey. On the contrary, I was thoroughly intrigued by his continually cheerful countenance, but I didn't want to overwhelm him with personal questions on his first day. Those enquiries could wait.

The first day passed without incident. Geoffrey seemed enthusiastic, hard-working and was quick to learn. He could get on with his job without fussing or stalling, asking only the occasional question when necessary. He was talkative, but not to the extent that you felt like telling him to shut up. We got on pretty well, although I could never shake the feeling there was something different about Geoffrey. Something really deviant. Naturally he was keen to make a good impression with his new workmates and the boss, but it seemed at times he was trying too hard to impress us. Was he in fact too good to be true? My curiousity was not able to overcome my timidity.

Could he be a Christian? He never mentioned Jesus, but as I myself knew full well, one did not need to be spouting off about Jesus all the time to be a Christian. The sensible preferred being quiet achievers for the kingdom of God as opposed to bible bashers who no doubt got the message across, but alienated people in the process. Joy was supposed to be one of the characteristics of Christians. Was it joy in Geoffrey's case? Or was it some sort of madness? What was joy anyway? I was a Christian yet I certainly did not walk around all the time wearing a big cornball grin like Geoffrey. Quite the opposite in fact. Did that mean that I was a bad Christian? Or worse, not a real Christian at all? Was I a fake? I pulled myself up on that one, dismissing the train of thought as paranoia.

The other problem I had was that if Geoffrey was a Christian how would I be able to bring myself to tell him that I was one too. That I was a brother. A brother in the Lord. To be honest I wasn't convinced that I wanted this man for a brother which was a terrible thought to have but, given our diametrical opposed dispositions, a confession by me that I was a believer may represent a loss of face for one of us. I was shocked by my own insecurity. Eventually I decided the possibility of Geoffrey being a Christian was too problematic for me, so I had to rule it out if only for convenience sake. For peace of mind I placed it in the in in-tray on my mental desk where it would be dealt with properly later. Or not.

One thing was certain though, I had to find a way to sate my curiousity about Geoffrey. I had to find out somehow, preferably non-directly, the reason behind the smile. This sleeping dog simply had to be disturbed.

All these things I pondered through the day and into the night. Not exactly tossing and turning, nor filling my every conscious thought, it nonetheless played on my mind.

One day at work I ran into Geoffrey in the toilet. It was a chance meeting, not in the big toilet down the hall which doubled as a smoking lounge, but in a smaller amenity located on the finishing floor itself. He was leaving as I was entering and we nearly collided, coming together in an uncomfortable moment in the doorway. It was that instant when somebody has to give way to the other, to yield ground either in retreat or to one side. Geoffrey, who was still sporting his Cheshire Cat grin, reversed back into the bathroom to let me in.

'Thank you,' I said appreciatively.

'No worries. You're probably in more of a hurry to have a piss than I am to get back to work' he said with a half laugh like the one you give when you are unsure if the other person is or will be amused by your comment.

He was right though. I was in a hurry and I didn't think he was particularly funny, so I headed straight over to the nearest urinal, unzipping my fly while I travelled. As I relieved myself, I realized that Geoffrey was still standing there which not only concerned me but also unnerved me. When waiting for him to say something - otherwise why didn't he just leave - proved fruitless, I said, 'So how do you like the job, all right?'

'Yeah it's pretty good.'

'You'd be hard pressed to find a better factory job than this one I reckon. What'd you do before here?' I asked seizing the opportunity to discover more about the smiling Geoffrey. What a relief to finally be able to ask a question. My shovel was poised and ready to dig.

'I was on the dole for a while,' said Geoffrey. 'Before that I worked in another factory. Before that. A bit of this and a bit of that.'

Pondering what the hell 'a bit of this and a bit of that' meant as I finished and zipped up, I remembered my dad saying to me when I dropped out of high school that I would have to find a job. If I went on the dole, he threatened, I would have to leave home. Given that choice, I got a job and had always been employed since. Not so with Geoffrey.

'You couldn't find a job or you didn't want one?' I asked, boldly preparing to take the high moral ground.

Geoffrey, unperturbed and apparently unashamed ,answered that he did not want to work.

When I finished washing my hands which I normally didn't do, I smiled to myself then suggested we get back to work. Although I was bothered by the fact he had taken government handouts merely because he was too lazy to get a job, I decided to leave the matter alone. My opinion of Geoffrey slid however with that revelation. He did have some character flaws after all. I reasoned that if I kept scraping at the gold plating, I would eventually reveal what lay beneath.

'Maybe we should get back to work.'

'Nah,' responded Geoffrey. 'There's nothing happening out there is there?'

'Not really,' I replied truthfully, still trying to work out why we were hanging out in the toilet like two old mates meeting by chance in the gents of the local hotel. Did I really want to be having this conversation with this person? In this place?

'Got plans for the weekend?' he asked.

'I'm working tomorrow and Sunday I go to church. That's all.'

The moment of truth had arrived. I had copped a little bit of flak from my workmates since my sudden conversion to Christianity which occurred not long after I had started working at Parke-Davis. The ribbing was mostly good natured and I took it that way. Trying hard not to be too preachy despite being very excited about the whole thing at the time, I made it clear that I was now a new person. My nickname, Religious Man, was ascribed to me at that time by Felix. I had toned down my zealotry, without watering down my conviction. I held my breath, waiting for Geoffrey's reaction.

'You're a Christian,' said Geoffrey. His smile widened, morphing into something much colder and darker. 'I'm a Satanist.'

He was still smiling when he said it. Surely, he was a lunatic. I could not believe what he had just said. If he wasn't mad, then he was just trying to be funny. No one would confess to being a Satanist. As far as I knew Devil worshippers only existed in the movies. What sane, rational person would choose to follow the Master of Lies and worse still, happily announce the fact. I was speechless, but after several uncomfortable moments, I found my voice. 'Are you serious?'

'Yeah. Why wouldn't I be?'

No way was this guy for real. It just could not be. I could not accept what was going on. Had to be dreaming. I knew that for sure. There was no need to do anything dumb like pinch myself to prove it either. Here was this perpetually cheery and easygoing bloke whom I hardly knew, proudly telling me that he was a Satanist. A disciple of the Prince of Darkness.

'I see,' I said profoundly.

'I'm fair dinkum. You follow Jesus. I follow the Devil,' he said matter-of-factly, making it sound so reasonable I almost agreed with him.

'Why?' I said, wanting to immediately get on the front foot. Although still stunned, I decided I had to try and convert the guy. I had to save him. It was my mission. God had divinely appointed me to be his warrior in this battle against the forces of darkness. 'Haven't you read the Bible? You're on the wrong side. The losing side. You picked the wrong team.'

'Yeah. I've read it, but I'm more interested in what's in the satanic bible. Hate conquers love and all that.'

'Hate conquers love?" I repeated incredulously. I laughed because I couldn't help it. Then I blasted away from zealous and entered angry. I felt like swearing at that point and really getting stuck into the damn fool. Hate conquers love? What the hell? Somehow by the grace of God, a minor miracle I'd say, I restrained myself. Totally exasperated, flabbergasted, but not wanting to show it, I simply shook my head and said, 'Let's get back to work.' This was neither the time nor the place to wage a holy war.

During the course of the following week, Geoffrey and I talked from time to time about religion which was, considering our opposing views the only thing we could discuss. A lofty spiritual discussion about eternal and divine matters is the pinnacle of social discourse. It had once been said that nothing in all the world is interesting…except religion. So we discussed and debated, argued and defended our respective faiths. And we did it with passion. Geoffrey told me more about the satanic bible and the local satanic church where he worshipped, and how he had recently attained the ranking of High Priest. He was obviously very proud of himself. I thought it was pathetic. Doubtless, he felt the same about me.

Apparently, he had a lot of power and was able to have any woman he wanted. *Have* in the biblical sense that is. He boasted of being able to seduce them easily into satisfying his sexual cravings. Rather than impress me, this disgusted me.

Geoffrey didn't appear bothered by my transparent doubt about what he was telling me. It seemed he didn't care at all what I thought of him, deliberately bragging about behaviour which he knew would offend me. Part of me could not deny at least the possibility that there was some truth in his words. If I believed in God, a living supernatural being, then I could not refute the existence of the devil, or deny his not insignificant power and capacity for evil.

The best defense against Geoffrey and his claimed ability to do supernatural works was to attack him with the truth of the bible. God's word, described as living, active and sharper than a double-edged sword was the only weapon at my disposal. He was a disciple of the Father of Lies so the truth had to be the best, most effective weapon against him.

Occasionally, I became discouraged because Geoffrey would simply reply to all my challenges by saying he knew what the bible said but he disagreed. He always remained calm, calmer than me and that damned smile never left his face. That frustrated me even more because I realized that pride had entered my heart and I was no longer always acting and speaking with the sole intention of glorifying God and defending the gospel of Christ. Sometimes it became much more personal than it should have. As the Godfather always said, it was not personal, it was business. That I did take it personally was something for which I may have received the admiration and respect of some, but I wanted to win so badly, I nearly forgot the reason the fight began and for whom I was fighting in the first place.

Through it all, the endless exchange of ideas, scriptures and beliefs, it became increasingly clear that Geoffrey had to be either insane, completely deceived and deluded or just plain stupid. His knowledge of the bible convinced me he had made an informed decision to follow the fallen angel named Lucifer. He was too rational to be demented so he must have been deceived. He had been blinded to the truth. What would it take to restore his sight? Obviously, a lot more than my feeble attempts at persuasion. Praying earnestly and scouring the bible for more ammunition for my dwindling arsenal was wearing me out. I was exhausted.

One Thursday morning as we were packing boxes on the frontline, Geoffrey and I got to talking about music. It transpired we had a common fondness for the music of Prince. He offered to lend me some of his Prince tapes to listen to and I offered him a lift home from work that afternoon, so I could pick them up. Looking back, it was a bizarre thing to do. What was I thinking? At the time I rationalized my decision to get chummy with Geoffrey by saying that perhaps by concentrating on common interests I would get more opportunities to witness to him. His conversion was still my prime objective. Most of the time. Sometimes it really was just pride. It was childish and foolish and not entirely how God would have wanted me to go about the task, but I could not help myself.

That afternoon, I drove Geoffrey home as we arranged, even though it was well out of my way. It wasn't that I was desperate to get those tapes, in truth I really did not like Prince as much as I had indicated. I definitely would not have called myself a fan yet there I was going out of my way to drive the devil to his den. I accepted when he invited me inside.

The High Priest lived alone in a smallish one-bedroom unit and the irony of such a humble dwelling did not escape me. It was decorated in bachelor style, sparse and masculine. Slightly untidy. There was nothing unusual or interesting about his place at first glance. I did not see a single candle, let alone hundreds of them nor was there a pentagram on the floor or on any of the walls. Montages of scenes from every horror movie I could remember seeing played on loop in my mind. Superficially, Geoffrey was an ordinary fellow. I knew he was about as far removed from normal as you could get. So far as to almost defy description. What I saw in his bedroom demonstrated his true nature conclusively.

Furnished with a queen-sized bed, a side table and a built-in wardrobe which was divided into three sections, it was a functional bedroom. There was a set of four drawers in the centre of the wardrobe with a large mirror above it set right back against the wall with sliding doors on either side. On the top of the drawers, which was effectively a table top, stood a tall red candle about twenty centimetres high surrounded by five shorter black candles, each about ten centimetres in height. A closer look showed that the candles were arranged around a pentagram which had been carved roughly into the wood.

On the sides of the wardrobe adjoining the mirror were numerous pictures of naked women and female body parts. All bare flesh shots, obviously pulled out of Playboy and Penthouse and other such men's magazines. Intermingled with those pictures were Polaroids of women. His conquests: at least a dozen of them. I took it all in, simultaneously, shocked and intrigued, before quickly leaving his bedroom to avoid being poisoned by the atmosphere of lust.

I asked Geoffrey for the tapes and made some weak excuse about how I had to hurry on home and start cooking because I was expecting my mum for dinner. He appeared to accept the reason for my quick getaway, but I had the feeling he was only amiable and tolerant to those who did the right thing by him. People would no doubt say he was a good bloke.

Driving home, I tried not to think about the altar to lust I had seen in Geoffrey's bedroom. I did not want to imagine the kind of things that had gone on there in front of the altar, on that bed, but those images of naked women infected my mind. Feelings of regret surged as I tried to fight off the thoughts of unholy desire which were beginning to run rampant in my head. I should not have gone to his home. I tried to pray, but as I did, all I could see was Geoffrey's smiling face. That devilish, lascivious grin had become a curse to me.

I never listened to the Prince tapes I borrowed from Geoffrey. At work, I only engaged in conversation with him when he instigated it. I did not go out of my way to talk to him or be near him. Naturally, working together meant there was still quite a lot of contact between us, but I tried to minimize it. Uncomfortable in Geoffrey's presence now, I sensed he savored my ill ease. Outwardly he maintained the unchanging good humour he presented to the world, but I saw him differently now. I felt I knew him well, too well and to me he was dangerous. He was a threat. Unfortunately, I was not as good at disguising my true feelings as he was. Our relationship had changed from the time I walked into his den of depravity. The battle lines had been drawn.

* * *

Felix turned eighteen and threw a big party at his house to celebrate. All his workmates were invited. Geoffrey arrived late, but not unnoticed. Though the party raged with music blaring and beer flowing, feelings of dread washed over me when I saw Geoffrey walk in with a very good looking, long-legged blonde. They were both dressed entirely in tight, black clothes. The girl had jewelry everywhere. Rings on all her fingers, bangles and bracelets on her arms. Necklaces, pendants and gaudy earrings. Most prominent was a silver cross hanging on a chain between her large, half exposed breasts. Geoffrey was also wearing several outlandish rings as well as a cross around his neck. It was inverted and broken.

His smile, once friendly and curious, now looked smug and self-satisfied: sinister. He oozed vile pride and arrogance, wanting everyone to see him and with whom he had arrived. Obligingly, the majority of party goers observed the late arrival of the distinctively dressed couple with fascination, perhaps even a little envy. As for me, the sight of Geoffrey and the blonde in black was grotesque. Was she already on his wall, or would she be there soon? What happened to those girls when Geoffrey finished with them?

So there he was, a macabre personification of evil, almost a parody. My response was to ignore him, but when he came straight over and sat near me at another table I had to acknowledge his presence out of courtesy. I could not think why he deserved politeness or respect, but I did not want to ruin Felix' party. An ominous dread whispered that trouble was certainly on the horizon. For a moment, I considered leaving. I should have.

Geoffrey and his vamp, who he failed to introduce to anyone, sat by themselves smoking and drinking, talking and kissing. Totally absorbed in themselves. She always fetched the drinks and lit his cigarettes which he smoked fairly continuously. From time to time they briefly stopped fondling each other to look around, but it was with detachment. They weren't interested in any one else although Geoffrey occasionally chatted to anyone who came within earshot.

What were they doing there? Why did they come? It seemed as if they could not wait to get their clothes off and have sex. Why couldn't they just leave and follow their lustful desires elsewhere? I was doing a lousy job of ignoring them. Fact was, I could hardly keep my eyes away from them. As much as I detested what I saw I just could not resist watching them and I'm sure Geoffrey knew it. No doubt that knowledge probably heightened his pleasure. Was I jealous? I felt sick.

Eventually I managed to move away, but I could feel Geoffrey watching me as I went. Every step. I went to get a beer and then I had a bit of a dance, if that's what you call it, to the sounds of Midnight Oil blasting out of the stereo. I was talking to Felix and a couple of other blokes standing around on the grass when Geoffrey and his goddess came over near us and started dancing. He was goading me. Felix encouraged Geoffrey and reminded him that if he got tired, any of the boys would be happy to take over with the blonde for a while. The dancing couple both smiled at the lewdness implied in the suggestion. I was beginning to lose it. I had to get away. I went back to where I was sitting before, hoping Geoffrey would leave me in peace.

An hour or so passed with Geoffrey following me around. Eventually I was able to completely ignore him and although I became bored with their antics, I remained aware he was always within earshot. It was as though he wanted to be able to hear whatever I said to anyone while simultaneously ensuring I could see every action and hear every word of his. Like he wanted to be close in case he suddenly decided he had something to say to me which he didn't want anyone else to hear. It was a very weird game.

The couple of beers I had consumed during the course of the night had taken the edge off my discomfort whilst not totally removing the sense of foreboding. A dark cloud hung over me ready to explode with thunder and lightning. I was sober but almost everyone else was tanked by that stage, especially the birthday boy and his mate from Hell.

Around eleven o'clock, I decided I'd had enough. The party seemed to be breaking up anyway. Some people were going home while others were moving onto the local nightclubs.

The dark and self-absorbed couple, Geoffrey and his woman,

were going out. They didn't say where and I didn't care. I was just relieved at finally being able to get away from him at least for the weekend. A couple of days of tranquility before I had to return to the finishing floor and labour around with a heavy load of spiritual oppression on my back in the form of the High Priest of Sutherland.

I climbed into my red and black Monaro which was parked nose first in the driveway of Felix' house, started the engine and reversed out onto the street. Two other people were in the car with me when I left. One was a friend, the other an acquaintance, and both had chosen me as their designated driver.

After selecting first gear on the floor shifter, I released the clutch and began to slowly move off up the road. Suddenly Geoffrey appeared in front of the car. I stopped to let him cross the road which he commenced to do while raising his hand and nodding in gratitude. Then he stopped. So, did my heart for a second.

Geoffrey looked at me and I looked back at him, but he didn't move. I didn't know what was going on. Why was he just standing there in front of the car grinning like a maniac? What did he want? My throat was dry as I waited nervously for him to move. I have no idea how long he stood there staring at me. It seemed like an eternity but was probably just a few minutes. However long it was, it was totally unnerving. I felt hot. My two passengers started yelling at Geoffrey, calling him names and telling him to move. Not surprisingly, he ignored them.

My mate beside me was really blowing his stack. He opened the door to get out and presumably use whatever necessary force to move Geoffrey off the road.

'Don't!' I ordered, again not wanting any trouble. 'He's moving now.'

'Fucking wanker. What's he doing?'

'He's moving now. Settle down,' I said, trying to contain what was potentially going to be a very violent confrontation. Temperatures were rising. The storm cloud thickened and began to rumble. I feared the worst.

'I should smash the little shit's head in anyway.'

'It's all right. Don't worry about it.'

Geoffrey seemed to move in slow motion and had almost passed my car when I did something inexplicable. Something for which, to this day, I can still not give a reason. Just as he reached the corner of the car I pressed the accelerator and let out the clutch just enough to make the car lurch forward. Next thing I knew, Geoffrey was on the ground.

Laughter erupted inside my car as Geoffrey, embarrassed and maddened, got up quickly and raced around to my side of the car. Grabbing a beer out of his woman's hand he put his face in through the open driver's door window right up close to mine. I could smell the overwhelming stench of beer on his breath. Frozen to my seat, I wondered what he was going to do and waited, expecting him to hit me. All Geoffrey did however was glare at me for a few seconds. My mate was yelling in my ear that I should hit him while I had the chance, but I couldn't move. He was no longer smiling. It was the first time I had seen such intensity on his face. In fact, I don't think I have ever seen such hate. He looked for all the world like he wanted to kill me. Seriously. It was almost funny in a bizarre kind of way.

Then he stepped back from the car and tossed some of the beer in my face.

'Smash him! Let's get the prick,' said my mate who was full of tough talk, but thus far no action. I didn't give him the chance to do anything because I took off almost immediately after receiving Geoffrey's lager shower. Abuse was flying out of the window, but I kept my mouth shut as I watched Geoffrey and his girl disappearing in the rearview mirror.

What had I done? Why on earth did I do that? One brief moment of insanity had almost certainly destroyed what little chance may have remained for me to reach Geoffrey and save him. Was he going to get me now? Put a curse on me? Pursue me like a mad dog? Would he try to hurt me? Kill me even? Whatever the outcome, I had crossed the line. Although I did not hurt Geoffrey when I knocked him down, not physically anyway, there was no doubt his super inflated Hell bound ego was damaged by my involuntary action. What if it had not been an accident, but the chance I had been waiting for all night? If that was the case, then I had much of which to be ashamed. I now had the rest of the weekend to ponder the situation.

On Monday morning, at work, I apologized to Geoffrey as soon as I saw him. It was a sincere apology, offered without explanation or excuse. How could I justify my action anyway? Not surprisingly Geoffrey almost fobbed off my apology as though it was unnecessary. There was neither light in his eyes nor a smile on his face, and I knew he would not forget it. And forgive me? Not a snowflake's chance in Hell. Forgiveness was a foreign concept. Forgiveness opens the door to Heaven, so the Devil wants that door permanently shut. No, Geoffrey would neither forgive nor forget. Now I was not only his spiritual nemesis, but a physical enemy: a marked man.

As the week continued I tried to maintain civility towards Geoffrey and act as if everything was cool between us. He had lied to me and now would not talk to me at all except for the bare minimum required for us to carry out our duties on the finishing floor. The enmity between us was palpable and suffocating. It was killing me. I absolutely dreaded going to work, everyday struggling to face Geoffrey and the hurricane of hate he was projecting on me.

On Thursday I took the day off, feigning illness. Although not physically sick, my soul was in agony. His hatred was oppressive, like a heavy weight forcing me to the ground every time that I tried to rise. I prayed all day for strength and for help and for some solution to this problem. I needed a way out and I knew that only God could provide it for me.

That afternoon, while I was drinking a cup of tea and watching television, Elijah the great prophet of God sprang to mind. The mighty spiritual warrior who challenged the prophets of Baal on Mount Carmel. Grabbing my Bible, I re read the story of Elijah from the Old Testament and God spoke to me through his Word. A challenge. Whose God is greater? Who is the Lord of all creation? The Most High? Who is the real God? I saw it all in my dreams that night and I was filled with hope.

The showdown on Mount Carmel was between the only remaining prophet of the one true God and the multitude of Baal's Prophets. Baal was an invention of the minds of men designed to satisfy their need for religion without forcing them to compromise their debauched and hedonistic lifestyles and customs. Elijah had opposed them from the beginning of his ministry but was in despair before God commanded him to challenge the prophets of Baal on the mountain. He believed that his enemies, being so great in number, would surely kill him and that God would allow Elijah a martyr's death. God had other plans though, and as I empathized with Elijah's predicament, I was shown the answer to my own.

Believing that no matter how hard I might try to convince any of my brothers in Christ of the likeliness, let alone the certainty of success in this endeavour, they would neither believe nor support me, so I kept it to myself. I was young in the faith, just a baby really, and I was without fear or doubt or wisdom. I gave no thought to the possible effects of such direct action. What if I lost? What if nothing happened? If God failed to show up? Naïve. Presumptuous. What if it was all my own idea and I only imagined that God wanted me to throw down the gauntlet to Geoffrey? Was it brazen conjecture on my part to believe that God would choose me to take on this high priest of Satan alone and defeat him? What did I have in mind when I thought of Geoffrey's defeat? Was it death? Embarrassment? A thousand such questions plagued me, but I was bereft of my senses, ensnared in a righteous fantasy.

The next morning at work I told Geoffrey we needed to talk and with transparent disdain and annoyance he consented to hear me out.

'I can't handle this anymore. We're spiritual and mortal enemies. Something must be done. I know that you hate me and wish me harm, so I just want to say that...' I paused, waiting for Geoffrey's reaction. There was none. He was listening to me, but there was not the slightest hint of emotion or interest in his face. I heard the quaver in my voice. 'I want to say that I love you with the love of Christ, and I want you to repent and follow God. Turn from your sin."

'Fuck off!' barked Geoffrey.

'This is your last chance. God has-'

'I said fuck off.'

'I challenge you in the name of Jesus to prove that your master, Satan is more powerful than my God,' I said loudly in a voice foreign to my ears.

Geoffrey actually cringed when I invoked Jesus' name which

really pleased me. However, his voice was no less hard or threatening.

'I could kill you right now. Would that be proof enough for you?'

I could feel my pulse pounding away in my temple as I digested Geoffrey's threat, but I pressed on. There was no turning back now. 'You call on Satan to demonstrate his might and then I will call on God to demonstrate his. Are you familiar with the story of Elijah on Mount Car-'

'Enough with the stories and the bullshit,' said Geoffrey, abruptly terminating another my sentences. 'I accept the challenge,' he said, sneering. Again I wondered whether he was mad.

'When and where?' asked Geoffrey as his devilish grin disappeared.

'The sooner the better right?'

Geoffrey eye's blazed with venom. I was undaunted. 'Bulli lookout at Mt.Ousley. Midnight tonight.'

Silently, he considered. The destination was a problem for him. It was a deliberate choice on my part to make it difficult for him to get to. Easy for me. Thirty-five minutes south by car. Geoffrey did not have a car or even a driver's license as far as I knew. There was chance of me offering him another ride anywhere ever again. Of course, on this occasion it would have been quite a sporting gesture, but this was not sport. This was eternity. Life and death.

Bulli Lookout offered a beautiful panoramic view of the city of Wollongong far below. It was the nearest and closest thing to Mount Carmel I could think of. Although fairly isolated, I was confident that if Geoffrey was as serious as he made out to be, he would find a way to get there. My confidence was growing, rapidly expanding as my faith ballooned. A small mustard seed had grown into a towering tree.

'Okay?' I asked a still pensive Geoffrey. I imagined I had him on the back foot.

'Midnight?'

'Midnight.'

'I'll see you there Christian.'

He meant it to sound contemptuous, spitting it out but I was thrilled. Surely my challenge had surprised him. Surely now I held the upper hand. There was nothing left to do but get through the rest of the day and wait for night to fall on Mt. Ousley. Geoffrey and I said nothing more to one another during the remainder of the shift. When working together, we worked in silence, each lost in our own thoughts and prayers.

Four o'clock rolled around and I went home. There was no need to confirm the details of the meeting. If Geoffrey didn't show up it would mean victory for me.

I was sitting on a large rock at Bulli lookout when Geoffrey arrived. My Monaro was parked deliberately in an obvious place out in the open: impossible to miss. However, I positioned myself out of view, but from where I could still see my car and the entry gate. I was invisible when a pair of headlights shone into the carpark and I knew that it was Geoffrey even before I saw his face. He was early. So was I. My heart began to beat faster. I swallowed hard as nervous excitement threatened to cause me to vomit.

It was a clear night, cool and bright thanks to a full moon perched in the cloudless sky. Geoffrey was dressed in black as usual and it struck me how much he must have hated having to wear an all white uniform at Parke-Davis: an amusing irony.

He walked quickly towards me and then straight past me to a portion of flat ground where the grass had died from being so frequently trampled upon by tourists, and all that remained was a bowl of dust. Geoffrey had apparently spotted that location early and decided it would be a suitable position from where he could do whatever it was that he intended to do. I was very curious. Having seen Hollywood style Satanic rituals I could only imagine what sort of show lay ahead. Would it be like the movies with smoke and fire and blood and demons flying around or much less dramatic? I was eager to find out.

First Geoffrey stamped down and smoothed out the dirt with his feet and then he knelt down and drew a pentagram with his finger. I noticed that he took some time and extra care with the star once he had drawn the outside circle. When he finished, Geoffrey stood in the centre of the pentagram facing east away from me, towards the panoramic view of the black ocean framed city. I could hear his voice, low and steady. A continuous droning sound as he went through all his preparations. I supposed he was praying or incanting or chanting or whatever his unholy church called their supplications.

Wondering how long all this was going to take, I stole a glance at my watch: five past midnight.

Smart remarks kept popping into my head, but I held my tongue, resisting the urge to call out to Geoffrey. Remembering how Elijah had taunted the prophets of Baal, suggesting among other things, that perhaps their god was busy on the toilet as they tried unsuccessfully to summon him, I felt like doing the same thing. I continued to watch in silent fascination.

Next Geoffrey removed his clothes. All his clothes. Fortunately, he had his back to me. His murmuring continued unabated, his voice undulating, loud then soft again. Quavering, almost melodic and mostly unintelligible. It sounded like an alien language, probably Latin I guessed. A dead language being used appropriately by a fool courting spiritual death. A dead man walking.

I was beginning to feel restless: bored, not afraid. Believing that God was going to show his power tonight both pleased and thrilled me.

The performance went on and on. Sometimes Geoffrey would kneel, other times he would lay prostrate, but most often he stood with his hands raised to the heavens imploring his master to visit Mt.Ousley. I wondered why he was looking to Heaven. A further half hour passed with all this business going on and I could no longer contain myself.

'It's taking a bit of time Geoffrey. Is everything alright? Is he busy or caught in traffic? Delayed? You know, unforeseen circumstances?' The thought of the Devil being delayed cracked me up and I began to laugh. To his credit, Geoffrey completely ignored me and continued his performance. My mood was lighthearted and carefree because it seemed pretty obvious the Devil would not be making an appearance this night. It was not necessarily the outcome I had anticipated. Without a confrontation between the forces of Good and Evil it was certainly an anticlimax. I sighed, disappointed; cheated.

'Geoffrey,' I said, 'That's enough mate. One hour gone. It looks like your master is not going to back you up this time. He's probably betrayed you. He's good at that.'

He stubbornly continued with his prayers and incantations oblivious to my jibes.

'Geoffrey,' I called, louder now. 'Geoffrey. Geoff. Geoff!'

He carried on as though he was alone. 'C'mon, man. Give it a rest. It's a no show. He's let you down.'

Suddenly Geoffrey fell to the ground heavily. Flat on his face, lying still as though dead. I thought about going over to see if he was all right, but before I could move I saw a dark shadow appear above his lifeless body. It was formless like smoke, shifting and swirling like clouds on a windy day. The moon still shone down on us, but the breeze had ceased. In the deathly quiet, I shivered with cold and sudden fear as I watched Geoffrey stand up inside the shadow and turn to face me. The dark cloud cloaked him, obscuring his features, clinging to him and encasing him. Then it spoke. I could not see if his mouth was moving, but the voice was definitely not Geoffrey's.

'Sorry about the delay,' said the Devil sarcastically in a deep, guttural tone. 'I was held up in traffic.' His laughter sounded like thunder, causing the hair on the back of my neck to stand to attention.

Now I was really freaked out. Satan was speaking to me and I didn't like it. Worse still, he was trying to be funny. I wanted nothing at all to do with the Lord of the Abyss. When he started to speak again, courage came from somewhere to fill me and I shouted back at him from pure instinct. 'Jesus is Lord! Jesus is Lord! In the name of Jesus, I command you to leave. Get lost! Get the hell out of here, in Jesus' name.' I kept on yelling my rebuke at the shadowy figure of the dark lord until I was hoarse. Then he was gone. Disappeared. Geoffrey crumpled to the ground like a puppet whose strings had just been cut by the puppeteer.

Still bellowing at the Devil long after he had vanished, I became aware of a power coursing through my body. I felt strong and bold. Invincible. The victory was won.

While I celebrated, Geoffrey was waking slowly as if from a deep sleep. Groggy and disoriented, he eventually managed to gain his bearings and struggle to his feet. After a brief search, he found his clothes nearby and obviously embarrassed by his nudity, put them on as quickly as he could.

'Do you know what happened Geoffrey?' I asked quietly.

After giving the question some thought he answered confidently, 'Yeah. I guess the Master showed up.'

'He did, but as soon as he arrived I told him to go in Jesus' name and he did. I guess that makes me the winner of this little contest of ours. Are you all right by the way?'

'I haven't seen God here tonight,' said Geoffrey defiantly. Driven by obscene pride, he was unwilling to concede defeat.

'I rebuked the Devil in Jesus' name. He's gone. I won. My God is the true God. The most powerful. The mightiest!' I said triumphantly.

'Cut the preachy shit. The Devil showed. Where is your saviour? The Christ. Where is he?'

Geoffrey was still blind. He had not seen therefore he did not believe. The Prince of Darkness had chewed him up and spat him out. Discarding his body when he was finished with it, throwing him down like an unloved rag doll.

A cool wind kicked up and blew into my back carrying my words quickly to Geoffrey. 'Repent! For the kingdom of Heaven is near,' I cried out.

'Repent this,' said Geoffrey as he gave me a one fingered salute. 'Fuck off loser. I'm outta here. My soul is the Devil's. I sold it long ago for power, and I have power,' screamed Geoffrey. Screamed like he was out of his mind, stretching the words to enhance them. He walked slowly away, turning back to me a couple of times, cursing me and swearing unspeakable profanities against God. I continued to plead with him and tell him that time was running out for him.

135

Suddenly Geoffrey burst into flames before my eyes. Horrified, I ran to him immediately as he fell to the ground and started rolling to try to extinguish the flames violently engulfing him. By the time I reached him only a few seconds had passed but he was already dead. Charred beyond recognition. The stench of his burning corpse made me gag. A furious supernatural fire had taken him. Geoffrey's horrific demise shocked and saddened me. All I could do was stand there and cry as I recalled the words of scripture saying that it was not God's will that anyone should perish.

Twelve

The Road through Hell

(first published in *Champagne Shivers, 2007,* and again in *short.story.me, October 2012*)

'Slow down!'

'Why?' said Pete, easing his foot off the accelerator slightly. 'It's three o'clock in the bloody morning. The coppers are asleep. Gimme that bottle!'

'It's dangerous,' replied his long-suffering girlfriend, Kelly, before reluctantly handing him the bottle. She was used to his penchant for speeding and criminal disregard for safety. An urgent reminder in the form of loud verbal abuse was usually all it took to bring him back into line, even if it never lasted very long.

'It's so dark,' she said.

'It's night time, stupid!'

They always travelled at night. In fact, they did everything at night. She didn't really know why, it was just the way they were. Living a life of occasional highs under a smothering blanket of darkness.

A sign appeared on the left of the narrow highway, shining briefly in the unearthly glare of the headlights. Kelly read it out loud in a tone of forced interest, as she often did, mocking Debra Winger's senile father in *Forget Paris*.

Welcome to Hell.
A New South Wales tidy town.
pop. 653

'Wanna spend a night in Hell honey?'

'Why don't you drive right on through to Heaven instead?' said Kelly, trying to sound flippant. She had never felt more afraid and it wasn't just the name of the town.

A shadow moved on to the road ahead and stayed out in front of them for a few seconds. Then it disappeared. Did she imagine it? It returned, quickly growing as though inflated by an invisible compressor, and began to form into a ragged sphere. What was it? Could Pete see it?

She pointed, but Pete was already looking, straining for a better view.

'What the hell was that?'

He flicked the high beams off, then on again to see if it was a trick of light. No trick. The shape grew larger still and was soon joined by another, then another.

Pete gripped the wheel in panic, his blood starved hands shared a ghostly luminescence which shone on his face, but he did not slow down.

'Is it an animal? I can't see. I can't tell!'

Kelly was frozen, suffocating behind a mask of awful terror as she watched a third shape ooze up from underneath the road. The three things maintained their speed and kept themselves just in front of the car before suddenly merging into one. The new shapeless entity was bigger than the car.

As they stared in dumb horror, a huge misshapen head extended from the centre of the black formless mass, followed quickly by two arms, then two long and powerful legs. It was running!

Kelly screamed as it turned to look over its shoulder at them. Accompanied by a wide toothless smile, two bloodshot eyeballs floated in a sea of torn flesh, gawking mischievously.

Madness gripped Pete, insane fear drove him to press harder on the accelerator as the monstrous apparition turned its whole hulking frame to face them. Still running, backwards now, it laughed at them.

'I'll kill you, get off the road, I'll kill you!' roared Pete.

'I'll kill you, get off the road, I'll kill you!' mimicked the beast, its disturbingly deep and raspy voice amplified inside the car.

In the same instant the running creature put up his open palmed hands and stopped dead in the middle of the road, the car crashed into a tree and split in two. Flung like worthless trash, the twisted halves of metal and plastic sped through the cold night air in opposite directions, carrying human debris with them.

* * *

The crumpled bodies of the young couple were discovered the next morning, on either side of a sign post which stood like a sentinel in a grassy field. The doctor rose from his knees and nodded to the police sergeant who pulled a blanket over the face of the woman. He looked at the sign and sadly shook his head as he read.

Welcome to Hell.
We have two graveyards and no hospitals.
Please drive carefully.

Thirteen

My Amygdala

Sometimes, when it's quiet, I can remember what my life was like before moving to Cedar Springs. When my thoughts had sharp edges, and my feelings were distinctly outlined by a shadow of self-control. Before the lines began to blur, running together like water colours in rain. A time when I was in control, or at the very least, when I confidently clung to the illusion of control as most of my fellow human beings do. Before moving to Cedar Springs, I was unhinging slowly, like a door which was being used as playground equipment. To say this move was important would be to grossly understate the fact. This move was life saving. This quiet and secluded house in Nowheresville had become my savior, and if my amygdala could have spoken, it would have cried with gratitude. Or would it?

The doctor had said it several times, as though I needed to know not only what it meant but how to pronounce it. A –myg-da-la. I was much more interested in what had gone wrong with it. I shook as I sat and listened: the lid on my anger barely restrained by the firm grip of my wife's hand on my arm. I had felt Alison's strength on previous occasions as it flowed from her hand through my body. It had been sufficient on all but two occasions. Now, as a direct result of the last of those occasions, she walked with a limp. And a proud scar bisected her left eyebrow as testimony to her bravery. I knew I should have run away from this woman who I had loved since the hormonal surge of adolescence propelled me towards manhood. If only for her sake, to protect her, but I was too afraid. Too scared to leave. Besides I didn't know where to go. I often wished that when my lips devoured hers, I could have sucked courage from her like a baby suckles nourishment from its mother's breast.

The doctor had worn an expression of practiced sympathy as he sighed and spoke to Alison. I remembered his exact words.

'We don't properly understand what has caused this damage nor do we have any means to repair it.'

A sudden dramatic sadness collapsed on me when I saw a single tear roll down Alison's cheek. I had wanted to speak, to offer some solace but I was incapable: paralyzed by the darkest melancholy. The realization that I would not get better was disturbing. My impotence as a comforter to my wife was humiliating. We both cried together inside a hopeless embrace.

Two months have passed, and I have not hurt Alison or myself. Somehow, I have managed not to break anything. I feel relatively calm. As calm as I ever am or can be. Lithonate apparently works well, to control the wild impulses associated with the manic phase of bi polar disorder, but I'm not bi polar. The doctor described my condition as something very much like it. He gave me a library of literature on bi polar and related mental illnesses, with a caveat that I was not bi polar and the research on the role of the amygdala was still in its early stages, so although some of the information may prove helpful, I should not count on it. I should not, he stressed, hang my hopes on it providing answers or solutions. I recall wanting to stuff all those brochures down his throat and watch him choke to death on them.

I never read a single word in those brochures because I cannot see how knowing what might be wrong with me, can assist me to carry on living with something less than the complete desperation that I feel most of the time. I take the pills I have been prescribed and I attended a series of therapy sessions. I also try to make healthy life choices, which for me means that I don't start drinking until after lunch, and I torment myself on an elliptical cross trainer, albeit infrequently. I have very strong and emotionally intense memory flashes, but I have learned how to manage them. The therapy sessions equipped me pretty well. I feel depressed, and then elated, then depressed again before a callous attack of one phobia or another leads me back down into the hole of abject misery. I am exhausted, so I sleep often, though never for more than a few hours. I live alone, and never leave the house in Cedar Springs. It is a fortress built to keep the protagonists in my private war in, rather than out. I am a menace, and I know it.

The telephone rings. Twice, then it stops. It rings again immediately, three times, then stops. When it sounds again, I pick it up and rest the receiver against my ear, breathing as quietly as I can though my heart is hammering in my chest, and I feel like I am suffocating.

'Bailey. It's me.'

'I know.'

'Then why don't you say anything when you pick up?'

I ignore Alison's question, partly because I figure she doesn't really want to know, but mostly because I don't know. She always contacts me using that agreed upon code, and every day

I respond with the same inexplicable paranoia.

'What are you doing?'

'Sitting.'

'Just sitting?'

'Uh-huh.'

Words were dancing through my mind like fairies in an enchanted forest: words with no discernible intent. I can't speak. I'm glad she doesn't expect me to. I feel hot and cold, feverish, as I listen to Alison talk about her day. She is trying to keep me connected but we both know that whatever binds a person to the society in which they live, has in my case, been terminally severed. I mumble and grunt in what I reason are appropriate places for such interjections. I am starting to experience heightened anxiety when I hear Alison say that she has to get back to work, but I don't know if it is because I am going to lose her again, or if some unspeakable evil is lurking at my door. There is always some hideous little beast waiting to pounce on me and tear me apart. That is what I fear now, as I say with as much sincerity as I can summon, 'I love you too. Bye.'

I hear laughter: the snickering of a mischievous child. Footsteps precede giggling. Stupid little girls hanging around outside the freak's windows trying to frighten themselves. Just having fun at my expense. Fun. Hilarity. I roar with amusement: a laugh so violent that I forget to breathe and am forced to the floor in a gagging fit. I laugh at myself. At the silly curious girls. At the absurdity of my imprisonment. And I laugh at my amygdala until my energy is totally depleted.

An alarm sounds, but I don't recognize it at first. Initially, I confuse it with the sound of my voice which I notice has become shrill and hoarse. The alarm is a reminder to take another pill, and although I have not eaten lunch, it is after twelve, so I can legally, according to my laws, wash the Lithonate down with a cold Carlton Draught. Great ads they make, I think. So funny. Funny? No, my laughter tank is dry. Clever. Who? Me or the beer ads? Pill? Yes please, and can I have fries with that? No, wait, on second thoughts, I'll take salad. After all, I'm supposed to be making healthy choices. Choices? Cigarettes. Do I smoke? I look at my watch and remember the Lithonate. I also notice that I have been standing still for half an hour. I feel a little better now.

I take my pill and swill my Carlton Draught in between puffs on a cigarette which surprisingly tastes stale. Maybe, I quit and forgot to throw these ones away. As I settle in my favourite chair in front of the television, my mind piggybacks my body into tranquility. My amygdala informs me, indirectly of course, that everything is all right for now. For now. This is my existence. I turn on the television and see straight edges and distinct shapes, and my hope is renewed.

Familiar voices soothe like Aloe Vera on sunburned skin. I know these people on the television, but they don't know me. I think my obscurity is an advantage, but I can't explain why. No one would ever ask anyway because I don't have conversations. When the need arises - and thank God that is seldom - I can fake it with the best of them. They're all fakers. I know that too. It's comforting to be certain about some things in my life even though those things are so few in number, I can count them on one hand.

What do I know? Upon which facts can I suspend my existence? I'm alive. I live alone. I don't really belong anywhere or with anyone. Alison loves me. I'm grappling with the vagueness caused by ineffective synapses in my brain, searching for the fifth thing. Hoping like crazy that I can seize it and even, dare I dream, make it to my other hand and then I will have really achieved something today. I take a breath and glance over to the bookshelf stuffed with dust covered silverfish boarding houses. I can't read anymore. I just don't enjoy it. I'm busy lamenting my loss of literary interest when I hear Alison's voice. Although it's unmistakable, the most recognizable voice in my life, I hesitate as I try to figure out how I could be hearing her. I do hear voices. That's not unusual, but I've never heard Alison. When I look at the television screen, I see her. She's doing an ad for a local pharmacy. Someone switches on a kettle in my stomach and I can feel the awful churning commence, the bubbling of emotions. I remember Alison studying for her degree, studying fervently, giving it everything she had. I recall criticizing her and calling her a dreamer. High school drop outs don't go on to university, earn degrees and get high paying jobs, I said. She cried whenever I was mean to her, and she cried when I inevitably apologized, but I kept on hurting her. I didn't mean to. I've never intended to hurt anyone. I smile, but it's a pathetic one like the seven hundredth cheesy grin you've had to force for the endless photo shoot at a wedding. I'm glad Alison and I never married.

I was well when we met, perfectly well and we were perfectly happy. We crashed headlong into love from the first night we met at a mutual friend's birthday party. We talked and laughed. We flirted, we connected – there's an overused word– and I remember wishing that I could stay with her all night. Spellbound, I was trapped in her intoxicating energy. By the time I started having trouble with my amygdala, we were so deeply in love and committed to one another that we thought we could win. Foolishly, we believed that we were strong enough to overcome anything. The fairy tale ending would be ours. We deserved it. We were so wrong.

Looking at Alison, I see a princess. But she's not my princess. She's beautiful, kind, generous and intelligent. She's dogged as well though, and underneath her sweet and soft veneer, is a warrior. But she's not my warrior. I realize I'm crying when I can no longer clearly see her face. The ad ends with a happy jingle and an invitation to visit the store for the lowest prices and the best service. I want to go to her. I stand up, but the room is spinning and I have to sit down. I won't be going to see her. I never leave my prison. I can't. Nothing is stopping me of course, except my own fear. I shudder and push my palms hard against my forehead. Can I reach my amygdala this way? Can I stop it? Can I crush this cruel dictator? I need some more pills. Did I miss the alarm? What time is it? Someone is yelling at me, telling me to get off my fat backside and do something useful. Be a man and stop wasting your life, it says. It sounds like my father, even though I never knew him. Or did I? I stand again, suddenly infused with anger. I want to hit something. Smash the source of that taunting voice. I feel hot as I listen carefully. Straining.

'It's only the size of an almond and you let it control your life,' says the voice.

I still can't tell from where these evil jibes emanate. I respond: 'Actually it's not a single entity. It's a set of neurons located deep in the medial temporal lobe.' Where did that come from?

'Good for you. You know your enemy.'

'It's enlarged,' I continue. 'Damaged, so that it doesn't function properly. That's why I suffer all these mental problems.'

'Did you know that it shrinks by thirty percent in males after castration?'

147

'Who are you?'

I realize I have walked into the kitchen during this conversation with an imaginary protagonist. A sense of déjà vu accompanies me. Maybe it's a good thing that my memory is faulty. When it works as it should, I have an overwhelming feeling that I have the same conversations every day, and do the same things. I don't know if this is true or not. It's not one of the five things I know for sure. That's right, the five things I know for sure. I recall trying to think of the fifth thing before I was distracted by the Warrior Princess on the television. Then it comes like a kingfisher dive bombing the surface of a creek for a feed: my amygdala is faulty, and it is to blame for my miserable existence. I am conscious of my shoulders sagging slowly under the weight of that depressing thought. I need a better one: a happy thought. I open the fridge. Everything is bright and fresh in there. so I stand and stare, allowing the cold air to refresh me and renew my hope once more. Then it comes to me like benevolent lightning from heaven. Fact number six: I like beer. It's been a great day. I did something good and I can't wait to tell Alison all about it, if I can remember when she calls.

Fourteen

The Devil Wears a Dressing Gown

~~~ ❧❧❧ ~~~

'No! I don't want to.' James' tone was increasingly defiant as he stood metaphorically face to face with his exasperated mother.

'C'mon James. It'll be fun. We'll all go together. C'mon,' said Michael, trying gentle persuasion as the primary anti-recalcitrance tactic. It was, after all, what the childcare gurus recommended. According to their collective wisdom there was no point in being aggressive and overbearing. You have to reason with children. They deserve respect and parents need to help their children see for themselves the benefits of obedience. Michael was not totally convinced that was always the right approach, but he had to concede that it did work occasionally, and it was definitely an easier way of conducting parent-child relationships.

Having apparently decided the discussion was over, James turned away from his father and started to fiddle around with some of his toy cars which were lying on the floor beside an overstuffed cabinet.

'James. Put your cars away. We have to go now.'

Michael was starting to boil on the inside. Despite hating himself for having a short fuse, he was powerless to halt the flood of negative emotions which seemed to have become more frequent since the birth of James' little sister, Alana.

His toddler ignored him, so he went over to him and pulled the cars out of his hands and repeated the order, 'Put your cars away! We have to go now.'

Having his toys taken off him by anyone at any time was sufficient cause for James to act his age. Three. First came the roars of protest then the tears. 'Want my car Daddy. My car Daddy. My car Daddy, Dad, Dad.'

'You can take a car or two with you if you change your clothes first.' Why was it always so hard to accomplish simple things? It sounded so reasonable to her, she was sure James would relent. After gentle persuasion comes insistence and when insistence only incites the predictable tantrum the next weapon in a parent's arsenal is bribery. It was a clever play. By including James' cars in the deal Michael had taken his son's mind off their destination.

James stopped crying and sat up on the floor, his face contorting dramatically through whatever mental processes were occurring. Finally, he consented and trotted off to his room. After fifteen long minutes, during which he frequently emphasized the return of his car, to make sure of the terms of the contract, he was dressed. Through gritted teeth, Michael endured his usual tricks like putting both feet in one leg of his trousers or shorts.

As he reveled silently in his ultimate victory, his wife Joanne entered the room.

'You told me to get ready. I'm ready. I don't see what the rush is anyway. He doesn't even know we are coming. What difference does it make if we are a little late?'

'We aren't a little late,' said Michael. 'We're a lot late. I don't want to be fiddling around here all day.'

'How do you know he doesn't know we're coming? Maybe he's sitting there right now wondering where we are. Watching the clock. Waiting.'

Stifling a giggle, Joanne answered sarcastically. 'Sure.' When Michael simply stood there, she continued, 'He's your grandfather. You know that not only is he not expecting us, but he won't even remember who we are when we get there. And five minutes after we've introduced ourselves he'll been asking our names again.'

Michael bit his tongue, before speaking with resignation 'Come on then. Let's go.'

* * *

Joanne was right again, of course. He wasn't mad at her though. He was just upset at the thought of seeing his grandad who until a few months ago had been a strong and agile - both physically and mentally - septuagenarian with a twinkle in his eye. At seventy five he was one of the younger residents of the Havendale nursing home and retirement village. The sudden downturn in his health had caught everyone by surprise, himself included. It was only seven days after his first fall, that they moved him out of his own self care unit and into the nursing home.

Harry had dismissed the first accident, brushing it aside by saying it was a freak occurrence, an isolated incident. Nothing to worry about. Stop fussing, he would always say. Michael had accepted his grandad's reassurances, albeit with some suspicion.

However, the second fall was much more serious and could

not be so lightly downplayed. On that occasion Harry hit his head on the corner of a coffee table on his way to the floor after apparently fainting. Two days of blurred vision and headaches followed. Five stitches were required to close the gash just above his left eye. Naturally he had every conceivable test conducted to ensure there was no permanent damage, and they kept him under surveillance in hospital for a full day and night. Ultimately the tests showed nothing. Harry seized on the negative results as an opportunity to remind his family that they were making much ado about nothing. He simply was not prepared to admit that there was anything wrong and the fact there was no hard, medical evidence to suggest otherwise, justified his opinion. Michael believed it was most likely false bravado.

A couple of days after Harry had been moved into the nursing home, he had a third fall which eradicated any lingering doubt.

'Sorry? What?' Suddenly Michael realized that Joanne was asking him a question and his response was suitably bewildered. 'What did you say? What was the question?'

The open front door admitted a view of the front lawn bathed in bright sunshine. Michal smiled. Outside was another world.

'No question,' said Joanne smiling sympathetically. 'I said for you to go ahead. I've just got to go to the toilet. I'll be there in a second.'

With his thoughts returned fully to the present, Michael ushered James towards the front door. 'Let's go mate.'

'Mummy go too? And 'Lana?' enquired James.

'Uh-huh.'

Reluctantly, James agreed to go ahead. It seemed as though sometimes he simply could not stand the thought of his parents being apart. Obviously, without being able to name it or describe it, he fully understood the concept of family and Michael intended not to disappoint him or disillusion him. It would be hard enough as he grew up to deal with the fact that his maternal grandparents no longer lived together or loved one another. Unfortunately, James' view of family did not appear to extend to include his great grandfather Harry whom he had only seen on a couple of occasions. Each time had been a very short visit and James had clung to Michael, more fearfully than he usually did in the company of strangers, for the duration of the stay. There was no reason for James to be so afraid, and it contributed the extreme awkwardness of these regular visits. Michael kept hoping things would improve, but the situation had in fact deteriorated.

Harry always talked to his eldest grandson pleasantly. Said hello, asked him how he was, and complimented James on his good looks, which he never failed to mention could not possibly have come from his father. Despite Harry's best efforts, James never warmed to him and it was so disappointing. Joanne was more philosophical about it, reasoning that James could hardly be expected to take a shine to a man with whom he had only spent several hours - a mere three hours out of his three years on the planet – but Michael didn't buy it; neither was he willing to accept it.

One possible solution was to visit his grandad more often and to take James with him. The expected increase in frequency of visits never eventuated and that really was something which Michael regretted, although not deeply enough to actually do anything about it. If there was one thing about which Michael could be, and often was, critical of himself, it was that his propensity for stalling. He was a chronic procrastinator. He was a 'gonna' rather than a 'doer'.

'Daddy's new car broke?' said James as they approached the

car.

'No, mate,' said Michael, patiently going through the details for the umpteenth time. 'We had to buy a new car because the old car was broken and could not be fixed. We don't use it anymore. The new car is not broken.'

'Daddy fix it? Sure, daddy?'

Michael marveled at James' confidence in his father's ability to mend anything. No matter how Michael might insist something was beyond repair, James would always counter with those words *daddy fix it, sure.* If only all things could be repaired as easily as James believed they could. For now, Michael was comfortable about fostering that illusion because he knew in time James would find out that his father was not perfect and there were things which could not be fixed; like Harry's rapid decline, and possibly James' troubling grandfather phobia.

'Yes mate,' said Michael, opening the car door, and helping helped James up into his seat, even though when he wanted to go somewhere he was more than capable of climbing in by himself.

It was both a wonderful thing and an annoyance to be so wanted, to be so necessary.

Soon after James was buckled in, Joanne came down the driveway to the car with Alana perched on her hip. She would probably need some help to get Alana secured in her seat. She was a real firecracker, full of beans, as they say. Small in size for her age but strong, active and healthy looking. Her brown hair was growing out straight and even, and she had big beautiful brown eyes, just like her brother. Currently going through a third wave of teething, Alana stuck out her lower jaw like a bulldog due to the irritation. When angry, she looked frightening.

James was growing impatient. 'Come on, Mummy. Daddy. Go out now.'

Joanne already looked weary and hassled although they had not even left the driveway yet. Michael suspected it was probably the way both of them looked most of the time. Organizing and preparing children for an outing of any size could be a very trying exercise. The logistics of mounting such expeditions were staggering.

'You all right, Babe?' asked Michael sympathetically.

'Yes,' she said quickly. 'No. Can you give me a hand please?'

Alana had reached a time in her life when the car seat was no longer an acceptable arrangement for travelling. She twisted and turned. Squiggled, squirmed and screamed, but eventually Michael and Joanne together succeeded in locking her safely in and they were at last ready to hit the road.

The forty five minute drive to Havendale was uneventful. Michael's thoughts were also on Harry and no matter how hard he tried to quell his nerves, the butterflies continued to dance in his stomach. Having had plenty of practice, he was usually able to avoid arousing his wife's suspicions about whether he was really listening to her or not. However, the T-shirt she had bought him for Father's Day made Michael wonder sometimes if he was as clever as he thought. The white T-shirt read:

'My wife says that I never listen to her
At least I think that was she says.'

By the time they arrived James had also fallen asleep. Looking at his son, Michael wondered how tired a person would have to be to be able to fall asleep in such an awkward position. The top half of his body faced the door while the bottom half pointed straight to the front of the car, except for his left leg which was bent and folded underneath his right leg. In between his head and the door was sandwiched a pillow and his chin rested on his chest. Michael noticed he had also undone his seatbelt. Something for which he would have to be reprimanded later. His immediate problem was how to get James out of the car. Would it be better to work out some way to lift his twenty kilogram son out without waking him, or just wake him up and save Michael's back?

When attempts to rouse James with a few gentle words failed, Michael tried to lift him. He grumbled and grizzled, acknowledging his father's presence, but he did not wake. It mattered not whether he was woken prematurely by someone or something, or whether he stirred from sleep in his own time, James was prone to be in a sour mood.

As he debated the issue with himself, Michael recalled the occasion of James' second birthday. A party had been organized by Joanne for James' little friends and their mums and dads. All the guests had arrived and were busy doing the things the party goers do: eating, drinking, talking, playing and, in the case of toddlers squabbling, but the birthday boy was still asleep. His morning nap had gone into overtime. After almost an hour, he stumbled out of his room groggy from deep sleep and got the shock of his short life. The room was full of noisy, lively people. It was too much for the little bloke, so he buried his head in Joanne's lap and cried. Eventually, James cheered up and joined the revelers, and before long he was tearing around the place, wreaking havoc. Once warmed up and in the right frame of mind, James was just as full of life as the next toddler. Cheeky, naughty, and possessive of his things, but he sure was a slow starter.

'C'mon mate. We're here. Get out now. Can you get down by yourself?' asked Michael, knowing full well what the answer would be.

'No!' moaned James. 'Up Daddy, up.'

Havendale sat sprawled among a forest of gum trees. With shaded, winding access lanes and footpaths, and neatly manicured gardens it looked like a holiday resort. Its residents were on their final vacation.

Michael sighed and looked to the heavens.

Joanne removed Alana from her seat without waking her. Then she stood with her daughter cradled in her left arm and a bag in her right hand, waiting for James and Michael.

The current all-purpose travel bag for the family was a Bananas in Pyjamas back pack which, aside from the fact it could not stand alone, contained many pockets and was a good size to use for either short visits or day trips. The kit included a change of clothes for Alana and pants for James in case of accident. Three or four nappies, Amolin nappy rash cream, baby wipes, a couple of bibs, a light blanket, a bottle of milk, breast or formula and one of water, a couple of spoons, a jar of a baby food, and a few toys, rattles and other brightly coloured objects designed to amuse Alana when she inevitably became restless.

'Let me take the bag, Babe,' offered Michael reaching out to relieve his overburdened wife.

'No. It's all right. I can manage.'

'Give it to me!'

'It's all right. I said I have it,' she said stubbornly.

So much conflict, fighting over who should work harder. How ridiculous. As Michael watched Joanne power on ahead, he was staggered by her mule-headedness. Why was everything such a battle.

'Your Mother is very pig headed.'

'Mummy not a pig, daddy. Don't say that,' said James.

Despite James' protestations which began immediately after his defense of his mother, Michael remained hopeful that perhaps this time his son would warm a little to Harry. This was a man whom Michael loved very much. He had a swagful of very pleasant memories of times spent with his grandad as a boy growing up. Trips to the zoo, to the movies and fishing in the Georges River where Harry once landed five large fish while everyone else looked on in amazement, staring into empty catch buckets. Later that morning Michael had actually hooked a toadfish. Thrilled to feel the first tug on the line and then to finally land his first fish, the disappointment of finding out the puffer he had just reeled in was inedible and had to be thrown back in to the river almost put him off fishing completely.

Harry was really good with his hands. From furniture to toys, his own workshop and all its fittings. Michael believed there was probably nothing his grandad could not build with a few pieces of wood, a handful of nails, and a hammer. He fondly remembered the set of cricket stumps Harry had made for him which he still had and looked forward to using, along with his size five Slazenger bat, to teach James how to play when he was old enough.

A man strong in character as well as physique, Harry was well liked by his peers. He spent a good deal of time both before and after his retirement, engaged in voluntary work with Legacy, an organization which looks after war widows and their children. Harry himself was a paratrooper in the second world war although he never spoke of it to Michael. In fact, Michael recalled very little conversation with his grandad.

Their relationship was more about doing and being together, than talking.

Michael had to wonder, as he continued his reminiscing, to what extent he had romanticized his childhood and his relationship as a boy with Harry. By contrast he recalled very little time spent with his own father during those same years. His dad was more of a shadowy figure. The mind can be deceiving, play tricks and distorting reality. Perhaps Michael, for whatever reason, had demonized, his own father while at the same time glorifying his grandfather. Maybe his dad was not quite the distant stranger, the absentee father, that he had believed him to be.

Pushing through the double glass doors with James still clinging to him like a cat stuck up a telegraph pole, Michael was struck by the coolness of the Havendale lounge. It was not a hot day. Low twenties, bright and sunny, yet the air conditioning was turned up high. Michael shivered, not just from the cold, but also from the thought that morgues were probably just as cold, if not colder, in order to preserve the corpses until they could be ultimately disposed of. He had heard it said that nursing homes were God's waiting rooms. and sadly. He looked around, inhaling the inertia of the frail and elderly. Amongst the weathered faces, he saw only a few flickering flames in a burnt-out forest of humanity.

Havendale was an unpleasant place to visit despite the best efforts of the designers of the facility and the staff who showed such diligent compassion to the residents.

He hoped to see Harry who, if by some slim chance remembered they were coming to visit him, should have been waiting in the lounge. The search was in vain.

'He's not here,' said Michael dejectedly.

159

'He'll be in his room,' suggested Joanne. 'I'll wait here.'

Visitors were generally advised to conduct their visits in the lounge as the bedrooms were small and began to burst at the seams with the addition of just one visitor. Not only were the rooms small, they were also cluttered, crammed with as many personal possessions as could be squeezed in. The rooms were, after all, designed to accommodate one person with limited needs and the sad fact was that many of Havendale's residents received very few visitors, if any at all.

Alana came to life and started to bounce up and down on Joanne's lap as she sat on a sofa in the lounge. Her cute, chubby, little legs were pumping with all the power they could muster. A few of the elderly folk seated nearby watched Alana bounce and clap her hands, smiles forming on their craggy faces. Those who could, leaned a little closer. Michael even saw one lady reaching out with both hands.

Noticing a familiar face among the nursing staff, he approached her to enquire after Harry. She was busy trying to coax an old chap to take his medicine and as Michael came closer he heard the stubborn gent say: "Don't trouble yourself, love. I feel fine today. I don't need the pills today. I feel good really. I'm all right. Don't make a fuss."

It sounded like he had attended denial classes, probably conducted by Harry. Michael observed the exchange with melancholic amusement.

'Mr.Emmett, please,' said Dominique, still using an even tone and exercising great patience. 'If you don't take your medicine, you could get very ill, very quickly. It might even kill you. Now you don't want to leave us yet, do you?'

He stopped shaking his head and looked Dominique directly in the eyes. 'Maybe, I do,' he said.

Exasperated, Dominique turned away sharply which brought her face to face with Michael.

'Mr Castlenau,' said Dominique, stifling signs of being flustered. 'What can I do for you?'

'I'm looking for Grandad. Harry? Where is he? In his room?'

'Yes, I believe so. I haven't seen him this afternoon, so I would imagine that's exactly where he is. Please excuse me.'

Dominique was unusually abrupt on this occasion and Michael suspected there might be more to it than just mule headed Mr.Emmett.

'James can you get down now please, mate?' Michael's arms had wearied of the weight of his son, so he lowered him to the floor, ignoring James complaints. Fortunately, James quickly accepted the ride was over and consented to walking beside Michael, holding his hand tightly.

As they walked down the corridor to Harry's room, Michael was aware that James was dawdling, but not for any reason other than he thought that it was fun. It seemed unlikely he was still worried about seeing his great grandad, because if that were the case, he probably would not be walking at all.

The door was closed so Michael knocked and then called out to Harry.

'Who's there?' came the gravelly voiced reply.

'It's Michael Grandad.'

'Michael who?'

'Your grandson, and James is here with me too. Can we com-'

'James who?'

'James Castlenau. Your great grandson,' replied Michael while slowly pushing open the door.

Harry was sitting on the bed facing away from the door, the grey ball of his head crowning the light blue checked dressing

161

gown Michael had bought him last Christmas. 'You're a relative of mine, aren't you? Come on in.' Said Harry, as he sat staring out through the glass door which opened onto a small grassy courtyard shared by several other residents.

'Up, Daddy. Up. Up Daddy,' said James, suddenly unnerved.

Michael picked him up roughly, as he did whenever he was annoyed with him.

'How are you Grandad?'

'Okay.'

'Did you forget we were coming today?'

'What time is it?' asked Harry, looking at his wrist where once a watch would have been.

'Nearly half past three.'

'Oh, I must have lost track of time,' said Harry. 'I knew you were coming today. For sure.'

Michael let the lie slip. Both he and Harry knew it was a bad one, but there was no point in pursuing the issue. It obviously hurt Harry's pride to be reminded of his forgetfulness.

'Joanne is out in the lounge with Alana. Can you come out?'

'Who's Joanne?'

James weight began to register in Michael's arms. He had answered this question before: many times before. 'My wife Joanne.'

'She's your daughter, right?'

Michael's shoulders dropped in relief which James evidently interpreted as a sign he was on his way back to the floor and out of safety. He dug his nails in, securing his hold.

Through all the small talk, Harry had not turned around and when he finally showed his face, Michael knew instantly why he had waited so long. At the sight of Harry, James tried to burrow his way into Michael's shoulder blade. Michael himself could not contain his shock: horror which overrode the pain of James attempts to use Michael's chest as a portal to another world.

'What the hell happened to your face Grandad?' demanded Michael. Without waiting for an answer, he added, 'Did you fall again?'

'Sorry. I should have warned you.'

'Yeah. You should have. Or someone should have.' Michael softened his tone and sat down on a chair by the dressing table. 'What happened?'

Harry's face was all swollen and puffy. Covered in red and blue blotches and welts, and his right eye was closed. He looked like he had been standing toe to toe with Mike Tyson for half an hour. James, eyes shut tight, pressed his face into Michael's chest. He could feel his son trembling.

'Would you believe an allergic reaction?' asked Harry sheepishly, pulling at the lapels of his dressing gown as though to protect himself from a chill.

'No.'

'Yeah. It's true. Apparently, I'm allergic to penicillin.'

'That's ridiculous. You're seventy-five and you only just found out now that you are allergic to penicillin. Get real.'

Harry shook his head. 'I don't know. That's what they said.'

Although Michael knew such a reaction to penicillin was possible because it had happened to Alana when she was six months old, he was stunned to think that a man could live for three quarters of a century and not know he was allergic to penicillin. Maybe he did know, but had forgotten, but surely his medical records would have mentioned such an important fact. It was courting catastrophe to rely on the memory of demented minds.

'I just saw Dominique in the lounge and she didn't say anything.

Did they change your medication? Yeah, they must have. Stupid question.'

'I don't know,' replied the old man thoughtfully. 'Anyway, it doesn't matter.'

'It bloody well does matter. It looks terrible. Does it hurt?'

'No,' said Harry. 'Bit itchy, that's all. No big deal. It'll get better. And who is this young fella you brought with you?' asked Harry changing the subject. 'Hiding his face? I'm the one with the ugly dial. You're probably a handsome young man with your mother's good looks.' Harry laughed.

Michael's heart beat a little faster as James came into focus. Harry came closer and gave James a playful poke in the ribs. James screamed.

Harry stepped back, mortified. 'I must have frightened him. What's his name?'

'James. And I reckon you did Grandad. You gave me a bit of a scare too.'

Michael could feel tears welling in his eyes as he looked at his grandad. He really did look terrible, even his checked dressing gown which was relatively new looked pitifully shabby. Michael thought how cruel it was, that he should suffer this disfigurement - albeit a temporary one - on top of everything else that was happening to him. Harry suddenly appeared to Michael as a weathered, worn out man, completely at the mercy of fate, unable to stem the ever faster flow of time away from him.

While Michael did not always understand, he held an unshake-able faith in a sovereign God which had long extracted his fear of death. He did not know however, whether or not Harry held any such convictions. Michael wondered again whether or not he should take the opportunity to talk to Harry about it, especially because of the guilt he felt about not having tried to do it earlier. Of course, he had thought about it many times but as was often the case with Michael, there was a vast chasm between the thought and the actual deed.

'Can you come out to see Joanne and Alana or should I bring them in here?' asked Michael, forcing his mind away from such philosophical wanderings.

'Bring them in David. Sorry.'

Michael overlooked Harry getting his name wrong, dismissing it as a triviality, but then then stupidly attempted to put James down.

'Get down for a minute and stay with Grandad,' he said. 'I'm going to get Mummy and Alana, okay?'

James screamed so loudly, both Michael and Harry jumped.

If James previously considered Harry as a stranger, he seemed to now think of him as some sort of monster: a devil in a dressing gown. He cowered, pressing harder against Michael's leg, pawing desperately for escape.

'We'll be right back, Grandad,' said Michael apologetically. 'I'm sorry about all this.'

Harry had turned away towards the window again and seemed not to hear or to care: hunching to make his head look like a burned-out sun setting in a blue checked horizon. As Michael walked through the door and back down the hall to the lounge with James clinging to him like clingwrap, he felt terrible. Really low. Sad for his grandad, worried for his son, and angry at himself. This potent concoction of emotions made Michael feel like running away, just like he used to do many years ago as an immature and irresponsible teenager. He just wanted to flee as fast as he could to anywhere.

'Come on down to his room, Babe. He doesn't want to come

out.'

'Why, what's wrong?' asked Joanne.

'He looks terrible. His face is all puffy and black and blue. He had a reaction to his medication. Apparently, they changed it, and nobody knew he was allergic to penicillin. Not even he did.'

'What's wrong with James?'

'He's scared of Grandad. His face. The way he looks, you know?'

'That's great,' said Joanne, rolling her eyes. 'This gets better all the time.'

Back at Harry's room, Michael knocked on the door again. 'We're back, Grandad.'

'Come in,' said Harry, thankfully not asking who it was this time.

'Here's your new little great granddaughter, Alana.'

Michael put James down and took Alana out of Joanne's arms. It worked out as a straight swap because James immediately climbed into the safety of his mother's arms. Alana continued to gurgle and blubber, stopping occasionally to give herself a clap.

Michael presented her to her great grandfather, who took her gladly as she gave him a cheeky smile. Harry smiled back warmly and spoke her name softly as he bounced her on his knee. Michael sighed.

'Sorry, I don't look the best, Alana,' said Harry. 'And thanks for not noticing. I'm a pretty handsome sort of a bloke underneath all this, you know?' He laughed and for an instant Michael saw a well and happy man: the healthy and exuberant grandad he had known all his life. The smile was quickly washed away though, by darker thoughts like a sandcastle swamped by a wave crashing on the beach.

James was still nestled securely in Joanne's arms, afraid to leave her embrace. Every now and then he stole a peek at Harry, but only for a moment before turning away again. Michael had seen that look on his son's face before. Scared and not wanting to look, but strangely unable not to.

During their recent trip to Thailand, Joanne's sister and her Thai boyfriend had taken them to Sampran Elephant Grounds, a tourist attraction located a couple of hours drive outside of Bangkok. The main show featured these huge beasts playing soccer, and doing handstands, or front feet stands in their case, and other tricks. They were accompanied by loud music and commentary in Thai. The final act was a recreation of an ancient battle between the Thai army and their traditional enemies, the Burmese. A very impressive mock battle complete with the bang of muskets, the boom of cannons and the metallic clang of clashing swords ensued. There was lots of shouting and mayhem, with the actors and the elephants resplendent in traditional costumes. James was terrified by it all, especially the noise of the cannons which really was very loud. Despite his fear, he could not take his eyes off the action. For the full ten minutes that it lasted, he had clutched little fistfuls of Michael's shirt.

His face bore the same expression now. A mixture of horror and fascination,

Harry started to cough. He quickly handed Alana back to Michael. When his hands were free, he pulled the lapel of his dressing gown up to cover his mouth and sat heavily in his recliner. The cough sounded horrible, and the poor man just could not stop. He mumbled apologies as he wrestled with the fit. When he eventually ceased, Michael poured him a glass of water from the plastic jug stationed on the side table. Having sated his thirst and eased the pain of a parched throat, Harry decided to stand again.

Michael rushed to his grandad's side to help him to his feet, and surprisingly the older man accepted the assistance. Harry reached out to touch James who saw it coming and cringed. Joanne gave an embarrassed laugh. 'He's very shy.'

Harry withdrew his outstretched hand and moved away to resume his spot, perched on the edge of his bed.

Michael knew Joanne was embarrassed and uncomfortable about James' bashfulness generally, but there was a difference between being shy and being scared, and this thing with Harry was in a different ball park.

'They changed my medication yesterday and look what happened to me,' said Harry, to no one in particular.

'Grandad is sick, James,' said Michael, trying to encourage his son to relax a little bit and maybe say something. James understood about people getting hurt and being sick. He also knew that sometimes people died as a result of their illness or injuries. Each time they drove past Sutherland District Hospital, where both he and Alana were born, James would tell how mummy was in there because she was hurt, and then she had a baby. He also, often remembered his grandmama's cat, Kaziah, with which he liked to play when he visited her. James knew that Kaziah had become sick and died, and that his grandmama was sad about that happening, and she had cried. Michael found it interesting that James talked about that event very dispassionately.

Michael was unsure whether James understood properly what had happened to Harry.

'Remember when Alana was little, James, and she was sick, and the doctor gave her some medicine which made her face go all red and itchy?'

'N-yes,' replied James softly.

'Well, that's what happened to Grandad.'

'Oh,' was all James said.

Breaking the following silence, Michael asked Harry if he had seen anything good on television recently.

'Yeah, I watched this show last night about…' started Harry, before pausing to grasp for the details. 'It was about…' Another pause. 'Oh yeah, a man who was travelling in Africa. It was good. Very interesting, but I missed the end. I must have fallen asleep.'

'Africa is on my hit list,' said Michael. 'I'd love to travel there. I guess we'll have to wait until the children are older.'

'It would sure cost a pretty penny. You'd have to save for years to be able to afford a trip like that.'

'We actually know some people who are living and working in Ethiopia.'

'Is that right?' asked Harry, with genuine interest.

'Yes. Working as missionaries. He's a vet. They live in a fairly rough rural area, quite a long way from the capital, Addis Abbaba. They're trying to learn the language, so they can share the gospel with the local people. You know, introduce them to God.'

Michael was very pleased with the direction of the conversation and sensed the opportunity he had been waiting for may soon present itself. However, Alana was getting restless, probably hungry or in need of a nappy change. He lowered his daughter to the floor and her mood instantly lightened. Michael would need to keep a close eye on his lightning fast daughter, with her spider like crawling action. This would not be conducive to good conversation. Nevertheless, it was better at that moment than trying to talk over the top of Alana's squeals of protest. On the floor she was, at least for the time being, relatively quiet and content.

'Don't they have their own God or gods?' asked Harry. 'The Africans?'

'Yes,' said Michael cautiously. He glanced at Joanne who was playing with James. When she noticed, she nodded, allowing Michael to continue. 'They have many gods. In fact, they worship all sorts of things. It's called animism. They worship animals and elements of nature, like the sun or the wind, for example. They believe there are various spirits which may live in a particular river, or rock, or tree, or even in an elephant, or a tiger.'

'But they kill elephants, don't they?'

'I don't mean all elephants, Grandad. It may be one especially large one, or a strangely coloured one. Like in Thailand, they consider white or albino elephants to be sacred and the rightful property of the king.'

'Thailand's in Asia, isn't it?' said Harry with a smile.

'Yes Grandad. Very funny. Anyway, it all depends. There are no national religions. They are all very localized. Each tribe will have its own set of gods and spirits to whom they pray. Not to ask for things. It's not like the kind of prayers we might say. Basically, they believe that if the spirits aren't properly respected and worshipped, they will become angry and bring misfortune on the tribe. So, whenever any natural disaster occurs, like a flood, it means that somebody in the tribe has done the wrong thing, either against his fellow tribesmen or against one of the gods. It's a religion based primarily on fear. The rituals too, have to be done exactly right. A failed corn crop probably means that the village shaman, or priest failed to conduct the planting ritual properly, and as a result the god of corn is mad.'

Michael again paused and looked at Joanne because he could feel her eyes boring into the back of his head. Although Harry was listening intently, and Michael was enjoying himself, Joanne and the children had reached the critical end of the tolerance levels. Alana, on the floor, squawking in frustration whenever Michael stopped her from doing or touching something she shouldn't have been. James, still remarkably in Joanne's lap, beginning to whine about going home. Joanne was plainly uncomfortable and wanted to leave. Michael didn't. More conflict.

'Hmm...interesting,' said Harry. 'What time is it? I think they serve dinner soon. That's good. I'm quite hungry.'

'That's good Grandad,' said Michael, turning around to see Joanne struggling to conceal her amusement. 'Have you been eating well? Still have a good appetite?'

'I'm eating a lot, but I wouldn't say that I'm necessarily eating well. No one cooks as good a feed as your Nana did.'

Not wanting to go down that nostalgic path, Michael gave Joanne a nod and she stood up. He noticed how frightened and unnerved James still looked.

'Grandad, we have to get going now,' announced Michael.

'Why's that? What time is it?'

'Nearly five.'

'Good. They'll be serving dinner soon. No one cooked as good a feed as your Nana, you know.'

'Yeah,' replied Michael, resigned to returning to mundane conversation. For a few minutes there, it had been as though there was nothing wrong with Harry's mind. 'One of my favourites was that trifle she used to make with custard and ice cream. Sensational.'

'So, we'll see you next time, Grandad,' said Joanne.

'Do you want us to walk you down to the dining room?' suggested Michael.

'No thanks, mate. It's too far. I'll have it in here and see if that bloke from Africa is on the box again tonight.'

'All right then, see you later, Grandad,' said Michael holding out his hand to Harry whose wiry wrist extended from the sleeve of his dressing gown. His grip was still strong, bellying his general failing health.

'Good bye...' said Harry, trying to remember his grandson's name. He could not, nor could he recall Joanne's or James'. Then he looked at Alana, now hanging off Michael's hip like a monkey.

'Good bye, Alana.'

Harry smiled warmly at Joanne and lightly touched her arm. He reached for James, but paused, before simply nodding and withdrawing his hand.

James wriggled to the floor, much to Joanne's relief, and began to walk on quickly ahead.

'Wait for us, James,' ordered Joanne.

Leaving the over chilled lounge area of Havendale, they strode out through the double glass doors, and into the warmth and sunshine of a November evening. They were leaving. Going home. The ordeal was over. James was his old self again, laughing and fooling around. Alana was a little grumpy as she was due for her feed. Michael wondered if she actually looked forward to that jar of purple mush called *apple and chicken dinner.*

Michael's thoughts returned to Harry, causing tears to well in his eyes again as he pictured Harry's blotched and swollen face. The swelling and the redness would disappear, but the sparkle would not return to his eyes. Michael had gotten over the initial shock of seeing Harry that way-in particular his face on this occasion, but James had not, and he could easily understand why. Now Michael felt he had made a mistake in bringing his family here. The one bright point in the gloom was that Harry seemed to enjoy having them there, and amazingly had established some rapport with Alana, who was not bothered at all by his appearance. Perhaps he was right to persist.

Next time, Michael decided he would come alone. Maybe bring Alana, but Joanne and James were clearly there under sufferance and were highly unlikely to ever be enthusiastic about trips to Havendale.

Joanne said she did not feel like cooking. Michael said he did not feel like eating. However, James was hungry, so they decided to grab some McDonalds on the way home. When they arrived, James was totally engrossed in his fries, and did not want to get out of the car. Eventually, they all made it inside. A depression smothered Michael as he prepared the children for bed.

'Be a good boy and go to sleep now. Grandmama is coming over to pick you up and take you out tomorrow. Maybe to a show. So, you go to sleep and when you wake up, you can get dressed and then Grandmama will come. Okay.'

James knew tomorrow as *sun up*. Night time was for sleeping and consequently he no longer consented to taking an afternoon nap. Sometimes he would sleep in the afternoon if he was really tired. Normally this would occur after he threw a massive tantrum, usually about nothing, and then fall asleep on the floor somewhere. Head down, bum up.

As was his custom, Michael asked James if he had had a good day.

'No, I don't like it, daddy.'

'You didn't like it? Why?'

'James scared monster. Devil. Me scared.'

'Okay, we'll pray about it so that you aren't scared of the devil.'

'Okay.'

'Lord Jesus...' began Michael.

'Nesus is lord,' interrupted James.

'Amen,' said Michael, before continuing. 'Lord Jesus, please make the devil go away, and protect James and make him not scared anymore. Amen.'

'Amen,' said James dreamily.

'Goodnight mate,' said Michael, before giving his son a goodnight kiss on the forehead.

* * *

Michael was a heavy sleeper and only became aware of the noises emanating from James' bedroom five or so minutes after they started. Joanne had woken up about the same time and was much more concerned than Michael initially. James was usually a very good sleeper. Although occasionally resisting going to bed in the first place, once there and settled in, he stayed and almost always slept through until morning. Even now as a toilet trained toddler, there were very few incidents of bed wetting, or any other such nocturnal disturbances.

Michael looked at the alarm clock beside Alana's cot at the foot of their bed. Two thirty a.m.

James was moaning as if he was in pain and Michael could hear him saying *no* over and over again in a voice foreign to him. It was still relatively high pitched, but lower than James' normal voice.

Speaking his son's name softly, Michael sat on James' bed and touched his face lightly with the palm of his hand. He stroked his hair and gently patted his back, trying to calm him down. 'It's all right, mate. It's just a dream. Not real. Just a dream.

Wake up, Daddy's here.'

'Daddy,' croaked James as he snuggled closer to Michael. 'Don't like it, Daddy. Bad. Devil. Don't like it.' A chill ran down Michael's spine. Then James fell quiet again as he drifted back to sleep. The nightmare was over. The last he'd had one was many months ago, after watching a particularly ghoulish episode of The Simpsons. The cartoon featured ghosts and skeletons skulking around. Some things frightened James, and he would say so. He was scared of dogs, especially when they barked, the sound of the vacuum cleaner which he called the 'baktina', and thunder. Other things literally terrified him, and words were not necessary to prove the point. The sound of a power drill really freaked him out. Usually, however, none of these things manifested themselves in his dreams.

As Michael returned to bed, having satisfied himself his son was again sleeping soundly, he could not shake the feeling that this dream must have been about Harry. People avoid things they don't like, or which frighten and disturb them. James' fear of the vacuum cleaner meant that whenever Michael or Joanne brought it out to vacuum the floor, he would take himself off to his bedroom and shut the door. But Harry wasn't a noisy machine, he was family.

* * *

Dawn welcomed Saturday and although Michael had recently been released from the tyranny of having to work an eighteen hour double shift every Saturday, he still rose before the rest of the family. Waking at four a.m. weekday mornings, Michael turned the alarm off on the weekend and usually rolled out of bed around six o'clock.

Alana was first up, followed by a groggy James, then lastly

Joanne. Harry did not rate a mention in their conversation that morning as they busied themselves preparing for a new day. Plopping himself down in the lounge chair facing the television, James quickly became engrossed in The Wiggles movie. He asked for a juice, and as usual had to be reminded to say 'please' when he asked for it.

As Michael slowly shoveled Just Right cereal into his mouth, he stewed about the events of yesterday and James' nightmare. Plagued by guilt and disquieted by the circumstances, he wondered how it could have come to this. It was an intolerable situation. Michael simply could not accept that seeing Harry could have such a profound effect on James, so as to cause him to have a nightmare. Or was that naivety on Michael's part? It seemed unavoidably clear that was exactly what had happened. He had to do something. He had to fix it. Make it right. But how?

A typical Saturday unfolded, including a visit to the local church spring fete, and the weekly shopping excursion to Coles. Thoughts of Harry, and of nightmares and devils, remained deep in the subconscious, where they belonged.

In fact, neither Harry nor James' nightmares rated a mention for the rest of the weekend.

* * *

On Monday, as Michael struggled out of bed, and roboted through his workday morning routine, he decided he would take James to Havendale that afternoon, to visit Harry. It was clear to him that James had demonized his great grandfather and that was something that needed to be sorted out immediately. Such thinking could not be allowed to fester.

Even though James had not, and in all fairness to him, probably could not have made the connection between Harry and the monster in his dreams, Michael knew they were one and the same.

'We are going out,' was all Michael said, but it was enough to satisfy James who happily climbed into his seat, ready to head off on another adventure. He really liked going out and would willingly go with just about anyone who showed up at the front door and offered to take him out. What he definitely did not like was staying at home, or more precisely, being left at home. Michael could not leave the house without James kicking up an almighty stink about it. To counter the dramatic protests that always arose upon his departure, Michael decided to take James with him wherever possible, even if it wasn't very convenient to do so.

When Michael steered their yellow Commodore into the driveway of Havendale, James seemed relaxed and chirpy. Obviously, he did not know where they were. However as soon as Michael parked the car, and the double glass entry doors could be clearly seen, James began to grumble: prelude to the tantrum.

'Back home, Daddy. Go back home now, okay?' James face was all screwed up as he pleaded with his dad.

'No mate,' replied Michael firmly.

Mantra mode kicked in: 'No, no, no!' wailed James. 'Go back home!'

Repeating the same words over and over again in a cycle of undulating volume, from a soft whimper he built to a climatic, screaming demand. Then he started kicking the back of the car seat. Michael was prepared for the tantrum so he was consequently calm and patient with James. All the while he was hoping the show would not go on too long or arouse the interest of passers-by. It would be unhelpful to have an audience for this particular performance.

Michael had called Harry during the day to explain the whole situation to him and ask for his help. A very apologetic and slightly confused Harry consented to Michael's request, once he had recovered from the shock of learning how he had inadvertently frightened his great grandson. Together they formulated a plan.

Turning in his seat to speak to his distraught son, Michael almost laughed when he saw James' face: contorted as it was by his disproportionate reaction. To counter the inappropriate urge to laugh, Michael got out of the car. This had no effect on the intensity of James' tantrum. With great patience, Michael waited a very long three minutes, before James began to quieten down.

Rubbing his eyes before sliding off the seat and onto the ground, James asked for a drink.

'All right mate. I'll get you a juice when we go inside.'

'No, Daddy. Now please. Me want 'Bena.' He had lost the last battle, but James had found himself a new cause to champion.

'I don't have any Ribena. I'll get you an orange juice inside.'

'No, Daddy. Me want 'Bena.'

Having failed to get his way with a full on display of toddler style defiance, James was now trying a more subtle method. Obstinance coupled with insistence and a dash of persistence. At its finest, an argumentative disposition could be brutally effective in wearing a parent down, but Michael would have none of it today. He was on a mission. 'Stop it!' he said. 'I'll give you a juice or you can have nothing. Let's go. Right now.'

Taking Michael's hand, James reluctantly trudged along beside his victorious father. Michael was feeling very pleased with himself at how relatively easy things had been so far. He knew, however, that had James not willingly lay down his guns, the battle would have raged much harder and much longer. Michael might even have cracked under the relentless pressure and aborted the mission. But no, as it stood things were progressing well.

They walked very slowly through the double glass doors of Havendale, across the floor of the lounge, and straight down the hall to Harry's room. Michael knocked gently on the door.

'G'day Grandad,' he said, smiling warmly as he pushed open the door and walked into Harry's room. He felt James' reluctance on the end of his arm.

'How...who's that there?' said Harry who was sitting on his bed as he was last time, facing out into the courtyard. Michael's face dropped when he saw that Harry was wearing that dressing gown. He had again forgotten they were coming and Michael worried his master plan might fail instantly. Harry was also supposed to have something special to show James. Something to arouse James' interest and take his mind off Harry's appearance. Succeeding in getting James' to the Harry's door was too much of an achievement itself to turn back now. The show had to go on. Michael cursed himself for relying so heavily on the time worn memory of an old man.

'It's Michael, your grandson.'

'Yes. How are you? Good to see you.'

'Grandad, can you get dressed please? James is here to see you and-'

'Yes, of course,' said Harry, a little flustered. 'Sorry. Had I known you were coming I would have got dressed.'

'It's all right Grandad. Don't worry about it. I'll help you.'

'Grandad,' said Michael patiently as he helped Harry out of

his infamous blue checked dressing gown. 'I told James that you had something to show him because when we spoke on the phone you assured me you would be able to find something of interest to him. You know, to act as an icebreaker?'

'Hmm' said Harry thoughtfully, as though he was hearing the idea for the first time.

'Anyway, let's get you dressed. James had a bad dream in which he says he saw the devil wearing a blue dressing gown just like yours. He thinks that you're the devil, or some kind of monster.'

Harry raised his bushy eyebrows.

'It's not your fault,' said Michael. 'No one is blaming you. I just don't want James to be scared of you. Last time, you know, seeing your face all puffy and red...well it freaked him out. You look much better by the way. Did I say that already?'

Harry nodded slowly. 'It takes so long to get dressed and undressed these days,' he lamented. 'Sometimes, I just can't be bothered. It's my bloody fingers, you know?'

'Don't worry about it,' said Michael. 'There's no rush.' As he and Harry wrestled with the dressing gown in an awkward dance, Michael was suddenly inspired. James really liked soldiers and planes especially. What if Harry had a photo of a B-52 bomber that he used to fly in.

'Do you have any photos of yourself from your army days?' asked Michael hopefully. 'Any shots of planes-James loves planes-or souvenirs?'

Harry thought a moment, stroking his chin when his face lit up. 'Yeah, I reckon I might.' He let his eyes wander around his small room. 'Where'd I put them?'

'One of your drawers over there?' suggested Michael. He glanced at James who was laying on the floor playing with an imaginary car. Hope swelled. Harry was coming to life and

James was safe inside his own world.

'Yeah…could be. I think I've got some old things in there.'

Michael left off unbuttoning Harry's pyjama shirt to go to the three drawer chest beside his bed. When he opened it, he was pleased to find an old shoe box. Where else would a bloke keep his collection of letters, photographs and other memorabilia? It was kind of thrilling for Michael as he carefully removed the shoebox from the drawer. He handled it as though it was the most precious and fragile jewel he had ever seen. Michael placed it on the bed and looked at Harry, motioning to remove the lid. 'May I?'

The older man nodded. He too had a look of wonderment on his face.

Inside was a bundle of letters addressed to Harry with Australian postage stamps on them. The envelopes, held together by a thick elastic band, were slightly ragged and yellowed.

'From your grandmother,' said Harry. 'She wrote me faithfully during the war. Unfortunately, a lot of them got held up somewhere and I didn't receive then until after I got back. Some, I reckon, just went missing. But what I did get was enough to keep me going. Like cold water to a weary soul is-'

'Good news from a distant land.' Michael could not resist completing Harry's sentence for him; amused by his grandfather quoting the Bible. It seemed at odds with the man.

'Yeah. I mean a bloke has his mates and they were good mates, good men. But we all missed our wives and girlfriends.' He sighed, as a fresh wave of melancholy washed over him.

Michael placed the bundle of letters on the bed beside the box. Next out was a collection of loose papers. One of which was Harry's official discharge, dated February 11, 1945. He had become seriously ill with a blood infection which followed an operation to repair a severe leg wound sustained during a routine bombing mission in Burma on Christmas Day, 1944. Ironically the injury was not a result of enemy fire, but of his own carelessness. It took many years for Harry to be able to admit the embarrassing reality behind his medical discharge.

Putting aside the rest of the papers and somehow managing to overcome his curiousity, Michael suddenly found what he was looking for. Photographs. Half a dozen black and white photos, also yellowed like the letters. Michael quickly shuffled through them before one particular shot grabbed his eye. James would love it.

'Can you show James this picture?' asked Michael, holding up the photo so Harry could see it. 'And spin a bit of a yarn about it?'

'Yeah,' said Harry laughing as he stared at the old photograph. 'I can do that all right.'

Michael could hardly contain himself as he watched all the lights blaze in Harry's eyes: the unmistakable and intoxicating sparkle of life. 'That's great,' he said. 'Let's get you dressed then.'

When they finished, Harry studied himself in the mirror, beaming. If nothing else went right today, Michael would still have thought it all worthwhile. Harry, happy and suddenly so full of life again, taking pride in his appearance. Surely the plan would work. How could James demonize Harry now? The way he was acting? The way he looked? How could James look at his grandfather this time and still see the devil in a dressing gown? With the dressing gown gone, Michael had never felt so confident that the devil was about to be sent on his way as well.

'Okay grandad, time to show James your photograph.'

'What paragraph?'

'Photograph. Photo. Not paragraph.' Michael was hoping

that Harry's long term memory functioned more efficiently than his short term. Hope springs eternal and it had gushed when Michael first found the old picture of his grandad, but the old man's intermittent recall ability was a worry. Perhaps all it would take to revive his recollection was to show him the picture and ask a simple question. A simple question might trigger a flood of memories. He put the photo in front of Harry. 'This photo.'

'James, Grandad has a picture to show you. Do you want to see it?'

James' imaginary car suddenly accelerated with a loud whoosh.

'Just have a look mate. It's a photo of grandad when he was a soldier and there's a plane in the picture too. Just look,' said Michael, trying not to get frustrated or appear belligerent to James. If he went to pick him up, he would surely trigger a tantrum, but as James was evidently intent on ignoring them, Michael had to do something. Just as despair crouched like a predator ready to spring on its prey, Harry spoke: unexpectedly, and prematurely perhaps.

'James, I used to fly in a big, big plane. Do you like planes? Daddy tells me you really like planes.'

'No,' lied James softly.

Harry moved a little closer. 'No? Your daddy told me that you really love to fly and you've already been in a big plane, and gone overseas. To Thailand?'

James wasn't biting. He wasn't even looking, but Michael watched amazed as James' imaginary car suddenly took off into the sky, launching as James got up off the floor. Sensing a breakthrough, Michael joined the attack.

'Grandad's plane is even bigger than the one we flew to

Thailand in. Much bigger. Look.'

Harry, still inching closer to his great grandson, held out the photo so James could see it. The frightened little boy remained still except for his eyes which reached to take in the picture. His invisible flying machine stopped dramatically in mid air. The scene showed Harry and several of his mates dressed in their flying uniforms, standing in front of the huge bomber which dwarfed them all. It was hard to believe that such a behemoth could actually get off the ground, let alone fly. The men had their helmets tucked under their arms and were standing proudly shoulder to shoulder. They looked brave and strong: utterly fearless. Directly behind Harry was the massive wheel of the mighty bomber.

'Look how big that wheel is James,' said Harry excitedly. He was close enough to touch James now, but he refrained. Michael marveled at the mastery of Harry's execution.

All this talk of massive wheels and huge bomber planes was more temptation than James could resist. He really did love aeroplanes. How could he not want to look at such an aviatory monster?

'Can you see that, James?'

'No,' replied James quietly, before suddenly reaching out to touch the photograph. Michael and Harry exchanged satisfied glances, then laughed heartily as James actually snatched the picture out of Harry's hand. Normally James would have got into trouble for behaving rudely, but on this occasion rousing on James was the furthest thing from Michael's thoughts.

'Big plane Daddy. Look!'

James kept his distance from Michael and Harry, secure in his own space, standing wide eyed, gazing at the photo in his hands.

'Yes, mate. Grandad flew in that in the war. A long time ago when he was a soldier.'

'Longer, longer?'

'Many years ago. Before Daddy was even born.'

'Oh,' said James. Then he slowly turned his head, very slowly to face Harry whose face had a child-like radiance. Almost in a whisper, James asked him, 'Dandad solder?'

'What's that, mate?'

'Dandad solder, sure?' repeated James. 'Fly big plane longer longer?'

Obviously unfamiliar with toddler-ese, Harry looked bewildered. Michael interpreted for him. Harry laughed once he got the translation. To James he said, 'That's right, mate.'

'Oh,' said an awestruck James.

'Come here,' said Harry, pausing as he tried to remember his great grandsons name. 'Come here and I'll tell you a story about this plane.' He had retreated to his recliner and sat down. 'Come on,' said Harry repeating the invitation to overcome James' obvious uncertainty. 'I won't bite you.'

With one word, James announced the success of the mission. 'Okay.' The devil in his dreams had been disrobed.

That night, after finishing the story of Teddy Bear at Play, Michael asked James if he had a fun day to which he replied excitedly that he had. He also wanted to know if they could go and visit Grandad again tomorrow.

'Not tomorrow, but later,' replied Michael as he ruffled James thick hair. 'Let's pray. Do you want to?'

'Yes. Nesus is Lord. Amen?'

'God grant James a peaceful night's sleep,' prayed Michael, before silently adding *and keep the devil in a dressing gown out of his dreams.* 'Please give him happy dreams.'

'Amen,' said James, with a twinkle in his eyes.

'Amen,' repeated Michael, pulling his son close to him and giving him a big bear hug. Then he kissed him lightly on the forehead and told him that he loved him. 'Goodnight son.'

Fifteen

The Darkness of Light

A sliver of light pierces the blinds and scars her eyelids. She
feels as though she has not slept at all, although she must
have drifted away into the blissful unconsciousness of
slumber at some point. Sleep eludes her despite her craving for
it. Even the pills, which she obtains as often as she can manage
with the increased scrutiny of doctors, only provide temporary
relief. The alcohol she washes them down with probably does
not help. This miserable cycle is all she knows, and she chose it,
so she cannot complain.

Not for the first time or the last, she sees Curtis' face. His
kind smile, the happiness which radiates from every pore in his
slightly tanned flesh. The smile which loves her, forgives her,
and encourages her. The same smile which she has persistently
tried to destroy. An oft repeated conversation wallows out from
within the recesses of her memory.

'A measure of politeness is not too much to ask for, is it?' said
Curtis. 'It's not that hard to smile and say hello.'

'I'm not a nice person,' she replied. 'I can't sweet talk. If you
don't like it, that's too bad because I can't change. I'm bad okay?

That's it.'

Curtis stepped close to her and placed his hands upon her shoulders.

'Don't say another word, or I'm going to leave right now. I have had enough.' She shrugged out of his grasp, ignoring the hurt in his eyes and focused on her own pain, comforting herself with the fact that she was bad, and she thoroughly deserved the misery to which she now clung. It was the only solid ground in her sorry existence: her anchor.

She turned away from Curtis and busied herself with the dishes which had piled up in the sink. She knew he had only not done them because he was respecting her wishes for peace and quiet in the mornings. Feeling his gaze on her, she said, "Leave me alone. I have to clean the house. That's what I'm here for: to serve you and to fuck you!"

She knows it isn't true. It wasn't true when she said it then or any of the countless other times she had said it. Curtis is a decent man: loving, honest and caring. He has only ever tried to help her. Despite his shortcomings, and the frequent and unjustified tongue lashings she has given him, he has remained faithful and gracious. She doesn't deserve him. He's too good.

Flinging, the doona off her and across the bed, she rises and enters the bathroom. Every step evokes a memory, every breath a painful reminder of her hopelessness. Curtis is already awake as usual, having risen early for his morning run. The sounds of breakfast making drift down the hall. It is normal everyday noise, but she will tell him to be quiet before she says good morning to him. Once finished showering, she dresses and ties her hair without once looking at herself in the mirror. She only ever sees disaster reflected in the glass: her figure gone, her face aging, her broken heart advertising its desolation through the windows of her tired eyes.

When she reaches the kitchen, Curtis turns to look at her and smiles. 'Good morning.'

'You're too noisy,' she replies.

Curtis shrugs, and approaches her. 'Give me a cuddle beautiful.'

In his arms, she feels warm. His passion for her burns her skin and eventually she has to break free, hoping she held the pose long enough to satisfy him in his delusion that they are happy and have a future. She goes to close the blinds Curtis has opened as he always does when he wakes. Knowing that no one can see inside their private world, does not stop her from believing that they can.

'It's nice outside,' says Curtis. 'A nice sunny day, and the air is fresh. It's a little stuffy in here.'

'I like my privacy.'

'You can have privacy without being in the dark all the time, and besides think of the money saved on electricity bills with the lights off instead of on during the day.'

Glaring at him, she attacks his parsimony. 'That's all you care about, isn't it? Money. Money. Money.'

Curtis appears ready to retort, probably along the lines of how she rails against him for leaving lights on and using the remote-controlled garage door to enter the house, instead of using the front door.

'You're stingy, and I'm sick of it,' she says. 'I like my privacy. It doesn't matter about the money.'

They have serious money problems because of her profligacy. She buys him things he does not need and pushes money through poker machines as though the notes grow on trees in their backyard. She does not even like those machines nor understand why she wastes money on them. Neither does Curtis, but he no longer says anything. They split their accounts some time ago, because she said she was tired of paying all his bills. She knows they are mutual bills, but she has never been able to bring herself to trust him enough to use the words 'us' and 'ours'. It is a mystery why he stays. She starves him of sex but is extremely proficient when she does consent. She makes him laugh sometimes, and she buys him nice clothes to wear, even though she knows he doesn't need them and they can't afford them. Even if they are struggling, it is important to her to maintain a good show of prosperity. Curtis doesn't seem to understand.

She remembers another all too familiar conversation, the like of which had been repeated so often, they could easily have played a recording and saved their strength.

'Our business is our business. Our problems are our problems. That was how I was raised. That is my family. Your family is different. What goes on between us, stays between us. It's not for your mum or your dad or your sister, or for the neighbours to enjoy thanks to your loud voice. I don't know how many times I have told you that I like my privacy, and if you can't respect that then get out of my life.'

Curtis held her gaze. Confident and calm as ever, he said, 'The neighbours can't hear anything, and they don't care anyway. They have their own problems.'

'Leave me alone, Curtis. I'm tired.'

She is tired all the time due to a lack of sleep, and the exhaustion caused by depression and anxiety, but this is also how she gets out of longer discussions with Curtis. She is not at all interested in his logic or his common sense. Her paranoia fuels her need to reject rationality. She's been treated so badly by the previous men in her life, that Curtis' genuine care for her barely registers. He rarely raises his voice or swears at her, and he has never abused her either with his mouth or his hands. It was a mistake inviting him into her life though, and she feels guilty for ruining his, on top of everything else she has done to underpin the deep vein of regret which courses through her bones. She is a lost cause and she knows it. The problem is how to make Curtis see that, and to get him out of her life. It doesn't help that on occasions, sometimes for a whole day or even a couple of days in a row they have a relationship which is world beating. They have experienced great joy together. The day they received a phone call from the real estate agent to tell them their application for the townhouse they really loved and wanted, had been approved. The time they went to a Big Bash League T20 cricket match and roared and cheered their way through three hours of action which led to an exciting victory for their team. Their trip to Auckland for New Year's Eve.

However, such times of joy were illusions, masking the truth of their pitiful excuse for a relationship. She is unlovable and growing increasingly annoyed by Curtis' dogged determination to love her. She's tried being direct with him, and simply swearing at him until she was blue in the face, but all that did was make him shake his head while tears rolled down his flushed cheeks. The next day he would be all smiles and sweetness again, and she would play along for a little longer. It is cruel. Very cruel, but it is Curtis' fault. If he cannot take a hint from the magnitude of her regular vitriolic tirades, then he can only blame himself for his unhappiness.

'On the subject of money,' says Curtis gingerly as though he is afraid of breaking something, or fanning to life the flames of her latent rage.

She rolls her eyes and sighs loudly.

Curtis shakes his head. 'Never mind.'

'My life is bad enough already, Curtis. All you do is take, take, take. I've got nothing, so don't ask me for anything, alright?'

'Okay. Don't worry about it.'

'I do worry. That's all I do. My life is shit, and you're not helping, okay.'

It's not a question, so she doesn't wait for his answer, but marches past him down the hall, and throws another familiar little quip towards him as she goes. 'I'll be upstairs.'

In bed, where she spends most of her time either on Facebook, or trying to sleep, she wonders why Curtis carries on with this charade. How the hell can she cleave him out of her life? What will it take for him to finally accept the futility of pursuing this relationship? Why won't he leave her alone? It's bloody-minded devotion, that's all. Not real love. He's using her for sex and money, and so she can cook and clean for him. She makes him look good. She's a readymade ego booster. He's probably addicted to that, and the overwhelming pulse of his masculinity derived from the multiple orgasms she fakes for him.

The next day, when she wakes up, Curtis has already left for work. He kissed her cheek and told her he loved her before he left while she pretended to be asleep. That's how it always goes. She readies herself for work and checks her phone: finding a love note from Curtis in her inbox. Kiss. Hug. Kiss. Hug. She doesn't bother replying.

Arriving home that evening, she opens the door, and notices Curtis' shoes are missing from the stand in the hall. The kitchen is spotless and the counter uncluttered. Her stomach constricts. Her hand trembles as she reaches for a single sheet of paper lying there. When she finishes reading the farewell note from Curtis which he has worded with typical craftsmanship, she scrunches it up and tosses it in the bin. His final message expresses loving concern for her and advises her to call him if she misses him, or if she wants him to come back. She misses him already, but as she closes all the blinds, blocking out the summer evening light, she knows she will not call. Then she goes upstairs and settles in the darkness.

The Darkness of Light is dedicated to Jessie in the hope that one day she learns to forgive herself, and finds some peace and happiness.

Sixteen

Gravel Rash

(first published in Raven's Light, April 2014)

'*D*on't fall and get gravel rash.'

The voice was unfamiliar, maybe imaginary, but the message was well known to him. From the first day he had pedaled free of the training wheels attached to his new bike, Brendon's mum had warned him and worried for him, with those words. All kids crash their bikes and rip up their knees. Brendon had the scars to prove his childhood bravado just like most of his friends. No big deal. He always assured his mum he would be fine, and usually he was.

Did he really hear someone say that to him just now? He was alone, wasn't he? Gravel crunched and jostled beneath the tyres as he rode through Lakeside Park on his way home from work. Had he started the trip after dark, and would have ridden the long way home ,but an extra fifteen minutes to avoid the park was fifteen minutes he wasn't willing to give up tonight. He had a date. Samantha Ewells had finally said yes.

Daylight was being folded away like a piece of paper soon

to be imprisoned in the darkness of an envelope. Brendon pedaled harder. He would probably make it through the park and reach the freeway before the black night began to reign but he maintained his pace, even ramped it up a little. There was no way he was going to be late home tonight. He had to make up time. That truck was to blame. The one which arrived late at the Toyota dealership, around the corner from the depot, to unload its cargo of new Camrys. The whole road was blocked for ten minutes as the driver made numerous attempts to reverse the truck into the lot. Brendon had sat there staring at it and tapping anxiously on the steering wheel. Wondering why him, why tonight and trying to not to think of having to make Samantha wait. She might not wait. He had cursed under his breath as he waited impatiently. Must have been a new driver. Inexperienced.

Now he was running late. Running out of time. This was an experience Brendon could have done without. He had heard stories about people going missing in Lakeside Park. Everyone said it was no place to be after the sun had gone down. The only ones to disregard the danger were the drunken fools and deviants who frequented the park in order to debauch and destroy themselves under the cover of darkness. Brendon would have happily avoided them for the rest of his life.

In the quiet of the dusk, the only sounds were Brendon's heavy breathing, a squeak from the pedals on each revolution, and the chuckle of the gravel underneath his tyres.

'Be careful of gravel rash.'

Brendon's first instinct was to stop and listen closely without audible interference, but fear kicked in and pushed him on. Was he hearing things? The gravel seemed looser, less willing to support and carry his weight, and he struggled at times to control the handlebars and stay on course. The night was black and heavy now. The acacias which lined the track leaned in closer to him, whispering seditiously. He flicked on his night light which was perched in the centre of the handlebars, but the battery was so low it barely reached the spinning tip of his front tyre. Hot, sweaty and panicking, he wondered how much farther to the freeway? He looked up for a moment but could not see through the opaque gloom. Suffocating gloom. That was what he felt. This was bad. Very bad.

'Don't fall. You'll get gravel rash.'

'Shut up!' yelled Brendon frantically at his invisible taunter. 'Shut up!'

Forcing himself to concentrate on controlling the bike, afforded Brendon some peace from the persistent paranoia, but someone was watching him. He knew it. Somehow keeping up with him. One of those perverted pariahs who lived in the park was teasing him, tormenting him. Must be that.

He felt the front of the bike dip suddenly and then rise again as though he had ridden through a pothole. His left hand was jolted free of the handlebar grip, but he quickly re-established a firm hold. Why was the damn freeway so far away tonight? He must be nearing the edge of the park. He encouraged himself, strengthened his aching legs. He imagined he could now see the headlights of vehicles flickering through the trees as they roared southbound along the F6. Then he realized he was sinking.

A violent and immediate stop catapulted Brendon over the handlebars and onto the gravel path. Having somehow managed to maintain a one-handed grip on the handlebar, he pulled the bike down on top of him as he fell, landed pedal first against his chest.

Too stunned to move initially, Brendon just lay there. Insistent and angry pain advised him he was still alive. A gush of air left his lungs as he exhaled, then he coughed for a minute or two, wincing with each contraction of his diaphragm. As he pushed the bike off himself, he felt the rough gravel nibbling at the skin around the back of his neck and calves. A strong sucking sensation against his right knee caused a new burst of pain as the sharp edges of the gravel cut his skin. He heard a sound close to him. Very close. A murmur. Low and indistinct. Garbled as though someone was talking with a mouthful of food.

No longer pinned by his bike, Brendon tried to wrest himself free of the disturbingly soft gravel, but the more he twisted the tighter he was held. If he could have he would have screamed for help but the only sound to escape his mouth was a pathetic mumble. If he could have he would have kept fighting his unseen enemy, but fear immobilized him. As the gravel swallowed him alive and crushed him, he lamented that truck blocking the road. If not for it, he would have been home now getting ready for his date with Samantha instead of dying alone in Lakeside Park.

Just before his head disappeared beneath the rippling surface of the gravel track, he heard the voice again, 'I warned you about gravel rash, didn't I?'

Seventeen

The Devil in the Driver's Seat

'*G*ive us ya fuckin' money. Now!'

The man in the passenger seat had reached around the security screen with his left hand, but John was able to fend him off while reaching for the driver's door handle, to try to get out and away. The passenger seat was far enough back to make it difficult for his assailant to reach John or get a clear punch at him. He had to get all the way forward on the seat and lean around the screen. The much-maligned polycarbonate shield was doing its job for the moment.

Suddenly, John remembered the alarm. He pressed it and began frantically to call out his destination. The base would be able to hear him and alert the police, along with any other cabs who may be in the area.

Unfortunately, John was only able to say the street name and suburb once. He had forgotten about the other guy in the back seat.

'What are you playing at? You think this is a game? Think that pissy screen will save ya?' taunted the guy, as he clambered from the back seat behind John to stand right beside the driver's door. 'Did you hit your alarm?' he said to John, before saying to his mate, 'I think he pressed the fuckin' alarm. We better get crackin'.'

The man reefed the door open outside, nearly ripping John's arm out of its socket in the process, as he tried to hold it shut. Not having time to release the door handle, John was pulled out of the cab and onto the ground.

A sharp pain followed. First in the head, then in the stomach and again, in his back. A warm wetness covered his face. More pain. This time, his arms. Again to his head. Blow after blow. John heard cracking sounds and thuds. He also heard the men yelling at him, but he could not understand or even hear properly what they were saying. His vision blurred. Black spots danced before his eyes. Was he going to die or just pass out? He felt himself being lifted. Then dropped. Eyes awash with blood, his peripheral vision darkened. The sound of doors slamming was followed by a final stab of pain in his leg which caused John to cry out with all the strength he had left in his body. His assailants scrambled into his taxi, driving over his leg as they tore off down the road leaving John crumpled and battered in the gutter as darkness engulfed him.

* * *

When he opened his eyes, John felt hung over. A heavy drinker in his youth, he had frequently suffered from seediness and headaches the morning after a night on the grog. Many people who knew him and how much he drank, called his consumption reckless. They wondered how long his body could endure the abuse, but he managed to survive adolescence and eventually learned to understand the word temperance and practice it. Many years had passed since he had drunk himself into oblivion, but he would never forget what the gut wrenching nausea of a rotten hangover felt like.

His throat was dry, and his eyes stung from the impact of the bright fluorescent lights. The worst thing about waking up this morning, if it was morning, was the headache. His whole head throbbed constantly with dull pain. John closed his eyes again and tried to calm himself down. Tried to wish away the pain of the hammer blows to his head and the memory of what caused them.

'Mr.Miles? Mr.Miles.'

Her voice was soft and comforting like his mother's voice. The way she spoke to him after he had a bad dream as a child. John slowly opened his eyes this time to lessen the shock of the light. On seeing the nurse, he momentarily forgot the pain. A beautiful young lady in white with a pretty, round face and a nice figure just like the nurses on television.

'Yes,' replied John with a croaky voice.

'How are you feeling?'

'Shit,' said John without thinking, because that was the truth. 'Sorry. I mean, not very well. "Excuse the French.'

Embarrassed at having used such language to the attractive woman in uniform, he smiled awkwardly and averted his eyes. To her credit, the nurse merely smiled and enquired further about John's condition. No doubt, she had heard such language before, and probably much worse. A special kind of people were nurses.

With his eyes better adjusted to the light, John now had a closer look at the nurse. Her name tag said Sharon. It was obvious that Sharon was naturally beautiful: auburn hair pulled back into a harsh bun and held in place with a butterfly pin, a fair skinned and make-up free face. After she had finished cataloging John's physical woes, he asked her for the time.

'It's five past seven,' she replied, after glancing up at a clock on the wall which John could have seen for himself. He wanted to keep her there by his side talking to him in that soft voice.

'What day is it?' asked John.

'Sunday. The eleventh,' said the nurse as she busied herself with tidying his bed.

'Have I been asleep all day?' asked John, rubbing his chin and feeling the rough stubble of three day's growth.

'Yes. They brought you in at about half past two this morning.'

'And you're still here working?'

'Knock off time soon. Anyway, yes, you have been sleeping all day. As you would. You took quite a beating it seems. You…'

John could have talked to her for hours. He wished that he was rich enough to hire her as his personal nurse. Every man should have a personal nurse to look after all his needs and to always do it with a smile. Some would say that was what wives were for, but that was just a fantasy. The reality, the post honeymoon reality was something altogether different in most cases. When the excitement and novelty of newlywed bliss wore off, the daily grind often erased all traces of romance and joyful servitude was buried under a mountain of selfish desires.

Her soothing tones and gorgeous appearance were hypnotic, morphine in the shape of an angel. The he thought of Cherie, his wife, and how she could also enchant him, he decided to cool the flirting. Who was he kidding anyway? Beaten up old John and goddess young Sharon? What a laugh.

'…and your leg is broken, although you probably can't feel that at the moment. I'll get you something for your headache.'

'Has my wife been in?' Mental pat on the back.

'You just missed her. She went home about half an hour ago

to get some of your things and something for you to read. She said you would get bored as soon as you woke up.'

Cherie knew him well. He only hoped she brought reading material to suit his taste rather than what she wanted him to read. She was persistent in her attempts to get him to read what she called *good stuff,* instead of garbage. John liked garbage. Nothing too heavy or serious like all that Christian propaganda she liked. A motoring magazine, Big League, or the newspaper would do him fine. Christian writing was fanciful and too otherworldly to be of any use or interest to him these days, especially the Bible.

'Thank you,' said John weakly as he watched her leave and realized that he had not been listening to her. Did she say when Cherie would return? He really wanted to see her, to touch her face and smell her hair.

He didn't feel as if he had been sleeping all day. More like he had not slept at all for a couple of days, as well as being beaten up. Sharon had not mentioned any damage to his face, but it hurt like hell. Having your glasses smashed into your face will do that. A mirror would have been useful to see how much disfigurement he had suffered. The odd scar might toughen his appearance without detracting from what his wife Cherie always said was a handsome face. Maybe nobody else thought so but Cherie's opinion was the only one that mattered to John.

On the other hand, too much scarring would make him look like a monster and he sure as hell didn't want to walk around scaring children. All he had managed to acquire so far in his twenty eight years was a few all-but-faded acne scars and another scar hidden by his eyebrow which was caused by a collision with a steel frame at work. He had never suffered any broken bones and his last visit to a hospital as a patient was when he was eight and had to have his appendix removed. Like many people, he had a dislike for hospitals because of the way they smelled and because they were full of sickness and disease and misery.

John shifted uneasily trying to scratch a nagging itch in his back. Funny that his main concern was an itchy back considering the scope and severity of the injuries he had suffered.

Finally, it had happened to him. Seven years behind the wheel of his red and white St.George taxi had resulted in him becoming a statistic. He had joined the chosen few. The victims list. John had always known there were risks involved in his job, particularly driving the night shift- which he only did one night a week out of the six days he worked, but no one ever thinks misfortune will befall them. The people in the news are always strangers. Now John had joined the ranks of those hard-working honest cabbies who had been robbed and bashed.

The bashing was the part John found hardest to accept. They probably wanted some drug money, so they robbed an easy target, but they did not have to beat him half to death. He would have handed them all the cash he had and the keys to the cab had they given him a chance. Why would someone want to do that to another person who has doing nothing to provoke them? To a bloke just trying to earn a living by providing a taxi service to those people without cars, or to those sensible enough not to drive themselves when they had been drinking? Why?

As he lay on the hard hospital bed staring at the ceiling he regretted his decision to continue working the Saturday night shift. He had decided to give it away and only work day shifts, but purely out of fear of the financial strain it would cause, due to Saturday night being by far his most profitable shift, he had changed his mind and returned to the hellish shift which always stressed him out. Not to mention the fact it was a constant worry for his family, especially Cherie. They wanted him to stop. Too dangerous they said. Cherie would always stay up to make sure that he made it home safely. Waiting and praying. They had been married for twelve months and she had maintained her Sunday morning vigil without fail.

John always confidently reassured his loved ones that the chances of anything happening to him were very slight. Truthfully, he never thought much about the inherent peril of his job. If a bloke was to worry about that sort of things all the time, or even occasionally, he simply would not be able to do the job. He would literally be too afraid to work. Prior to this attack, John had only ever felt threatened once or twice by passengers in his seven years behind the wheel. Only once was he the victim of anything even approaching assault, apart from verbal abuse which he received quite regularly. That was just a bit of a shove. Nothing serious.

Sharon returned with a couple of Panadeine tablets for John's headache. She was followed closely by a doctor, and behind him, lurking just outside the door to the ward, were two police officers. It was nearly question and answer time. John would be asked to recall the events of those wee hours of that Sunday morning in minute detail for the attending officers.

The doctor finished his observations then assured John there was nothing wrong with him that would not heal fully in time. Taking the pretty young nurse with him, he left the room. John watched as he chatted briefly with the police. Gesturing and nodding accompanied the muffled conversation. John tried to make himself more comfortable by sitting, but a sharp pain in his side argued against it. The police came to John's bedside.

'Mr.Miles?' said one of the officers.

'John'll do. Just call me John.'

'John, we need to ask you some questions. If you feel well enough to help us, we would appreciate it.'

'Of course,' replied John, even though he really didn't feel like it.

'We will need a detailed written statement later. You can come to the station when you are feeling better and we will take care of that for you. For now, if you could just tell us briefly what happened.'

John took a moment to gather his thoughts. Both officers were watching him with a look of concentrated compassion. The male of average height with short cropped hair and noticeably large ears was asking the questions. He towered above his female partner, a petite brunette with a youthful, plain face. She was poised with notepad and pencil at the ready to take down John's statement. For an instant John thought that he might laugh, as they looked odd together. The stereotypical brawny six-foot law enforcer had become an oddity in recent years, due to a relaxing of recruitment parameters. Desperately needing new recruits, the police service lowered its physical standards while at the same time ironically lifting academic standards.

He restrained himself, took a breath and began to tell his tale.

'Two blokes from Sutherland. Off the rank. Going to Hurstville. It was about one thirty Sunday morning. We arrived at their home. Well, what I thought was their home. It was dark. No lights on in the house we pulled up in front of, or any of the surrounding houses. That didn't surprise me given the late hour. I tell them the fare and then they demand my money. They start yelling at me and before I could hand it over the guy sitting beside me starts hitting me. It was pretty clumsy because of him having to get around the screen and he never got a square

205

hit on me, but he distracted me long enough for his mate, who I'd forgotten about, to get out of the back seat, pull open the driver's door and yank me out onto the road. Then they both started laying into me.'

John paused, breathless. He had been speaking more quickly as the story unfolded and wondered if he might have lost the brunette notetaker. She was scribbling furiously long after John had stopped talking.

'Did you get a good look at the guys?' asked the male officer, his expression and tone unchanged. Police could be like robots sometimes.

After licking his dry lips, he covered his mouth and coughed. 'Not the guy in the back. But the guy in the front had blonde hair in a sort of shaggy style like he never brushed it and...'

'Is this him?' asked the same officer, interrupting John by producing a Polaroid snapshot.

John was amazed. 'Yeah, yeah that's him...how?'

'Luckily we had a patrol car cruising the area and they were able to respond very quickly to your emergency call.'

'Unluckily for me, they weren't in the same bloody street,' said John with a straight face.

'The two men were apprehended whilst trying to flee on foot after running your taxi off the road and into a fence,' droned the officer.

'Wow. Like I say, though, what a shame they weren't intercepted before I had the shit kicked out of me.'

Ignoring the comment, the officer continued, 'Both men have been charged with the theft of your taxi and resisting arrest. We'll of course add assault to the charges once we have your completed statement.'

'Right,' said John. He scratched his head and winced as he felt the rough texture of stitches.

'How much money was stolen?'

'They got my money bag. Around twenty dollars worth of gold coins. Plus...I dunno...maybe six or seven dollars in silver. Notes from my shirt pocket. About sixty dollars there and one hundred out of my wallet. That's how much I had. I don't actually know what they took. Did you recover my wallet?'

'Yes. They had taken the money out and left your wallet there beside you.'

'Oh, but they didn't get my pay-in money. Two hundred bucks stashed away in my sock.' John remembered how stupid he felt when he first started putting his money in his sock. Despite being strongly advised to do so he always felt it was overly cautious. Nevertheless, he trained himself to do it and now was very thankful he had. 'Where is that now?'

'I suspect it will be with all your personal belongings.'

'Yeah,' said John, smiling at the success of that little trick.

'So,' began the petite officer thoughtfully, 'That was a total of one hundred and eighty dollars cash, right?'

'Yep. Sounds right. Your maths is probably better than mine.' There was no reaction and John was seriously starting to think that maybe these two officers were automatons. 'What about my phone?' he continued.

'It was still in the taxi.'

'Good. So, I guess all they got was the money and a shit load of trouble from you blokes,' said John, still managing to find some humour in the situation. He realized he had referred to the female officer as a bloke, but she didn't seem to notice. Like nurses, she had probably heard that before. Which was worse? Being a policewoman or a nurse?

'We'll be in touch regarding your statement, John. We wish

you a speedy recovery, and thanks for your time.'

'Thank you,' replied John. The two officers disappeared through the ward door leaving him alone with his thoughts and his pain.

The following week in hospital recovering and undergoing a series of tests to ensure that all was well with his brain – no permanent damage - had messed with John's head. Bored and frustrated, even though he understood the necessity of staying. The doctors didn't want to see any complications arise or any evidence of serious head trauma any more than John did himself. Cherie had been in every day, as had other family members and a few of his mates. Their visits broke the monotony, but the tedium was beginning to break his spirit. Finally, they released him.

Receiving the advice of his doctor to take it very easy for at least three to four weeks, and gratefully accepting a script for painkillers, John left the hospital on a rainy Sunday morning. Cherie arrived promptly to pick him up and take him home. This day should have been a happy one, but the gloomy weather matched John's mood. Soured by both his physical wounds and the damage to his soul, he felt transformed. Different. Bent right out of shape.

* * *

When John started working again six weeks after his release from hospital, Cherie was convinced there was something seriously wrong with him.

'John,' she began hesitantly, 'I don't know how to talk to you anymore. You're always biting my head off. I'm trying to help you, but..'

'But what? I'm fine. I just don't want to go to church or read the bible. That's not going to help. If God cares so much why'd he let this happen to me? Can you answer me that?'

'No, but if you're fine why don't you go back to work?'

John shook his head. 'I'm not ready yet.' Glaring at her, he added, "Just drop it okay? Stop trying to help me.'

* * *

John's pent up rage began to manifest itself in a series of unpleasant incidents which started during his second week back behind the wheel of his red and white St.George taxi. These episodes were merely the tip of the iceberg: minor demonstrations of a seriously dangerous mentality. John had become a thin skinned and belligerent time bomb.

Passengers could be both the best and the worst aspect of the taxi driver's job just like every other service related job or any job where a person had to deal with other people. People were the best and the worst of life in general. Prior to the assault he had been able to easily suppress irritation and treat all but the most antagonistic of passengers with customary politeness. Self-control was just one of the casualties of the vicious assault he had suffered.

One slow Wednesday morning, circumstances were mounting an offensive on John's disposition. Australia had lost the cricket test match against the West Indies and there wasn't much work around. Several passengers in a row had left the windows down when they exited the cab and although it was a trivial thing, it still got on John's goat. The taxi rank was seemingly always full of idle cabs and a plethora of private cars using the designated rank as a drop off zone. The static on the radio was driving him mad and no matter his position on the rank the maddening crackle continued unabated. Everything was annoying, and he felt like he had no control over anything in his life.

A lady came up beside John's cab, leaned over, looked in through the passenger window, and began to move her mouth. John gestured for her to open the door as he could not hear what she was saying, but she kept on opening and closing her trap as if she believed that either she was shouting at John or that he had bionic hearing. Exasperated at being an unwilling participant in a game of charades, John leaned across to open the door ignoring the security shield which stabbed into his side as he reached for the door handle.

'Are you vacant?' she asked, stepping back a pace as the door swung open.

This was the crucial moment. The split second in which one has to decide how to react to what someone says or does. Civil or sarcastic? Normally John would have chosen the right path of politeness, but as he was feeling as far from normal as the earth is from the sun, and the day was going badly anyway, he accelerated down the highway of sarcasm.

'Well I'm not here for my health or to get my jollys mam.'

Why would a person ask an empty taxi parked on a taxi rank with his roof light on to show he's available for hire, if he was vacant or not? What else would he be doing there? This lady was not the first to ask what had to be one of the stupidest questions of all time.

She seemed not to understand so John simply said yes, which instantly satisfied her. Next, she closed the front door and got in the back seat. John wound his window up and turned the radio down so that he could hear her. Unfortunately, she had a soft voice which John certainly did not blame her for, nor was he hard of hearing. It was just one of the drawbacks of the security screens: they blocked a bit of sound and made communication difficult at times. Small price to pay according to John. That view put him in a minority as most drivers complained loudly and incessantly about the inconveniences the screens caused. Many passengers also questioned their value and even though the screen had not saved him, John was still glad it was there. Being in a foul brewing tempest, even this private conversation gave him the shits. He wished the lady had sat next to him in the front seat to make it easier. He wished there were no old ladies.

She told him where she wanted to go and asked if he knew the place. John replied confidently that he did because there was not much that he didn't know about his local area. A few minutes into the estimated ten minute journey, John ascertained that the silence indicated his passenger was not the garrulous kind so he turned up the radio. Silence in the cab, especially with a fare on board was not something that John enjoyed at all. However, no sooner had he turned up the volume when he heard a small voice emanating from the back seat. Briefly John considered ignoring her, but he thought better of it. He sucked in a sharp breath and held it briefly.

'I'm sorry, mam. You'll have to speak up. I can't hear you.'

'Sorry,' she said in only a slightly louder voice, 'I asked if you were having a busy day?'

That was the most frequently asked question, and the taxi driver's most hated one. 'No, I'm not.'

'Oh!' said the lady, obviously a bit taken aback by John's abrupt answer.

'Is that all then? Can I answer another dumb question for you?' asked John.

'I was just trying to make conversation,' she replied. 'Sorry.'

'If you wanted to talk to me, why didn't you sit here in the front seat? And why did you wait three minutes after I had turned the volume back up on the radio before opening your mouth?'

No sooner had the words left John's mouth when he realized he had overstepped the mark, but in truth he was enjoying himself too much to care. How could this be fun? Deep inside he knew the woman, like many other passengers, simply wanted to be friendly and without knowing the driver, in this case John, they start off with an easy general question or a remark about the weather. He did not act according to what he knew because the freedom to be able to say whatever was on his mind was suddenly exhilarating. When he considered the hundreds or even thousands of times he had bitten his tongue just for the sake of civility and talked about nothing just to keep his passengers amused, he reckoned he had earned a measure of payback. Nothing wrong with being honest.

'So,' continued John, 'just sit there quietly until we get to your place - yes I know where it is - and let me listen to the radio. Okay?'

There was no reply from the passenger.

John turned into the nominated street, slowed down, and waited for instructions. He also turned off the radio. When he reached the end of the road without having heard so much as a peep from the lady in the back he stopped the cab, turned his head around and said to her.

'Did I get the street wrong?'

'No. No we're here. Well, just back there a little bit actually.'

'Why didn't you say something? I don't know your house. You didn't tell me the number. All you had to say was stop here please.'

The lady ignored his question.

'How much is the fare, please?' she asked obviously upset and eager to leave as quickly as possible.

'Eight fifty.'

She handed John a ten dollar note, and after receiving the change, said, 'You are a very rude man.'

'Thank you mam.'

'And I'm going to report you.'

'No worries. Did you get my authority number? I'll write it down for you if you like.'

'I have it already.'

'Good. Off you go then. See ya.'

After she left the cab, John stayed put for a few moments. Normally being told that he was going to be reported to the complaints department did not bother him because on the few occasions he had been threatened with such, nothing had eventuated. John made sure that he avoided provoking passengers in any way. Previous threats had vanished purely because they were spurious charges. John knew he was not at fault and consequently was not concerned about any further action against him. This time was different. The woman's complaint was entirely justified. He rubbed his chin thoughtfully.

The next passenger offered John a one hundred dollar note to pay an eight dollar fare without the slightest attempt at an apology. When John told her that he was unable to change it she miraculously found a tenner in her purse. It was just one of those days. Even the weather was seemingly conspiring against him. An overcast day, hot and humid inside the cab but cool and windy outside. Too cold for the air conditioner and to blowy to have the windows down. It was a matter of good fortune, or the grace of Cherie's God, that only one of his passengers fell victim to his sharp tongue as it expressed the emotion of a charred heart.

Usually John reckoned he could count on having a good day following a particularly bad one. It was very rare indeed to have consecutive bad luck, bad mood days. However, when John woke up late the next morning having forgotten to set his alarm clock, he knew it was the beginning of another twenty-four hours of disaster. He needn't have bothered dressing as a heavy coat of impending doom pressed down upon his shoulders.

Ten thirty arrived and John had only taken seventy dollars in four and a half hours work. This would be, barring a miracle like a sudden rush of business or a return fare to Wollongong, another shift where John would be forced to give more money to the owner of the cab than he could put in his own pocket. Another shortfall in the budget. More juggling of the finances would be needed to avoid missing the fortnightly rent payment. That was the whole problem with this job and why he had returned to work the Saturday night shift. There was too much difference in income between the good days and the bad days, and it was too easy for a good day to become a bad one.

The weather was humid again and the cab's air conditioning system was on its last legs - barely functioning. Pulling onto an abnormally vacant Caringbah rank, John only had a short wait for his next fare. Was this the beginning of rush hour? Perhaps the day could be salvaged after all but probably not. John told himself to calm down. False hope was the creation of fools.

A male passenger approached John's cab. He was a large man, tall and solid: a typical Pacific Islander. Once seated in the front seat, he directed John to make a right hand turn off the rank as a female climbed quietly into the back seat behind him. John had not seen her and in fact had nearly pulled off the rank as she was sitting down. The lack of response from the man in the front indicated they were probably together: his wife or girlfriend. There was obvious tension between the two, but that was not unusual. People's relational problems were a part of the daily parade. Communication breakdowns. Animosity. Resentment. Treating each other with disrespect and sometimes even disgust. John's cab was like a laundromat on Saturday morning, filled with other people's dirty laundry.

John made the turn as requested out onto the Kingsway but had only travelled a hundred metres when the guy told him to pull over. Reluctantly, John obeyed, and waited with increasing annoyance as the man and woman began to argue. Then the man got out and went into a fast food shop. The woman stayed where she was so John left the meter running. Assuming again that the man would return, to continue the fair. People were generally poor communicators and John was often forced to make assumptions.

'Sorry about this, mate,' she said softly.

John did not respond.

The gruff Islander came back to the taxi, opened the door, leant in and asked how much the fare was. Then he told the woman to get out, which she did without a hesitation. John was bemused and irritated but not concerned, despite the man's overtly aggressive demeanor and tone.

'Three twenty thanks mate.'

'Can you change a twenty?' he asked.

'No I can't,' said John through gritted teeth, wondering why the guy needed change for a twenty when he just came out of a shop.

'Well fuck you then,' he replied before slamming the door shut. 'We didn't fuckin' go anywhere anyway, eh!'

John turned the meter off and watched as the guy walked around to the driver's side of the cab thinking to himself how ludicrous it was that he had just been told off for not being able to change a twenty-dollar note. There was no way he was going to get into a blue over such a small amount of money, not even for the principle. John nonetheless felt that perhaps the big unit intended to pay after all. Or maybe he was just coming around to pour out some more abuse. This curiousity kept John there when he should have driven off immediately after the bloke refused to pay. The woman had already alighted so what good could possibly come from hanging around?

Against his better judgement, he turned off the radio and wound down his window. Without warning the man spat directly into John's face. Recovering from the shock, John quickly wiped the disgusting spittle off his face as best he could, using his hand and shirt sleeve. Then he exploded. The volcano which had been threatening violence for a couple of days, now erupted with maniacal force. He was like a city whose walls had been broken down. Unable to fight on his terms, but only react in desperation as the enemy attacked.

John burst out of his cab, slamming the door into the animal's knees. He was an animal. Had to be because only animals spit. Too large to fall, the angry Islander merely stumbled back a few paces into the path of oncoming traffic. John heard the screeching of brakes, and out of the corner of his eye saw the braking car in a cloud of burnt rubber smoke. John lunged, throwing a full punch at the stunned giant which connected with the side of his face, albeit with no noticeable effect.

The man returned a heavy fist, but he was slow and John was easily able to avoid the blow while counterpunching into his stomach. Unfortunately for John there was too much blubber there for his strike to cause any pain. The Islander grabbed John with his left hand and tried to line him up for a punch to the head.

John's gaze was directed for the first time to the giant's bandaged knee. He struck out for it with his right foot. The impact loosened the bigger man's grip on John who took careful aim and stabbed his foot right into the other's knee as hard as he could. So hard in fact that John lost his own balance and fell onto the road. As he fell he heard the man cry out and scream obscenities. That was all the encouragement John needed to quickly regain his feet and press home his advantage.

The spitting animal lay on the road clutching his knee. Mercilessly John stomped down again on the knee for a third time. People were yelling at him to stop. Telling him it was enough, but for John it was not enough. With his bloodthirst unsated, he leaned down, and planted his fist right on the nose of the humbled giant. There was a crack. Blood gushed.

Straightening up and looking around, John became aware again of his surroundings. Traffic had stopped, and a crowd of onlookers had gathered staring in amazement. Summoning one last burst of angry energy, John roared out to the crowd. 'This prick spat in my face because I couldn't change a twenty.'

He jumped back into his taxi and tore off down the road. In the rearview mirror, John watched the Islander's partner rush over to him. It never mattered how much of bastard a man was, there was always someone to cry for him, even if only his mother or his pathetic, gutless girlfriend.

Blood surged through John's veins as the rush of adrenalin drove his heart to pump faster than was safe. Where to now? Should he keep working? What should he do? Maybe pack it in for the day? No keep going. Have to make the dollars. Have to keep going. Eventually John convinced himself and he arrived at the next suburb, Miranda, without having been aware that he was still driving. The riot in his mind began to slowly disperse.

There would probably be a complaint filed about this incident. John chuckled to himself then immediately questioned whether laughter was appropriate. He was nervous and frightened by his own behaviour. It was either laugh or cry. Even if they didn't get his taxi license plate number, or his driver I.D. number there was a galaxy of witnesses who would more than likely side with the passenger and present a sympathetic point of view despite John's parting words. The passenger had most certainly provoked the incident, but John knew he was not without guilt. Taxi drivers are expected to grin and bear it whenever they are insulted or mistreated. They are taught early on in their training and know from their own experience that reacting to rude or aggressive passengers only causes the situation to escalate. Responding in kind was not only foolish but could also prove dangerous.

John, however, was unable to endure anything negative at all from his passengers anymore, let alone a physical assault. He simply could not control his feelings. Every passenger had to pay for what those guys did to him, but that was crazy. What about the old lady who was trying to be friendly? She did not deserve John's sarcasm. This guy had spat on him- in his face. In John's eyes, definitely constituting a physical attack, but he shouldn't have retaliated. At the time, there was no way on earth that he was going to accept such treatment lying down. He had not even considered turning the other cheek, not for a nanosecond. Now he wondered what good it had done. Violence begets violence and hate begets hate. As much as John tried to calm himself down, anger boiled in his bones: machine gun rage, spraying bullets indiscriminately.

For the rest of the shift, John basically ignored his passengers. Using the bare minimum of talk necessary to complete the task of taking them where they wanted to go and getting paid. His mind was fully occupied with the incident in Caringbah. He replayed the event over and over again, endlessly in his mind. Knowing that eventually he would be called to give an account of his actions, he tried to figure out a reasonable defense. Running through every detail and adding self-justifying embellishments where necessary, John constructed the story of what happened in just the way he wanted it to be told. He had done the wrong thing, but there was no way he was prepared to come straight out and admit it.

Somehow finishing his shift without further trouble, John arrived home and offered nothing but grumbled answers to Cherie's questions. She yanked him out of his pathetic indifference with a direct question. 'What happened today John? What's wrong with you?'

'Nothing,' replied John dismissively.

'Look at me,' said Cherie, letting anger infuse her words with venom. 'Open your mouth and talk to me properly and tell me what happened. What's wrong with you?'

John noticed her flushed cheeks and the anguish in her voice and was surprised by sudden feelings of sympathy for his wife. He knew he had been treating her poorly. It was not deliberate, but he was aware he was shutting her out of his life, and although he knew that was wrong, it was like everything else in his life at the moment: out of control.

'John?' said Cherie, interrupting his thoughts.

'I…' said John, before pausing to rehearse the story again as he had practiced all afternoon.

'I had a fight with a passenger this morning.'

'What? A fight? You mean like a fist fight or just an argument?'

'He spat in my face, so I got out of the cab and hit him.'

Cherie stood and listened, incredulous as John told her the whole story. Whenever he paused, she pushed him, probing for details and struggling to come to terms with what she was hearing. When he finished his tale, he added, 'Something is wrong with me babe. I'm shitty all the time. I'm losing it. I can't control my temper.'

'That's painfully obvious,' replied Cherie, frowning, suppressing tears.

'I mean everything ticks me off. Everyone. Everything. I can't help it and I can't trust anyone or talk to anyone. I feel like some sort of outcast. I try to be friendly and polite, but I just can't. Sometimes I can't even be bothered trying. I forget how. I don't know who I am.'

During the silence which followed, John stared at the floor, unable to meet Cherie's eyes.

'You are blaming all your passengers for what those men did to you, aren't you?'

'I don't know if blaming is the right word. I don't know if that's what this is about. I just don't know. I'm just…just angry all the time. What am I gonna do, babe?'

Cherie suggested he stop working for a while and that maybe he had started back at work too soon after the attack. John protested by saying there was no way they could afford for him to stay off work any longer. The six week lay off had already consumed all their savings. She countered that perhaps she could take on a full-time position at the restaurant where she now worked part time. Maybe that would enable John to stop work for a while. Just to get his head together. John did not like that idea either.

'I have to work. I can't just sit around all day. That would be worse.'

'We need to pray,' said Cherie hopefully. 'And ask-'

'What the fuck is that gonna do?' said John, helplessly exploding again. 'You know I don't go for that stuff, and where was God when I was having my head kicked in by those pricks?'

He watched his wife's face crumble, lips trembling, eyes glistening. He regretted his tone, but she should have known better than to go there. Religious discussions were an impossibility between them now. They could argue very well about God and the church and John enjoyed baiting her, but it was all terribly unconstructive. So she just quietly went about the business of trying to love him or convert him or whatever she was trying to do. Occasionally she would ask him if he wanted to go to church with her, but he always refused and told her to stop asking him. He was just not interested.

The irony of the situation was not lost on John who had been a committed Christian when they met. He had started to fall away and lose his devotion even before he was assaulted that night. Stopped going to church over what he perceived as being the immoral politics of the church and a personality clash with the new minister. Had stopped trying and had even given up on making excuses for himself or for the church. Being a Christian, a follower of Christ required commitment and effort. Commitment to other interests, including sport and watching movies, had usurped John's dedication to God. Being so badly beaten that night had simply reinforced his diminished respect for God. It was the final nail in the coffin in which his faith was buried.

'I'll pray for you then John,' said Cherie as she moved forward to embrace him. 'I love you.'

'I love you too,' replied John rather too quickly. It sounded hollow and half-hearted and the truth was that he had very little room left in his heart for love: filled as it was with the bile of bitterness.

The conversation ended there. John grabbed himself a beer from the fridge and sat down to watch television until dinner. After eating, he watched the box a while longer before having a shower and going to bed. He did not say anything at all. Not to Cherie. Not to himself. Not even to the television as he used to do in happier days.

A few days passed. John managed to push the memory of that morning in Caringbah away to the back of his mind. Neither the police or the taxi base had contacted him, so he felt safe in assuming that the spitting animal had not filed a complaint or pressed charges. He was possibly too ashamed to lodge a complaint and was perhaps willing to accept some of the blame. Maybe his sweet girlfriend had talked him out of taking the matter any further. Whatever the reason, John believed he was probably in the clear and the pleasure he gained from that belief was doubled by a couple of busy, relatively trouble free shifts in a row.

Although he was not overtly rude to anyone, John was at best indifferent. Every now and then he would strike up a bit of a conversation with a particularly genial passenger, but by and large he kept his own counsel and used words sparingly: both in the cab and at home. The struggle within raged on.

One week later, John was sitting in his cab in the parking lot of KFC Miranda. It was just before eleven o'clock and he had stopped for lunch. Parked facing the street, John watched the passing parade of people and cars as he munched on a chicken fillet burger. A bus stopped in front of him at a red light. Inside was a group of teenaged boys fooling around as teenage boys are prone to do. One of them apparently decided to target John for a bit of fun. He looked out the window directly at John, pointed his finger, then turned to his mates and started laughing. It was just a bit of fun for the sake of impressing his friends: not a personal attack, but John gave the young man the finger and mouthed a few choice swear words, making sure that the kid would be left in no doubt as to what John thought of his antics. The teenager responded in kind and John blew his stack again.

Jumping out of the cab, he leapt over a flower bed, ran the short distance to the stationary bus and banged on the door and demanded the driver open it and let him in. The shocked driver was unaware of what had been going on behind him, so he told John in the strongest possible terms to forget about it before putting the bus in gear and moving off as the light turned green. Undeterred, John frantically looked around for something to throw at the bus. There was no way he was going to let that little prick get away with being such a smart arse.

Seeing a fist sized rock near the gutter, he picked it up, took aim, and pitched it at the glass separating the smirking boy from the outside world. His stupid grin disappeared in a flash when he realized that the projectile was coming straight toward him. He ducked his head just as the rock impacted the glass. John cursed as the window merely cobwebbed. Damn safety glass. Immediately aware the window had not shattered and that he was quite unharmed, the teenager bobbed his head back up, moved to the back of the bus, and gave John the finger one last time for good measure.

John went back to his taxi and finished his burger, seething: huffing through each mouthful. He drank some Pepsi then lit a cigarette and laughed to himself like a lunatic. What a fool he had just made of himself. During the laugh he forgot to exhale and began to cough: the gagging, hacking kind of cough that smokers do so well. There had to be some way of reeling in his temper. It seemed that now he had let the tiger out of its cage, there was no stopping the carnage. Someone was going to get hurt. John sucked on his cigarette and worried himself into a fierce headache.

Later that day he picked up two passengers from their home in Yowie Bay. Neither of the two men responded to John's greeting when they got in the cab. One of them told John they wanted to go to the train station. Nearing the destination John moved in to the left hand lane just before a roundabout preparing to drop them in a bus bay opposite the station entrance. That was where most people got out to save the time it would take to go past the entrance to the station, turn around and come back again.

Almost in the roundabout, the man in the front told John to turn right and stop on the corner. Instantly annoyed, John nonetheless made a risky right hand turn from the left hand lane; the wrong lane. As there was insufficient room to stop the cab right on the corner without blocking traffic, John travelled another fifty metres to where he could stop safely. Twice during that fifty metres the man told John to stop.

'I heard you the first time mate,' said John without trying to hide his irritation. 'I couldn't stop right on the corner. It wasn't safe. And thanks for not giving me any warning to turn right either. Everyone else gets out up there on the left. In the bus bay.'

Silence from both men. John was annoyed they did not respond. He was in the mood for a fight. Another rage was brewing.

'How much is that?' asked the man in the back.

'Four sixty.'

A ten-dollar note came from the guy in the back while the one in the front seat got out.

'I don't have much change. I'll have to give it to you in coins. Mostly silver,' said John without attempting an apology. He did have sufficient change but was trying to raise the ire of this arrogant passenger. A slight grumble was all it took. 'Why don't you let me keep it then if you're worried about carrying so much change,' suggested John sarcastically.

'I doubt it. Hurry up please. We have a train to catch.'

'Do we now?' mocked John. 'You'd probably wait ten minutes for a five-cent piece, wouldn't you, ya arrogant prick.' John dumped the coins in the man's hands, causing some of them to fall to the floor. 'Sorry dear.'

'What's your number? I'm going to report you,' he threatened, as he scrounged around on the floor for the fallen coins.

'Oh no,' said John, feigning a fearful tone as he jumped out of the driver's seat and raced around to the other side of the cab.

The guy got out, stood up and repeated his threat to report John before adding, 'What's your problem?'

'What's your problem?' roared John the tiger, madly directing his self-hate at the innocent man. He knocked him to the ground with a double handed shove to his chest. The man dropped his money again as he crashed on to the seat of his pants. Red faced with anger and humiliation, he stood up quickly and ignoring his money lunged at John. His mate joined the battle immediately after John decked the man a second time with a right cross to the side of his head.

'You want some too?' yelled John as the other man approached. 'Fuck off after your train. Hurry up or you'll miss it.'

One last parting glare followed from the two men before they turned and walked away. Defeated. Humiliated. The bloke that John did not get to lay hands on put his arm around his mate's shoulder as they walked, leaned close to him and spoke into his ear. Presumably, words of comfort. John felt powerful, shouting after them, 'Fucking poofters!'

He bent down and picked up every single coin that the guy had dropped during the altercation, then got into his taxi and drove back to Miranda rank still seething, to await his next fare.

It was all one-way traffic for John, a highway to Hell: venting his anger and asserting his authority in a pitiful power display. Anyone who rubbed him the wrong way copped sarcasm at best, and at worst, invective laden abuse. It did not matter whether they deserved to be abused in John's view or even if they had provoked him at all. With each successive episode, his remorse was drowned with maniacal glee. He was really enjoying himself. The dominance was addictive and exciting. All the while, his conscience burned, and his heart blackened.

Fifteen minutes after he arrived on the rank, a lady got into his cab, said hello, and asked to be driven to Cronulla. John had been watching a group of teenaged boys being questioned by police just prior to the lady getting in. She referred to them in her first statement after they pulled off the taxi rank.

'It's criminal,' she said. 'Those bastards shouldn't be allowed to do that.'

'What's that?' asked John, only half interested.

'The police!' Her voice increasingly manifesting the great offence she perceived. 'Corrupting the minds of the young. They are all dishonest and dangerous bastards.'

'The police? You can't say that,' protested John.

'I can. They are. All corrupt. I don't trust them. They'll probably take the boys away, lock them up and brainwash them.'

'Yeah, right,' said John sarcastically.

'You don't believe me?'

She obviously really believed what she was saying and was further upset by John not accepting her truth, not joining her outrage.

'No,' said John. 'It's bullshit.'

'Well, let me tell you something.' She began to rave, repeating the same stupid and baseless accusations against the police and authority in general over and over. One paranoid conspiracy theory after another. John tuned out and let her ramble on. Occasionally, he nodded or said yes or uh-huh. There was no point arguing with her or even trying to say anything. She wasn't listening. She kept on talking as if this was the very last opportunity she would have in life to speak. Finally, and thankfully, she stopped, either out of breath or bereft of ideas, and asked John for his name.

'I can't tell you. You might report me to the police. You might be one of them. They'll come and arrest me and take me to some dark room with a spotlight shining in my face and force me to confess everything.' John was pleased at finally being able to say something, but he knew that sensible conversation was quite out of the question with this weirdo, so he attempted to amuse himself.

'Stop the cab!' she ordered. 'Let me out immediately.'

John was happy to oblige. 'Six eighty thanks.'

'What?' she asked, already half way out the door.

'The fare is six dollars eighty,' repeated John.

'I don't like you.'

'I don't give a shit,' he snapped. 'Just pay the fare and piss off.'

The look of shock on her face was priceless. Like she had just seen a flasher open his raincoat. For a moment, she seemed dumbstruck, frozen of mouth and of mind.

'Pay the fare. Six eighty,' insisted John, while staring at her.

She gave him a five dollar note then fumbled around in her bag for some change. He probably would not get a tip for this job. Eventually she found a handful of coins and slowly counted out exactly one dollar and eighty cents. Handing John the money, she said, 'I don't like your vibe.'

'My vibe?' John's eyebrows jumped to the top of his forehead, nearly escaping to the open sky. 'Whatever the hell vibe is, I don't care. Like I said. Piss off now. Off you go. You're wasting my time.'

And go she did. The rest of the shift passed without further incident.

John arrived home to find Cherie had gone out. Initially he was relieved because her absence meant he would not have to answer her questions. In which case he would have to tell more lies to keep her off his case. Nor would he have to force himself to engage in civil conversation when he felt so far removed from civilization that he may as well have been a leper living in the Nullabor Desert.

Going to the fridge to grab a cold beer, John noticed a piece of paper held in place on the fridge door by a Home Sweet Home fridge magnet. It read.

Dear John,

I've gone to stay with my mum for a while. I don't understand what's happened to you, but I know you've changed. I can't stand to be ignored by you and lied to. pushed aside as if I don't mean anything to you. You have shut me right out of your life. I'm hurt. Really hurt. Hurt by the knowledge that you can't or won't share yourself with me. Your thoughts and feelings. A relationship without communication is a joke. That's why I left. I'm not leaving you, not yet. But I've decided to leave you alone for a while. I love you John. I just didn't know what else to do.

You seem to want to be left alone so I'll give you what you think that you want.

Don't call me until you want to talk. I mean until you really want to talk to me. Like a husband should talk to his wife. Believe me I just want to help you. I want the man that I married back again. Where is he?

Cherie

John pulled the note off the fridge door, letting the magnet fall to the floor. He opened the door, picked up a beer, twisted the lid off it and took a long deep drink of the ice cold lager. Then he plopped down on a kitchen chair and re read the letter from Cherie. Not really knowing how he felt about this development - which did surprise him although it shouldn't have - he merely sat there alone in the kitchen for a while, drinking his beer.

She had not left him, but she was gone. What was that supposed to mean? John detested riddles. Cherie was gone. His wife was gone. Quite suddenly John choked up with a torrent of emotions. There was a knot in his throat as he tried to stem the tide. His eyes burned as tears forced their way out and ran down his cheeks. At first, he tried to fight but there were too many pent up feelings to resist: like a flood swollen river overwhelming its banks. Too much repressed rage and bitterness, and now remorse. He had shut his wife out of his life. She had knocked on the door of his heart, wanting to come in and share his pain. but he had slammed the door in her face and broken her nose, forcing her away.

Giving up the struggle, John allowed the weeping to turn to sobbing, and then to unrestrained wailing. He cried like he never had before, but finally, after what seemed like an eternity of heart wrenching grief, he stopped. Physically and emotionally exhausted, he slumped on the kitchen table with his face on the letter from Cherie. Eventually he stood and went to the sink to wash his tear stained face. He also drank some cold water straight from the tap to soothe his throat. 'She's gone,' he whispered. 'What do I do now? She's gone.'

Sitting back down at the kitchen table, he lit a cigarette, drew deeply, then blew the smoke out slowly. It was very satisfying. He felt clean, the crying acting like a hot shower on an aching body. Still sad and disappointed with himself, he realized he had let bitterness take control of his life. He had let the devil climb into the driver's seat and could blame nobody, but himself for his foolish and destructive behaviour.

As he put the cigarette to his lips for a second drag, he heard a voice. A quiet voice. A gentle voice. Louder than a whisper, but surely inaudible. Perhaps it was his imagination, but no, there it was again. John knew he was not hearing things. The voice was real. He turned around to confirm he was alone. There was no fear. He was not afraid at all. Instead, an odd feeling of serenity, an aura of tranquility in the voice flowed over him. It was at once compassionate and authoritative. A voice not to be ignored, like a parent calling their wayward child to order. John listened carefully.

'It's alright, my son. You can start again. I can give you a fresh start. A new beginning.'

'Is that you dad?' John called to his father who had been killed by bowel cancer when John was just twelve years old. But he never talked to John that way. Never talked much at all. 'Dad?' he called again in vain.

John continued to puff on his cigarette, contemplating the

words and wondering about their origin as a sense of happiness and hopefulness covered him like a blanket on a cold winter's night.

Then he laughed. What was he thinking? In-bloody-sane. Crying and softie bullshit. He had to pull himself together. 'A new beginning, eh?' This was too intense. He needed a change of scene and a large amount of alcohol. 'How about a few coldies at the local,' he said, feeling like his old self had suddenly returned. He would drink in celebration, not to drown his sorrows. He felt delirious. Drunk, although he had consumed just two bottles of beer.

His friend Mick was home when John telephoned, and he agreed to meet him at the local hotel, the Caringbah Inn, in half an hour. John showered, put on some fresh clothes and walked up the road to the pub, feeling high and manly: resolutely intent on being tough.

His ever exuberant drinking partner arrived just as John had downed the first of many beers he planned to drink. The two men sat there drinking and talking about nothing in particular while watching a replay of the NRL match of the round on the big screen television. John quickly got plastered. Mick, on the other hand, took it a little easier because he had to drive home, unlike John who could stumble and stagger the few hundred metres down the road to his place.

'So how you been?' asked Mick. 'Haven't seen much of you lately?'

Mick's wife and Cherie were pretty close. Permission for him to go out for a drink would have had strings attached. John suspected as much but had been pleasantly surprised he and Mick had stayed in safe conversation territory. Until now. If Mick decided to push, John would be forced into the danger zone. 'I'm great. I told ya, just great.'

'What are you doing here in the middle of the bloody week then?'

John tried to avoid his friend's glare of inquisition, but he'd seen it before. Rare though it was, once unleashed, Mick could be unrelenting. He felt his resolve evaporating.

Mick pressed in. 'What's going on?'

'Cherie left me. Left a note on the fridge. I'm all fucked up Mick. I'm falling from one disaster at work to another. I tell ya, one of these days I'm going really hurt someone. I just can't control myself. I'm so pissed off with myself and with everybody else.'

'Well congratulations on the show you been putting on then. Why didn't you just tell me on the blower that Cherie had split, and you needed to talk?' He smiled. 'I knew it already, you dopey bastard.'

'I don't know.' It was an honest answer. John wondered why he found it so hard to share his problems with Mick whom he considered his closest friend.

Mick finished his beer and held the empty glass towards John to ask if he wanted another one. John nodded and quickly sculled the contents of his glass before burping and reaching for a cigarette. He had not intended to come and discuss all this with Mick, had not wanted to, but it was too late now. They were into it and John was starting to feel emotional again. He wondered if maybe he should make a run for the door to avoid displaying the waterworks in front of Mick. Before he could make up his mind, Mick returned.

'All right,' said Mick, laying down a couple of foam crested schooners on the table. 'Talk to me. I'm all ears.'

John shifted uneasily in his seat as he began to recount the whole sorry tale. Trouble at work and trouble at home. Nothing but trouble almost every waking hour. Mick initially found it all a bit of a laugh, but as the violence increased the humour evaporated. John could see shock and disbelief, even disgust written all over his face. John smoked continuously as he talked and when he finished his eyes were red and his voice hoarse.

Mick did the manly thing, making a joke and calling John a sissy before telling him to snap out of it. 'She'll be right, mate.' They changed the subject, steering the ship of conversation back into calm water, but John felt like he was rowing a leaky canoe towards a waterfall.

In the middle of a moaning session about the poor quality of refereeing in the NRL, Mick shifted back to John's problem. Offering the only help he could think of, he said, 'Mate, why don't you call me when you start to feel your blood boil and I'll tell you a joke or something. Might save ya from falling into the shit again.'

With an unconvincing nod, John agreed.

At half past eight they traded a few more insults and said their good byes. 'Call me anytime you need to,' said Mick, 'and do whatever you need to, to get Cherie back. You'll really have fucked up if you lose her.'

John thanked his mate before beginning the walk home: very slowly, enjoying his state of inebriation. By the time he arrived at the front door, he had forgotten about the note from Cherie, his emotional outburst, the voice he'd heard and Mick's parting words of advice. The dark and quiet house drained away his euphoria as quickly as it had come on that afternoon following his mini breakdown. His thoughts returned to Cherie as he fell into the cold and empty bed: a hollow ache in his heart. In a few minutes, he was asleep.

The next morning John woke up with a hangover and a feeling of dread. His shift started with the first few passengers in the morning paying for their small fares with twenty-dollar notes which sunk his float by taking all his change. Then he had a couple of no shows in a row before settling down on Miranda rank for a full hour waiting for another job. He tried to read the paper to calm himself down and ease the boredom, but his anger festered. When he did finally get another fare, she was rude and argumentative, accusing John of trying to take her the long way to get more money out of her. He really hated being accused of attempting to rip people off. He was no cheat. Just an honest, hard-working bloke who resented immensely any suggestion of greed. As a result of her accusation, he verbally abused the woman and enjoyed doing so.

'Why don't you shut up. I think I know the fucking quickest way to go. In fact, I probably know half a dozen ways to get there. And don't you fucking accuse me of trying to rip you off, ya stupid bitch. How about that?' John paused as if expecting applause or some form of congratulations for his tirade. When none came he continued, 'Just shut up and let me drive you, ya cow...'

That barrage was enough to silence her, but John kept on berating her anyway. Beyond what was reasonable. Like the worst kind of abusive alcoholic who fed off the fear and humiliation of the person they were abusing, John totally loved it. Blinded to sensitivity or reason: fatally wounded animal lashing out in hostile instinct. He stopped to take a breath and found he had run out of things to say, completely exhausting his rage, for the time being anyway. When he finished the woman, was crying, but John didn't care. That was the problem. He simply did not care anymore. Not about himself, not about his job and certainly not about other people. Worse than this revelation was the knowledge that it was not a problem he intended to fix. John figured he was probably as low as he could go. Probably.

'Maybe next time,' said John, in a normal tone, 'You will think before you open your mouth and start making false accusations.'

Wordlessly, the poor woman paid John and got out of the cab without waiting for her change.

* * *

At eleven o'clock John stopped for lunch. Having managed to calm down a little, he ate his sandwich and read the Telegraph. After this short break, however, his day went from bad to worse. The next couple of hours yielded a paltry five fares. John barked at all his passengers, drove erratically and swore at everyone who got in his way and slowed him down.

Travelling at around fifty kilometres per hour down a left hand turn lane towards a set of traffic lights showing a green arrow for a left hand turn, John saw a woman running across the road out of the corner of his eye. He didn't slow down. Neither did she. Nor did she turn her head to look when John honked his horn loudly and continuously. She appeared deaf as well as stupid and reckless. A collision was imminent. Unavoidable. John jumped on the brakes which locked, causing the tyres to squeal as the car skidded to a stop, while John turned the steering wheel as hard as he could to the left to avoid the woman who was now right in front of him. She had finally halted her mad dash, shocked to find herself literally within centimetres of being flattened by John's taxi. Pausing for the briefest of moments, she then completed her careless crossing without even a glance at John or any attempt at an apology. John slammed his hand repeatedly against the steering wheel.

A half hour later John, still ropeable about his recent near miss, approached another green light at speed. He noticed the car facing him waiting to make a right hand turn. John had the right of way and the other driver apparently seemed well aware of that because he had stopped there; indicator flashing, waiting for a safe gap in the flow of traffic to turn.

Suddenly that car was right in John's path and this time no amount of skill or luck was going to avert a serious impact. John hit the brakes and watched in slow motion as the cab crashed into the side of the car, the force of the collision pushing it across two lanes and into a power pole. John was dumbfounded. Incredulous, that the driver of a now bent and banged up grey Volvo had not seen John coming and had turned right in front of him making the collision impossible to avoid. Did he have a death wish?

Taking a few moments to make sure he wasn't hurt, John then got out of his taxi, quickly surveyed the smashed up front end and proceeded directly over to the other car. Amazingly the bloke was not hurt either despite extensive damage to his car.

'What the hell was that? Didn't you fuckin' see me right in front of you?' roared John standing right up in the face of the dazed man. 'Do the words *give way* mean anything to you? Why'd you fucking do that? Why?'

John was screaming at him now. He pushed him to the ground and continued to berate him. 'That was so fuckin' stupid man. What's your problem? What the hell is wrong with your eyes dickhead?'

Still recovering from the shock of the accident, the man didn't respond. Not that there would have been any use in responding anyway. To his credit he stood up quickly. Lifting his hands with open palms aimed at John he begged for calm.

'Sorry mate,' he said, 'I'm really sorry all right? Calm down.'

'No it's not fucking alright.'

'Just calm down. I didn't mean it,' said the man shaking his head and shaking in his shoes.

John could hear the tremor in his voice. 'I don't give a shit if you meant it or not. I'm pissed off.'

'Take it easy. Are you okay? Are you…?' He was slowly stepping away from John who was following him with intimidating gestures; fists closed tightly.

'Do I look okay to you, you stupid prick?'

John punched the man in the face. Then punched him again, and a third time. He was lining up a fourth blow when someone grabbed his arm from behind restraining him. He was strong. Too strong. Turning his head John saw a large bearded man holding his arm. As devil mad crazy as he was, John was not able to break free of the man's Herculean grip.

'Calm down mate,' said the man. 'It was an accident.'

'It wasn't a fucking accident at all. Let me you go ya prick. Who the fuck are you? Let me go!'

Attempting to wrestle free, John was soon set upon by another body and then another. Though he thrashed and struggled with superhuman strength, he was unable to resist being forced to the ground. The heavy landing knocked the wind out of him. Gasping and grunting, he attempted one last surge to break free, but it was futile. Needing to catch his breath, he lay there quietly letting the sweet smell of the soft grass fill his nostrils.

The next thing he knew, he was hauled roughly to his feet and brought face to face with a somber looking police officer.

'Have you finished mate?' asked the officer using a tone of voice usually reserved for a parent remonstrating with a tantrum throwing toddler.

'Looks that way officer.' It was the cleverest thing John could think to say.

The extra manpower which had contributed to John's crash to the earth was in fact two police men. John looked around and saw the bearded man who had initially stepped in to protect the other driver standing with a group of onlookers on the footpath. The object of his rage was standing beside his wrecked Volvo being questioned by another officer. Other police were on the scene diverting traffic around the accident site. The ubiquitous tow truck drivers were also present. Little clumps of passers-by had formed and were quietly discussing the drama among themselves.

'You need to arrange for your cab to be towed and then we want you to accompany us to the police station,' said the officer.

'Me? Why? He caused it,' protested John, throwing his hand toward the other driver.

'The other driver has admitted fault, but you had no right to assault him.'

'Bullshit, I didn't,' argued John.

'I reckon you should shut your mouth now and do as you're told before you get yourself into any more trouble. All right?' The policeman was taller than John and had a stare from a pair of deep set blue eyes that could have busted down a brick wall.

'Yeah, okay,' said John, finally showing some contrition and sense. The officer was obviously not about to put up with anymore foolishness from John. The question was whether John was willing to put up with anymore of his own nonsense. He knew he was embarrassing himself and not only digging a deep hole in which he would be buried, but already shoveling dirt to fill the hole in.

John walked over to his cab which had been pushed out of the middle of the intersection to the side of the road. Gathering his personal possessions into his bag, he began to see and think clearly for the first time in many days. No matter who he tried to pin the blame on, the fact was he was entirely at fault. From the first shift after he was beaten to a pulp until this, possibly his last shift ever, John had sought after and welcomed trouble into his life. He called the fleet manager and explained what happened, asking if he had a preferred towing company and smash repairer.

As he crossed the road back towards the policemen, he noticed a paddy wagon and hoped that he would not be forced to ride in the back of it to the police station.

John recalled the time he and a group of friends had been herded into the back of a paddy wagon by police who had discovered them in possession of a stolen car. They had stolen it and were parked that night at Greenhills Beach getting drunk as usual on cheap wine, when their plans for the night were interrupted by a patrol car. They feigned being asleep but were ordered out of the car and asked to explain what they were doing. Pitiful lies and smart mouthed remarks had resulted in the police swearing and threatening them. They were all scared witless and the next few hours of being interviewed by the police and explaining to their shocked and embarrassed parents had been a nightmare none of them would ever forget.

It was striking to think that fifteen years had passed since that first, and until now only, encounter with the boys in blue. Fifteen years and here he was again. In trouble with the police for his own stupidity. Nothing learned. In the grip of the strong arm of the law with no excuses or reasonable explanation for his behaviour.

Having arrived at the police station in the back seat of a Holden patrol car - no paddy wagon thankfully - John finished the interview with the police then completed and signed a written statement. He was permitted to leave but needed a ride home. Cherie was the first person he thought of naturally enough, but he wasn't sure if he should or even if he could telephone her. Recalling the note she left him, and her warning not to contact her until he was ready to talk caused hesitation. With his thumb hovering over the keypad of his mobile phone, John asked himself if he was ready. After a final deep breath, he made the call.

'Hi Cherie. I need a favour, and I, I want to talk to you.' Bad start John. Why did he ask for a favour first?

'What's the favour?' asked Cherie, slowly after a deafening and intolerably long silence.

'I'm at Miranda police station and I need a ride home. Could you...'

'What happened? What's wrong?'

Cherie had switched from caution, almost indifference, to alarm in a flash. It was a good sign.

'I was in an accident.'

'Are you all right?' There was that soft and caring tone of voice which he had missed so much.

John was relieved her first concern was for him. For his health. It would not have been surprising if she'd reacted with coldness. That would have been very reasonable given John's erratic behaviour during the previous few weeks. Fortunately, mercy appeared to have triumphed over judgment. Sympathy was what he heard in Cherie's voice, and exactly what he needed.

'Yes. I'm fine. Can you come and pick me up please? I really want to talk to you. I miss you baby. I'm ready to talk.'

After another uncomfortable pause, albeit a shorter one, she answered. 'Okay, I'll be there in ten minutes or so.'

'Thanks,' said John sincerely, before hanging up.

He spent the time waiting deep in thought, figuring out what he was going to say to Cherie about the note and about how he felt. What should he say? What shouldn't he say? Then there was the unknown and therefore frightening question of what she would say to him. How would she react? John knew he simply had to tell the truth, the whole truth this time. He would definitely need to ask, maybe even beg, for Cherie's forgiveness. This was his chance to make everything right. To start again.

It was only then a thought was triggered, and John remembered the voice in the kitchen. Had that been Cherie's God talking to him. Must have been. He was not drunk or insane, and definitely not prone to hearing voices in his head. It had to be real. He had dismissed it quickly, but there was no denying what had happened. Pondering his chances of a new beginning, he recalled the words he heard offering him exactly that which he now so desperately wanted. He felt his heart melting. That reassuring yet authoritative voice. That quiet voice he had heard so clearly as he sat at his kitchen table a broken man. Who was it that once said that a man had to be right at the bottom before he would look up?

John smiled and tossed a thank you into the air to whoever or whatever had opened his eyes.

Cherie arrived, embraced John with intensity and brevity, then silently walked him out to the car and drove him home. On the way, he recounted all that happened with the accident including the part about him assaulting the guy who caused the accident. Cherie listened dutifully without commenting. John watched her face continually looking for some reaction and he saw a tear escape from the corner of her eye. How he loved that face and wished he could kiss those cheeks and taste the salt of her emotions. How it sliced his heart to know he was the cause of those tears.

At home, sitting together on the couch, they held hands as John explained how he initially felt afraid when he recommenced work after he was assaulted, and how that fear had somehow transformed into a frightening cocktail of guilt, bitterness and anger. John exposed his feelings to his wife in a way he had never done before. It was humbling but it felt good. Very good. Cherie breathed words of forgiveness and love into his ear, before husband and wife cried together, washing away the bile that had poisoned their marriage. The One with the quiet voice looked on with great pleasure.

Over a ten year period, alternating between part time and full time (seven twelve hour shifts each week), I drove a taxi in Sydney. It's a tough way to earn a living. The Devil in the Driver's Seat is dedicated to all cabbies, past and present, especially those who have been victims of abuse, robbery or assault.

Eighteen

The Death of Isaac

(first published in Forge Journal, May 2016)

*T*he stone-gray sky mourned his awakening as Abraham pushed open the tent flap and stepped outside. He groaned inwardly as he stretched his back and looked to the majestic escarpment. Normally bathed in the warm glow of sunrise, it inspired him and encouraged him. Today, however, a silver fog bearded the mountain range while dense white clouds cascaded over its crown. Abraham sighed and scuffed the rocky ground with his sandaled foot. How he missed the oak groves of Mamre, the Hill country where he had pitched his tent for fifteen years among the tribes of the Amorites.

Mamre: where Yahweh had spoken to him, promising he and Sarah would, finally, after decades of heartache and broken dreams, have a child and this child would be the father of many nations. On feeling the light touch of Sarah's hand on his arm, Abraham did not react. She had joined him outside the tent, moving quietly and gracefully to stand by his side to greet the new day as she did every day.

'Yahweh mourns this day, my husband. He weeps in the colour of the sky. He is sad.'

Abraham turned his head towards the western sky where Nanna was falling with the rising of Utu. These were ancient reflections, habits he had never been able to shake. Though he knew the astral Deities of his forefathers, and his former life in the Chaldees, to be shadows of Yahweh, he could not help but worship them when he could see them, and the majestic trails they traced in the Heavens.

'I have an urgent matter to attend to today.'

'Urgent?'

Yahweh has spoken to me again.

Sarah gasped. Yahweh and his messengers were benevolent, but she nonetheless feared them and often wished they were more like the gods of the Babylonians who were completely disinterested in the affairs of men, and only inclined to action when they were angry, displeased with the sacrifices presented to them. An, Enil, Enki and Ninhursag. Sarah knew their names and despised them, but at least their cruelty was predictable. This Yahweh was always surprising them and requiring outlandish acts of obedience like the relocation from Ur decades earlier. Eight hundred kilometers north west along the Euphrates River to a foreign and inhospitable land. A place called Haran.

'I must journey with Isaac to Mt. Moriah where I am to present a burnt offering to Yahweh, and worship him there.'

'It is a long journey for you and the boy,' said Sarah. She would rather have kept her son at home with her but she would not argue with Abraham. 'When will you leave?'

Just then, two of Abraham's servants approached. They were leading a donkey which had a large pair of baskets joined by a leather strap, draped across its back. One of the men was carrying an axe. Bowing their heads as they neared, they slowed and finally stopped.

'How much wood do we need, Master?'

'Fill the baskets if there is enough,' replied Abraham, before turning to Sarah and saying, 'it is a three-day journey and we will leave this morning.'

'Does Isaac know?'

'My son will do as he is told to do.'

With that Abraham quickly entered the tent and gently roused Isaac from his slumber. He gazed on the angelic face of his twelve year old son and sighed.

'Isaac,' called Abraham. 'Rise my son. We are to journey together to the Land of Moriah. Rise, eat and bid farewell to your mother. We will be gone for six days.'

The boy obeyed his father and prepared himself for the trip while Abraham supervised the loading of the wood and other provisions onto the donkey. He had chosen this particular beast for its unusual endurance and docility. While all asses were designed for hard work and did not tire easily, this was one exceptional. It would serve them well.

* * *

Sarah watched her husband work, as she simultaneously fussed over Isaac.

'Tell me the story mother.'

'There is not time for that tale and you have already heard it so many times. Do you not grow weary of its retelling? Do you not know it by heart?'

'Please, mother. There is time. Shorten it as you see fit.'

Sarah smiled at the boy. She had never been able to deny her only son anything, and so she began.

'Your father was sitting at the entrance to the tent in the heat of the day. When he looked among the Terebrinth trees he saw three men approaching. He ran to greet them, fell to his knees and lowered his face to the ground. They accepted his offer of hospitality and he hastened away to get me to prepare some food for these mysterious guests. He gave them water and bid them sit and rest. Your father was surprised when one of the men asked him where I was, and used my name. His spirit quickened within him as he recognized these men as Yahweh's messengers. Though he had not seen them before, somehow he knew them.

One of them told your father that he would return in one year and at that time I would bear a son.'

'What did you do when you heard those words?'

'I laughed.'

Isaac laughed. 'You laughed at Yahweh's servants, and denied it when they asked you why.'

Sarah smiled. 'I was already an old woman, and your father too, almost one hundred years walking the earth. It seemed impossible. Ridiculous to think that I could have a child. I can still hardly believe it. You are our miracle, Isaac. The proof of the power of Yahweh, and the one through whom He will fufill His promise to your father, made forty years ago in Ur.'

The boy was too young to understand how he could be so important and Sarah could see the innocent ignorance in his eyes as he rose from the ground and bowed to her. He liked the story because his mother had laughed and then named him, Isaac which means "laughter."

'Go, my son,' she said simply. 'Your father awaits and is anxious to be on his way.'

'Did he speak to you of the purpose of this journey?'

'Only that he must go and worship Yahweh on Mt. Moriah. I think the significance of you being required to accompany him, should not be overlooked. Do you understand, my precious Isaac?'

'Yes mother.'

* * *

Abraham's heart was heavy as he watched Isaac leave the tent and walk towards him. He had not told Sarah exactly what Yahweh had said. He had deliberately left out the part about presenting Isaac as a burnt offering. Thankfully Sarah had not asked from where he was to get an animal for the offering. Her curiosity had faded with the passage of the decades, and so had his. In its place, a resigned complacency had settled whereby they knew and accepted mystery without needing to, or even wanting to, understand it. They were secure in their unawareness. They also trusted each other to speak or not speak. To act or to remain passive. Love and dedication were fuelled by a passion undiminished by the years albeit expressed less exuberantly.

After a final inspection of the donkey load, Abraham gave the command for the party of four to begin the journey. Abraham preferred silence but Isaac was more garrulous due to his youth and the excitement of adventure.

'Tell me the story of my cousin Lot.'

'The night after the angels had visited us with news of your imminent conception your mother dreamt of Lot. It was a dark, ominous dream. She feared that he and his family may have been in some trouble. She said she saw them running from an unseen enemy, then they were frozen in time, like pillars of salt.

I told her that I had been anxious for them as well. I had heard some ill tidings from some of the Hittite traders. One of whom told me, as we completed our deal, that he had decided to bypass Sodom because of the increasing violence on the streets there. He said it was a city of wickedness beyond measure. He used the words filthy and depraved.'

'Depraved and wicked?' Isaac shuddered.

'Evil, my son. Evil.

Lot had chosen to move into the city for a reason known only to himself. From the fertile plains of the Jordan he had transferred his family and was, it appeared, in mortal danger. I feared for my nephew and family but felt impotent against such evil as was described in the hearts of the Sodomites. I wondered had Lot himself been corrupted? I had heard whispers of him being seen at the City Gate which was indicative of a possible leadership role. How enmeshed was he? Anxiety boiled in my veins.

The following day, around the midday heat, the three visitors appeared again. Once more, I greeted them properly and bid them rest, and prepared food and water for them, but they seemed to be in a hurry. They were polite yet obviously distracted so I asked what was troubling them.

One of them said he had heard many complaints about the people of Sodom, and that they were going to investigate. I heard an edge to their voices as they explained that if they found Sodom to be a cesspool of obscenities, they would have to do something about it. The implication in those words was unmistakable and terrifying, and I felt compelled to do something, if only for the sake of my nephew and his family.

I ran after them and stood before them, hands clasped in supplication. I was trembling as I issued a challenge to their in-tended carnage. I knew that Sodom was overrun by wickedness but I reasoned that not all of its inhabitants could have been worthy of death.

'Are you going,' I said to them, trying to control the shakiness in my voice, 'to destroy the good people along with the bad people? What if there are fifty decent people in Sodom, will you still annihilate them all?'

Yahweh himself answered me and said that if there were fifty righteous men in Sodom he would save the city. I pressed him further and asked what he would do if he found forty righteous men in Sodom. He replied that for the sake of forty he would not destroy it. Foolishly, I continued to bargain with the Almighty, and asked if he would restrain the extermination if there were just ten righteous citizens of Sodom. Without displaying the faintest trace of annoyance at my impertinence, Yahweh said that if there were ten righteous people in Sodom he would repent, and leave them be but, he said, but my child Abraham, there are no righteous citizens there. Not one. They have all turned away from decency and goodness. They have become like beasts following whatever vile impulses and wanton lusts come upon them. They are lost by their own choosing, and I cannot tolerate them any longer. That is what he told me and I was sickened and shocked. So much so that I crumpled to the dirty ground like a tent without poles.

Isaac had heard the story before, but just as Sarah's story about laughing at Yahweh's messengers always made him laugh, so this story of the merciless obliteration of Sodom never ceased to grieve him. Abraham knew this and they had discussed it many times. He had continued to impress upon Isaac's young mind the need to trust and obey Yahweh, regardless of how he might feel. Did the story of Sodom prove that Yahweh was cruel? Then what of His kindness in granting them a miracle child? Isaac still wanted answers. He still believed that there were answers for all the questions he could ever think of, and he invariably expected Abraham to provide those answers. Abraham knew how frustrated Isaac felt when his only answer was that he didn't know, or that he didn't understand. Abraham had never lied to his son, never pretended that he was omnipotent or omniscient. Life was characterized by suffering, and the sooner the boy understood and accepted that fact, the better off he would be.

It was at this point that Abraham's mind disengaged from the present. He continued walking on autopilot, satisfied that Isaac would remain quiet for some time as he again contemplated the ramifications of Sodom's destruction. Abraham was considering the command of Yahweh to go to Mt. Moriah and to present Isaac as a burnt offering. He had heard of such practices in Babylon and Mesopotamia but he knew that most people considered human sacrifice, especially of children, abhorrent. Why would Yahweh command him to sacrifice his son? And why, of all his many sons, Isaac? His beloved, the child of the promise. The more he thought about it the more he became convinced that he had misheard. But pondering Sodom clouded the issue. If Yahweh was not concerned for the hundreds who lived in Sodom, why should he care about one child? His feet felt leaden, and he suddenly stumbled and landed on the ground with a grunt.

'Father,' cried Isaac, kneeling beside him. 'Father, what's wrong?'

'Sometimes I think I have lived too long.'

'Nonsense,' said Isaac dismissively. 'Rise and let us continue our journey to Mt.Moriah. Yahweh has called us, so we must go. He will strengthen our legs and our resolve for his glory.'

Is it glory, thought Abraham as he struggled to his feet with Isaac's assistance, for this God to want your death at my hand?

Why? If His desire is to examine my faith then why not some other way, and have I not already proved myself over and over again? Abraham was complaining bitterly but thankful at least, for having sufficient control to contain his rambling inside his head. He knew, of course, instinctively, that there would not be, could not be, a greater test of obedience than to surrender the thing he most loved in all the world, his precious son. Somewhere in his mind, logic was prevailing against the tide of stormy emotion: resentment. If Yahweh was merely applying a trial with his command to sacrifice Isaac then perhaps he would repent at the last minute, or soon. At some point in this journey, he would speak once more and commend Abraham on his submission, then send him back to Gerar. Yahweh could change his mind. Just because he did not repent from the massacre of Sodomites, did not mean that he would not repent on this occasion. There was still hope. There was always hope. There was only hope.

'Come father,' urged Isaac, 'You appear as an old man, yet you are still young and strong. Take some water and let us continue.'

Abraham drank from the bronze horned vessel that Isaac handed him, then poured a little of the cool water on his head. He was aware of the two young servants standing by, watching pensively to see if he would be able to continue. The donkey brayed impatiently. Even the ashen sky seemed to hold its breath until finally, Abraham placed his hand firmly on Isaac's shoulder and nodded. Although undecided with respect to the dilemma he faced, Abraham determined to forge ahead and allow events to unfold as Yahweh ordained them. The days and nights which followed were peaceful, and with favourable weather conditions the four made good progress towards Moriah.

* * *

251

On the third day, Abraham looked and saw the place in the distance. Without being specific, Yahweh had told him he would know the place when he saw it, and this was confirmed now. It was further evidence of Yahweh's faithfulness yet also another nail in the coffin of Abraham's hopes that He would change his mind about Isaac. In fact, Abraham was now convinced that Yahweh would actually require him to murder his son.

Leaving the donkey with the two servants, Abraham told them that he and Isaac were going further on to worship Yahweh, and then they would return. He pronounced the words from an arid throat but did not believe them.

'Gather a load of wood, Isaac and carry it on your back. I have the flint to start fire and a knife for the sacrifice. Let us go.'

'But Father,' said Isaac, 'where is the sheep for the burnt offering?'

Abraham realized this was probably a question which Isaac had wanted to ask many times during their journey, but had thought better of it, preferring to trust his father implicitly. Now, however, as they were so close, he could restrain himself no longer.

'We have all we need, except the actual animal to sacrifice.'

Not knowing what to say, Abraham opted for silence and merely gestured for Isaac to do what he had been told to do. He wondered if he should share his heart with his son, or continue to try to protect him from the ugly, fatal truth. He wondered if he had the courage to do what was required of him. An eruption of pain burst inside his temple and he automatically reached for it, to sooth it, to fix it. Isaac's back was turned to him so he did not notice the latest physical assault against his father. Abraham fought hard against his feelings, the strength of which threatened to overwhelm him at any moment. A tsunami of doubt rolled over him and he tripped on some loose stones. Somehow managing to keep his feet, he waved away Isaac's look of concern and they continued walking: together but each alone with his own thoughts.

'Here, my son. Lay down your load and let us build an altar.' He looked around. 'There should be enough stones here to build a low platform.'

Abraham watched his son carefully. As there was still no sign of a sheep, no miraculous appearance of any beast for the offering, Isaac hesitated. He probably felt guilty for being disobedient, and for doubting but was powerless to help it. Abraham knew the brute force of emotion. The battlefield between emotion and will was littered with the corpses of good intentions. He decided there was nothing for it but to carry on the work, so he selected a large base stone and laid it down. Then he found another and laid it on top. Soon Isaac joined his labour and in no time they had constructed a crude altar. Taking wood from the bundle Isaac had toted, Abraham began to lay out the pieces in an orderly fashion, alternating larger branches with smaller twigs for kindling so that the fire would start easily and burn well.

'Father?'

Abraham straightened and gazed into his son's eyes. Tears burned his own eyes and blurred his vision. When he attempted to speak, he coughed the word, Yahweh, out of his mouth like a curse. Not good enough, he told himself.

'Yahweh himself will provide a sheep for the offering,' he said before immediately averting Isaac's eyes. 'Continue. We must finish.'

Once the altar was complete, Abraham stood and stared at it. Isaac, although bemused, participated in this strange, previously unheard part of the ritual. After several long minutes, Abraham called Isaac to him.

'Isaac. Come let me bind your hands and feet.'

'Father?'

'I will tie your hands and feet, then lay you on the altar.'

'Why?'

The pent up confusion and rage he felt towards Yahweh exploded from Abraham's lips. 'Do as I tell you Isaac,' he ordered, then cringed inwardly as he witnessed his son wilt in front of him. It was possible, until that moment, Isaac had thought his father was joking. Abraham quite clearly demonstrated the error of that thinking. He approached Isaac holding the cords with which he intended to bind him. Isaac remained motionless and silent. When Abraham took hold of Isaac's hand, he shook free of his father's grip.

'No father.'

Abraham tried again and this time Isaac pushed him. Suddenly Abraham felt the volcano inside him, and he shouted for Isaac to submit.

'No father. I will not be your sacrifice to Yahweh. Have you lost your mind?'

Abraham stepped close to Isaac and grasped his son by the shoulders. Isaac grabbed a handful of Abraham's tunic and the two were thus locked in a stalemate. Though still a child, Isaac was able to match Abrahams' strength long enough for his father's endurance to weaken. They glared at each other as though the intensity of their eye contact could win the struggle for them. Abraham had no passion for this fight though. Surely his son was right when he suggested that he had lost his mind. He loved Isaac and could not deliberately harm him let alone draw the blade of a knife across his throat to drain him of life.

Finally, Abraham released him before slumping to the ground: abject, defeated.

He could feel the heat of Isaac's shock and simmering anger. Abraham kept his face to the ground. Mortified. No words were spoken. Failure. He had not wanted to kill Isaac and consequently had not tried to. Isaac had disobeyed him for the first time in his short life. Defiant to the point of violence. A primal scream of resistance into the face of authority.

When Isaac turned and trudged away, Abraham rose from the dirt and dusted himself off. After waiting a few minutes, he followed until he reached the place where he had left his two servants with the donkey. Isaac had walked past them apparently without offering any explanation.

'Did Isaac speak?'

The two young men shook their heads simultaneously.

'Go and collect the wood from the altar, bundle it and load it onto the donkey's back. We are going back to Gerar.'

* * *

Later that day, Abraham saw Isaac walking ahead in the distance. Thankfully he had a good sense of direction, and he also appeared strong which heartened Abraham. Before too long he hoped to have the opportunity to explain to Isaac what had happened, to try to justify what he did. He was a smart child, and would understand and in time, he hoped, forgive the wrong done to him. On the other hand, Abraham hoped not to speak with Yahweh, who he knew must be angry with both of them. Abraham's greater concern was with the welfare of his son. Looking again, he could no longer see him and he knew the boy should eat and rest.

Addressing one of his servants, Abraham said, 'Hurry ahead

and catch up with Isaac. Ask him to stop and rest with us. Ask him, don't tell him. Ask him to eat with us tonight and suggest he will be free to walk alone again on the morrow, if he wishes.'

While the servant raced off in pursuit of Isaac, the other man helped Abraham make camp. Before they had finished however, the servant returned with his chest heaving, and barely able to talk.

'Where is Isaac?' asked Abraham.

'He has fallen and is injured.'

'Why didn't you bring him here?' Abraham was too frantic to wait for an answer. He said to the other servant. 'Go with him and bring Isaac to me now.'

Abraham used the unbearably anxious wait to beseech Yahweh, to beg his intervention, to save his boy. There was no time for apologies, no time for remorse. His son was hurt but he did not know how seriously. Surely, the Almighty would be merciful. Abraham wept hot tears as he waited in the fading light of dusk.

* * *

By the time, the servants returned to camp, night had fallen so their approach was obscured. They came quietly and laid Isaac down beside the fire. Abraham was by his side in an instant cradling his unconscious son, weeping prayers, oozing misery.

'Master,' said one of the servants softly. 'The boy has bled profusely from a head wound. He has shown no sign of life since we reached him until now. I'm sorry, master. He is dead.'

Abraham moaned as he tightly hugged the limp, lifeless body of his beloved son.

Nineteen

Megapixilated

༄༅ ⚬⚬⚬ ༄༅

(first published in WiFiles, 2014)

T he image captures the true essence of the person: as the soul bleeds into the frame, the pixels incarcerate the unwary. Darius Umbete knows this truth. It is both frightening and exhilarating to think of the eternal imprisonment facing all upon whom he focuses his lens. The unsuspecting victims of his art. Another candidate stands before him now.

'How much is it?'

'$495,' replies Darius half-heartedly. He is the only salesman in New South Wales, perhaps even in the whole of Australia, who does not require a sales pitch or a personality. Darius knows photography. Cameras, lenses, auto exposure, auto flash, back-lights, catch lights, APS, CCD, latitude, length, compensation value, pixels and the list goes on. He smiles at himself.

The customer smiles, albeit cautiously and asks, 'Is that negotiable?'

Darius stares at him. The camera is already too cheap and

this man clearly too incompetent for such a superb piece of photographic technology. Too much of a simpleton.

'Maybe, you'd like to see a less expensive model. This one's probably more than you need, anyway. Overkill, you know?'

'Overkill?'

Darius laugh and the man's bemused look intensifies. 'You only want to shoot family and friends, don't you? And capture some scenery when you're on vacation?'

The man nods, and Darius recalls the first time he shot a friend. He hadn't known at the time what he was doing or what he was capable of doing, even though he'd seen his father do it. It was terrifying. He gulps hard, feeling a cricket ball in his throat, and reminds himself that he has, since that awful day, never again photographed anyone he loves or even anyone he likes.

The customer is staring at Darius as though there is something wrong with his face. He resists the urge to take a clumsy swipe across his countenance.

'I said, okay. Show me another one.'

As he returns the Nikon D5100 to the display case, Darius hopes that he only imagined irritation in the customer's voice. The crap that he has to endure from Neanderthals like him is more than he can bear at times. He grabs a Panasonic DMC LX5 and summons a quantum of patience.

'This one is two hundred dollars less and has many of the same features as the Nikon. It only offers 10.1 megapixels though. Whereas the Nikon gives you 16.2.'

With a childlike brightness in his eyes, the customer says, 'More megapixels means better pictures, right?'

Darius almost calls him a philistine, but instead manages a cordial affirmation. 'Precisely.'

After the man decides to purchase the Panasonic, Darius asks him if he would like a demonstration of some of its features. He declines with abruptness: reeking of arrogance. Darius is offended and insists that a brief tour of the device will stand the customer in better shape for photographic adventure than if he simply goes home and reads the instructions. 'They can be a little confusing you know.'

The customer is unconvinced but hasn't left yet. Darius knows that is because, although he has taken the man's money, he has not handed over the camera. He presses on, attempting to filter out the urgency from his voice. Why doesn't anybody properly appreciate what cameras do? Why don't they understand the power in their hands? A feather touch on a small button kidnaps a moment in time. He has seen it. He has done it. His father showed him how. He spent every spare moment teaching Darius about photography, and not merely instructing him in the mechanics but instilling him an awe of the deep, dark magic of the camera. He remembers the first time his father shot an animal and how he forced him to watch the disintegration of life, piece by piece, cell by cell, pixel by pixel. Darius had felt both mortified and enchanted.

'Look, I need to get going. Thanks for the offer but I'll figure it out.' He reaches for the bag with his camera in it. 'How hard can it be?'

Darius forces a smile and reluctantly hands it over. 'If you have any problems, give me a call.'

The pleasantries end, and as soon as the happy customer turns away, Darius' smile dissolves. He's sold another camera, but he doesn't give a dingo's kidney about sales figures. He sells loads of cameras and he earns juicy commissions and bonuses on a regular basis. That much is easy. The problem is he knows that the cameras he sells will not be treated with the respect they deserve. They will be underutilized. Dishonoured. Most of the cretans to whom he sells cameras do not deserve such high-quality equipment. Darius thumps his fist against his thigh, and glares down at the counter. He sees the coiled sales receipt then glances at the computer where the customer's details are still on display. His jaw loosens.

Darius offers to stay late and close the shop. This offer is generously accepted by his colleagues who see their job as a means to an end. Darius also sees it that way, but his end is dramatically different to theirs. By the time he has rung off the till, secured the shop and activated the alarm, he has already rehearsed his plan dozens of times. He has the address and he has his camera: a custom-built model which he started to assemble following his father's premature death when Darius was fourteen. It had taken more than a year and had caused him incredible frustration. The money had been a problem too especially after his mother caught him stealing from her purse. Other sources of funding presented themselves. Finally, he had completed his project, having employed everything his father had taught him about the power: how to summon it, how to harness it and how to use it. He had shot twelve people before he even started working at the camera shop which was two years ago now. Five more people had since fallen victim to his camera. As his obsession grew, his control waned. The passion which raged in his veins, barked and howled inside his head like a rabid dog. It boils.

He feels it now. His body is humming with the power, struggling for freedom, to fulfill its calling. Darius walks faster. He has the customer's address and he knows the street. It isn't far. Soon he's standing on the lawn, staring at the house, shaking and sweating, reaching for his camera. His thoughts lose coherence.

He feels nothing as he walks to the window. He sees the man at the dining table with his family: a picture book cliché. Darius wants to take a photograph. He knocks on the front door and waits. He doesn't know who will answer. He doesn't care. He raises the camera to eye level and feels its energy vibrating through him, rattling his bones. Light appears in the viewfinder as the door swings silently open and Darius stops breathing as he hits the capture button.

The flash illuminates the doorway and temporarily blinds him but then he sees it happening. He's seen it before but it never becomes less thrilling. Pieces of a woman disconnect from her body and flutter away, like dust beaten out of a pillow. Little bits fall towards the ground but vanish before they reach their destination. Cells break down. Skin melts like cheese in a pizza oven. A woman. Her clothing evaporates thread by thread. It takes so long, Darius feels impatient again, and tired. It's a woman. He has shot a woman. Not the man he wanted. He realizes he must leave. The show is almost over. She is nearly gone but if he stays too long he may be seen. He can't be seen. Darius rushes away into the night clutching his camera in one hand and his head in the other. He feels cold now, and weak. Very weak, but still a whisper of triumph blows in his ear: an ecstatic resonance in his twisted mind.

Twenty

P.D.S.

*T*hey say the devil is in the detail, but they never tell you what he's doing there. It's a throw-away line: a platitude, warning about hidden agendas and crooked conspiracies. Does the devil care that people are so flippant with regard to contracts? Why should he? Ignorance isn't bliss; it's simply ignorance, and stupid people habitually stumble into danger. Matthew Price pondered these mysteries as he lay on his bed in a torpor. The afterburn of over-proof rum scratched the back of his throat and he swallowed suddenly to suppress rising vomit. He mumbled the words, *the devil's in the detail*, and closed his eyes.

The room swirled around him. Or maybe it was his head. Without the smothering embrace of alcohol, he might have been afraid: scared his heart would explode in his chest. Fearful his next breath would be his last. Price wanted to wake up, but he couldn't. His eyes were taped shut and his arms and legs pinned to the bed. In the alcoholic fog, he could see humour in his predicament, but his attempt at laughter was a spluttering, gagging cough. Stupid people habitually stumble into danger.

He wasn't sure if he was going to die but reasoned he deserved it. More than that, he craved it. God, let this be my very last fuck up. Please.

Time slowed and Price relaxed. The fear ebbed away almost imperceptibly as he floated back through the last hours, days and weeks of his wretched life. There was no need to ask where it had begun because he knew. He could pinpoint the exact moment when the virus had infected him, the disease gripping him with the stabbing pain of its talons. Lust. Plain and simple. Price giggled for half a second before the over-proof fire scorched his throat. It was the awkward laugh of a school boy. The one that erupted from his acne framed mouth the first time he saw snarling women staring from the pages of Swank, displaying exposed and contorted bodies.

Over time Price came to hate those pictures: their vulgarity and the power they held over him. He measured every woman he saw against them, and in turn felt their judgement upon him: as if just by looking at him, they could tell he was a pervert. Part of him accepted that reality, but he detested that part as well. Each girl for whom he felt any attraction was going to satisfy the wild desires inflamed by those pictures and she had to be pursued. That's the way his mind worked in effortless evil. As long as the hunt held promise of reward, he chased with vigour but the reality was eternally unsatisfying. He never got the girl and he could never figure out how they resisted. Why they resisted. Fantasy honeys in cyberspace, fell over themselves to please him, but the young ladies he interacted with in the real world were merely polite and friendly at best, indifferent at worst. Matthew Price's life was characterized by a relentless and unrequited desire for sexual gratification. That lust had brought him here: paralyzed and alone on his bed.

The endless battle against his rabid emotional drives left Price exhausted and in desperate need of anesthetic. His chosen escape was a cocktail of marijuana and alcohol which he consumed in darkness with the television and computer switched off. Fast and angry heavy metal music provided the background noise in which he lost himself. Mostly it was just the music: crazy pounding drums, thumping bass and guitars alternately grinding, gnashing, and then screaming. Some lunatic yelling or growling unintelligible lyrics adding to the cacophony. Price loved it. He didn't know what the hell they were on about, but he loved it. He felt it. It caressed him, occasionally whipped him.

One afternoon, having returned from work more angry and frustrated than usual, he loaded a glass with rum and coke then switched on the computer. Music or porn? Porn was normally the first option, but some nameless demon urged him to type 'possessed' into the Google search box. Following the links, Price came to the website of a heavy metal band and he hit play on one of their sample tracks. As the violent torrent of music exploded from the speakers, Price rolled a joint, finishing his rum, before lighting up. He closed his eyes and let the percussion volcano spew hot lava into his tormented brain.

'Take what you want.'

He opened his eyes very slowly and listened carefully. A voice had spoken clearly. The clarity was unnerving as the music played on and the singer screamed and beneath it all; lurking inside the noise was the voice. 'Take what you want.'

Price heard himself speaking aloud. 'What do I want?'

'Take what you want,' repeated the voice.

'How? What are you saying?'

The voice did not respond immediately. Price was going to

ask again but he was interrupted.

'Take what you want.'

Suddenly, he needed to know what the song was saying. What were the lyrics? Did they include the line, take what you want? Was that the hook? Price Googled the lyrics for the song he was listening to. It was called P.D.S. Product Disclosure Statement. Price smiled.

You know you want it. You deserve it.

Here's the deal. I'll show you how to get it. I'll give you the power.
Make the deal. Get what you want.

Take it.

Staring at the words as if they were another one of the impossibly beautiful and well -constructed women he both loved and hated, Price took a deep toke on the joint and closed his eyes once more. He was used to the whirlpool effect, the sudden weightlessness, so he found it reassuring. In the spinning, silent blackness he listened. From within the void of irrationality he heard the voice again.

'Name the girl. Have the girl. Sell me your soul and your desperate thirst will finally be slaked.'

'What do I have to do?' asked Price knowing, in that sweet moment, he would gladly do whatever was required of him.

'Just say yes.'

'Yes,' said Price.

Three letters to seal his fate. One word to give him what he longed for, ached for. An instant in time, from which he could trace his descent into the depths of madness.

When Price woke up, he was still sitting in front of the computer. The room was dark and cold air had crept in from the winter's night outside. Disoriented, he temporarily forgot about the deal and decided to do something about the hunger gnawing his stomach. It was half past eight when he trudged into the kitchen and began to rummage through the fridge and the pantry. It was twenty-five minutes to nine when he remembered.

As frozen as the pie he had just extracted from the tiny freezer compartment, Price sucked in a painful breath then coughed it out violently.

A picture of Sandy from the office flashed into his mind. She was hot and single. He had her phone number though she had, after the first call, warned him never to use it again. Price's breathing was erratic, and he was sweating as he grabbed his mobile phone from the counter and brought up Sandy's number from the directory. Just before he pressed the call button he stopped.

'Think first,' he said out loud. 'Easy boy. Slow down. Calm down.'

Miraculously it worked; as if those words had suddenly been imbued with magical power. He dialed the number and asked if he could come over to see her and she said yes. That was the first time Matthew Price got what he wanted, but it was certainly not the last.

What he had not reckoned on was how monotonous it would soon become. Not only had the thrill of the chase vanished, but the pursuit itself was a distant memory. Price asked, and he received. It was too easy. At first, he stuck to single girls. Anyone he encountered who took his fancy received the two questions: Are you with anyone? Followed by, would you like to be with me? Before too long he ran out of single girls and it was against his policy to spend more than a couple of weeks with anyone. Even that was really stretching it. The physical enjoyment of the act of sex was the first casualty. When Price decided he wanted a girl and then imagined being with her, it was exciting. Being with her in that moment when clothes were coming off and hands and mouths roamed naked bodies frantically was also exciting. He never failed to rise to the occasion, but the actual mechanics of foreplay and sexual intercourse were getting stale. There was something missing.

By this stage, Price was drinking more heavily and more regularly, but he was oblivious to the landslide. Blindly obsessed, he considered how to revive the fervour, to reignite the flames of passion. A variation to the game presented itself to his twisted thoughts. If ask and you shall receive had lost its flavour, what about don't ask, but still receive. And what about women previously beyond his wildest imaginings? Advertising models and television personalities. Movie stars. Price closed his mouth and swallowed hard. The possibilities lined up before him like ripe in-season fruits at the market. He smiled salaciously.

In his medicated melancholy, Price licked his lips and savoured the soothing wetness of his tongue and the saltiness it captured. His eyes rolled languidly in swollen sockets underneath heavy dark lids. Some part of Matthew Price was enjoying this rapture. He reveled in the sense of disconnectedness, and emptiness. Hollow emotion. Another part of him was drowning. Neither one knew if what he was experiencing was real or not. A vein rose, irate in his temple and throbbed its disapproval.

The AAMI girl had been lucky enough, at least in Price's eyes, to be his guinea pig. Having seen her beautiful warm smile welcoming him from bus shelters and roadside billboards, he first contacted AAMI, and then the advertising agency. Naturally, they would not give out her name or her number. Undeterred, Price left his, together with a short message, and waited. Susan Trajzceski telephoned him later that week and thanked him for his kind words of adoration. She invited him out for coffee. And that took care of advertising models. There were more of course, but Susan remained special to him as she turned out to be a beautiful person as well which was seldom the case with others. Price had never known love. Never experienced it. Never seen it. He doubted he would recognize it even if it whacked him in the face, but it was a fairy tale which persisted through every conceivable cultural funnel into the collective consciousness of society. Love. Perhaps that strange and irresistible mix of emotions he felt for Susan was the very thing people dreamed of and searched for, in some cases all their lives. Whatever the feeling was, Price found it disturbing and it made him anxious when he considered Susan. There was a nagging disquiet concerning the lack of choice involved in their relationship. In all honesty, it could not rightly be called a relationship. He ended it and felt noble for having done so.

Despite the setback, and the painfully obvious disadvantages of his new resolve and power, Price pressed on. He was resigned to the fact he would never know true love and though that knowledge was eroding his soul, he hardly noticed thanks to the selfless comfort provided by his closest friends: the green weed and the dark rum.

A shiver coursed through Price's inertia and his head flicked from side to side. Lights flashed on the screen inside his eyelids and he tried to blink to escape the stinging pain they caused. His left arm twitched and bounced on the bed beside him like a decapitated snake. Though he wanted to lie still, he could not. He had no control over his body and his mind was panicking. The bright lights swirled and formed pictures of women, then broke apart and reformed. Faces. Smiling. Snarling. Pouting. Body parts. Glimpses. Peephole views. Naked. Price watched the parade: a testimony to his perverse obsession. He imagined himself blinking furiously to disperse the images, but they appeared and disappeared at will. He pictured himself resisting the sordid seduction. He pretended to take offence, to be horrified and distressed, but Matthew Price was loving it.

Suddenly and shockingly aware of the pleasure he was receiving from this bizarre and sleazy experience, Price tried to scream. He wanted to protest, to escape this torture. It wasn't right. It wasn't good. It was overwhelming.

'You got what you wanted,' said the voice from within the shadow in the corner of his eye. "Foolish. Stupid fucking moron. 'You got what you wanted.'

'I didn't know what I wanted.'

'You knew.'

'I didn't know. I thought I did, but I was wrong.'

'You knew.' The voice was a growling whisper of accusation. 'So wrong.'

Price could feel his arm flapping against the side of his body and he concentrated on it, trying desperately to make it heed his commands. He reasoned if he could regain control of just one body part at a time he would be able to stop this. Stupidly he hoped. The more he cursed himself, the more he wanted to believe that he could overcome. Desire. He wanted to believe. He wanted to love and to be loved. Desire. To give and stop taking. Purity of thought. Price allowed the rapid infusion of hope to flood his mind. He welcomed the turbid water as though it was his saviour. His only hope. When his arm stopped its crazy dance, his mouth suddenly opened, and a rush of air surged out, dragging a guttural cry behind it. He heard the primal scream and noticed his arm was still. *Someone* had switched the lights off. The scream faded.

The voice said, 'You knew what you wanted,' but Price did not hear it.

I was caught in fractional sexual addiction for decades, most of my adult life. In 2016 I did a course at my church called Valiant Man. It was a watershed moment in my life because for the first time I recognized the truth, and exposed my mind to light, thus beginning a journey away from the darkness of sexual impurity and addiction. P.D.S. is dedicated to men everywhere who are fighting against the demon of lust.

Twenty-One

The Devil's Marbles

*'d heard countless stories of cars breaking down in the middle of nowhere: stranding their occupants. Australia, like few other countries, features a hell of a lot of nothing in its interior. Long, lonely stretches of roads which blister during the scorching day as they streak the outback regions of a vast and empty nation. Motorists attempting these long drives are warned to prepare, to make sure the vehicle itself is up for such challenging conditions, and to ensure adequate provisions of water. Particularly in case of an emergency, like disconnected kangaroo body parts embedded in the engine bay.

My Mustang was fine. More than fine. Newly purchased and recently run in, this was her first true test on open roads where neither officer friendly or any of his electronic assistants were present. The truth is I would have been on the road even if she was falling apart. It was not a break down, nor an accident, however, which brought my journey to a halt. Sheepishly, I must confess to the true cause. A simple overestimation of my ability to drive long distances. I stopped because I was dog tired.

After several microsleeps which merely resulted in a series

of short violent shudders accompanied by plumes of red dust as the Mustang ran off the asphalt, I decided I might die if I kept pushing myself. There was no reason for haste. I allowed a week for the journey to Adelaide where a new job awaited, hopefully. I'd give myself a few days, or longer to settle in, find some accommodation and get my head around my dramatic change of fortune.

Nearly twelve hours into my journey from Darwin, and roughly an hour after beginning to battle that dreaded drowsiness, I roared into Warumungu Nature Park, and its most famous attraction loomed ahead. The Devils Marbles - known as Karlu Karlu in the local language.

After visiting Alice Springs, and the awe inspiring sacred sites at Uluru and Kata Tjuta, I had developed a bit of a fascination for Indigenous culture and in particular their connection with the land. I did some reading about Karlu Karlu before my trip, and always intended to visit this internationally recognized symbol of the Australian outback. Arriving at the Devils Marbles as the red hues of dusk caused the gigantic boulders to glow, I sat and thought. Located at the crossroads of four different Aboriginal language groups, the boulders were said to be, in the dreaming stories of the traditional owners, the product of balls of hair and spit left behind by the Devil Man, Arrange, as he travelled through the area making a hair belt for himself.

In the few moments before sleep overwhelmed me, I wound the driver's seat back, found the least uncomfortable position, and turned my thoughts to myself, where they were too often.

I had a good, secure job in Darwin. I loved where I lived in a city apartment with views of the harbor, close to work. Loved my church, loved the extraordinary weather, loved my life. I was alone though, and that is something I've never liked. My previous girlfriend had gone south along with our relationship, and after three months I was climbing the walls a little. It might just have been wet season fever, but I wanted some company. Someone to share my home with, and my heart.

One evening I walked up to Mitchell Street to find a quiet place for a drink. Tap Bar was relatively uncrowded, and I knew some of the staff there, so I walked in. Searching for a seat as I headed for the bar, a pair of legs caught my eye: long legs. Eventually I discovered the body to which they were attached and was pleased to see a young blonde in a tank top and shorts, de rigeur in Darwin, especially for tourists. I detoured via her table, sat down opposite her and introduced myself with an outstretched hand.

'G'day,' I said.

She looked mildly surprised which suggested to me I was not the first guy to take such liberties.

'Salut,' she said with a smile.

'Can I buy you a drink-' I paused to allow the insertion of her name, raising my eyebrows.

'Nathalie,' she obliged. 'Oui. Merci.'

As I walked away, I wondered if she spoke English. Anyone who had been through the school system in Australia knew basic French. I for some reason had hung on to a few additional phrases which thus far in my life, I had never used for anything other than my own amusement. If Nathalie could not speak English, then a very short conversation was on the cards. I returned with her drink, Kahlua and Coke, and an Iron Jack for myself, resumed my seat and raised my glass towards her.

To cut a long story short, this majestic and magical woman told me her story, and I drank too much, and fell in love with her. I know what you're thinking, but it's true. I was besotted. I would have wrestled a crocodile for her if she asked me to. Guys do some seriously crazy stuff when their command centres are located below the navel. Nathalie had been orphaned and had a large sum of money, her inheritance, locked up in a French bank account as per the conditions of her father's will.

'I just need one thousand euros to unlock the account,' she said, moving her chair around closer to mine. 'If I find the right man to help me and take care of me, I'll be his. And so will the money.'

I remember laughing, and also the hurt look on her pretty face. Drowning deep inside those sparkling green eyes, I did something which Vulcans would find abhorrent: I abandoned logic. We flirtatiously chatted some more, until I ran out of money. As it was getting late, I began to say goodbye, even though I wanted to invite her home. Nathalie beat me to it. On the way back to the Mantra Hotel, where she was staying, I told her I would help her.

In the morning, I should have been appalled by my lack of control, but instead of being ashamed and asking God's mercy for my sin, I justified myself. Having just spent the night with a rich goddess, I was euphoric. I gave Nathalie fifteen hundred dollars Australian, for which she was obviously thankful, exuberantly so, gushing about how I had made her dreams come true and was the most wonderful man in the world. She flew out of Darwin two days later and I never heard from her again.

Two weeks down the track, I was still wearing my embarrassment and self-loathing on my sleeve, and I had become an everyday drinker as a result. I couldn't sleep, so I got bombed every night. I might have expected to draw some attention for my behavior at work, but unbeknownst to me, I was on the verge of redundancy. When the boss informed me their contract had not been renewed and therefore neither would my job be continuing, I decided to get out of town and look for another fresh start. When I was ready, I loaded up the mustang and split, feeling more sorry for myself than ever.

Getting back to what happened at the Devils Marbles.

Waking from sleep, courtesy of a coughing fit produced from the desert in my throat, I decided to get out, stretch my legs and importantly drink some water. I didn't have any snacks left so I was pretty hungry. What happened still makes no sense to me at all, and no matter how many times I tell this story, I remain ignorant of the truth. I'll tell you what I remember, but I honestly don't know if it actually happened.

Night reigned, but there was a full moon so I could see The Devils Marbles clearly, radiant in the lunar luminescence. I walked towards them, feeling quite disoriented and dizzy, as though the short nap had exacerbated my weariness rather than curing it. I continued forward without registering the spherical shape of the two largest stones, nor their gravity defying position on rock pedestals. In between these two boulders, I saw a man. It could have been a shadow. In fact, I was sure it was a shadow…until it spoke to me.

'Since you are God's son,' said he in a sonorous and vaguely sinister voice. 'Command these stones to become bread.'

Befuddled as I was, by sleep and hunger, I didn't immediately recognize the line from Mathew 4, but I did take exception to being singled out as God's son.

Cleverly, I replied: 'Are you talking to me?'

'I know you're hungry,' said he. 'Make these stones into bread so you can eat.'

Once again, with a touch of comic genius, I looked at the giant stones and said, 'I'm not that hungry.'

I watched the shadow for evidence of something less ephemeral, but the light was devious. The shadow appeared to be waiting for me to do its bidding. Of course, it was a ridiculous suggestion, and whilst on the verge of replying with another witticism, I suddenly recalled, in a moment of clarity, the story of Jesus' temptation in the wilderness.

'It is written,' I said confidently, '*that man cannot live on bread alone.*'

The shadow flickered, then vanished, only to reappear on the top of one of the marbles. 'Join me here,' it said and without any voluntary effort on my part, I did. 'Look down and out and what do you see?'

'Desert,' I said, although I did note that we seemed to be much higher than I would have thought, judging the height from ground level.

'Since you are God's son, throw yourself down, for it is written *I will command my angels concerning you, and they will take you up in their hands, so that you won't hit your foot on the stone.*'

Now, there were a couple of things going on here. I told you I felt groggy initially, but that had worn off and by this stage of the encounter -let's call it that- I felt quite alert. I was thankful to have actually read the Bible and I knew this story. I'd read it numerous times without ever imagining, naturally, that I myself would face a similar temptation to Christ. To be honest, as you've probably gathered from my tone, it all seemed pretty comical. God had spoken to me in dreams before, so I considered the possibility that what I was experiencing was merely an extremely vivid dream. That in itself was odd. I had never before wondered whether I was having a dream while I was having one.

The shadow must have taken my tardy response as a sign I had not heard his question, so he repeated it.

'It is also written,' I said, '*Don't test the Lord your God.* And in any case, I'd be more worried about my head striking the ground. Not my foot.' The shadow flickered and vanished. After I spoke these words I felt the distance between myself and the ground increasing at an alarming rate. I was still on the rock. I could feel it under my feet, so either the boulder itself was stretching heavenward or the earth below was falling away. The acceleration made me feel sick, and when I came to a sudden stop, I ejected the contents of my stomach towards the distant ground. After recovering from the violence of vomiting, I noticed a myriad of lights where once had only been the moderate, moon lit undulations of the desert.

'Look,' said the shadow, reappearing beside me. 'Observe the glory of all the kingdoms of the world. Their power and wealth. I will give you all this.' His arms, now of disproportionate length, extended in either direction from his body. 'It can all be yours if you bow down and worship me.'

'Look,' I said. 'I feel a little sick from that doped up elevator ride. Can I get back to you on that offer?'

When he failed to answer, I sighed theatrically, and said the magic words, 'It is written: *You will worship the Lord your God and serve only Him.'*

The shadow flickered and disappeared, and in his stead stood two men in shiny white outfits – okay, I made that up- two very ordinary men dressed like national park rangers, lifted me gently and carried me back down to the ground. There was a camp fire going and some aromatic steam escaping from a pot over the fire. One of the men said to me, 'There you go mate. Take it easy.'

I stuttered through the whole alphabet until finally managing to join some letters and construct a sentence; part of a sentence at least. 'But what about-?'

Both men looked at me, beaming. One whacked me on the shoulder good-naturedly and said. 'Keep going to Adelaide. She'll be right mate.' Then they disappeared.

Every time I have told this story, without fail, I am told by every Tom, Dick and Harry who hears it that it was a dream. The thing is when I arrived in Adelaide, checked into a hotel and went to the local for a beer and a feed, guess who I met there? She was cashed up too, I'll tell you.

Twenty-Two

Written Off

(first published in Necrology Shorts in 2012)

He stands stooped before the brick wall which stretches over two hundred metres either side of him, and stares at the graffiti. An exuberant splash of colour and meaningless symbols, it is messy and pointless, he thinks, like his life. Sniffing to prevent a flood of mucas from his nostril, he removes a packet of cigarettes from his pocket, extracts one and lights it. He continues to stare at the wall, oblivious of the world and more importantly to his uncle who walks up beside him, assuming an identical stance.

'Whatcha lookin' at?'

Peter gestures half-heartedly towards the wall and says, 'What's it mean?'

Ron smiles and turns to study his nephew. 'Nothin'. Kids with nothing betta to do.'

Following a strange silence during which Ron probably wonders what is wrong with his nephew, and Peter wonders what is wrong with himself, the two men walk the length of the wall to the right, turn the corner and enter the yard through a wrought iron gate.

The sign says, Outback Wreckers and Peter snorts at the irony. It's a five hectare automotive graveyard located on Llandilo Rd, Londonderry in the outer western suburbs of Sydney. When he was younger, Peter used to laugh at the idea that the western suburbs of Sydney qualified as the outback in his uncle's opinion. Nowadays, he doesn't find anything funny.

Ron leads him into the office and motions for him to take a seat as the fly screen door smacks shut behind them. Choosing the first available chair, Peter slowly lowers himself onto it as though he is dipping his body in a hot bath. He winces and shifts his bodyweight until he is more comfortable. Aware of Ron fiddling around at the sink with a kettle and some coffee mugs, Peter simply sits quietly and waits. The surface of the small dining table is stained and scuffed.

'How ya been, Pete?'

'Alright,' he lies. Pain is his ever-present companion. Heavy doses of codeine keep the physical pain in check, but nothing can dull the blade of emotional torture.

Ron grunts dismissively as he places a steaming mug of coffee on the table in front of Peter.

'Ya mum says otherwise.'

Watching his uncle take a seat opposite him and thoughtfully sip his coffee, Peter wonders what his mum hopes to achieve by this arrangement. He has to hand it to her though because since the accident she has never stopped trying to help him. She loves him and he knows it, but her love is desperate and suffocating. That's what mothers do, he supposes, they love with sometimes frightening passion, as though their love is the ultimate force for good in the universe; as though it was omnipotent. He's grateful but she's wearing herself out for nothing because he is beyond help. No one else wants to accept this truth.

'She reckons,' continues Ron, 'that by spending some time down here with me and working here at the yard...'

Although he doesn't finish the sentence, it doesn't matter. Peter hears the skepticism in his uncle's tone but does not blame him for that. Without a better plan, or any plan at all for that matter, Peter has agreed to his mum's latest tactic. That she has chosen a wrecking yard as the location for his redemption seems like sending an alcoholic to a pub to get sober. Sick irony. Perhaps there is madness to her method, perhaps she is just mad. He sighs. Somewhere deep inside him, where an innocent seventeen year old used to live and laugh boldly in the face of life's challenges, there are good memories. Peter can't often reach them though as they are like deep wells scattered around a vast desert, and his doesn't even have the energy to search for them let alone draw water up and drink it. He's dying of thirst.

Ron nods with the wise understanding his sixty two years has given him.

'Anyway,' he says, 'You're always welcome here.'

'Thanks,' replies Peter without looking up from the table.

A finger of sunlight pokes through the dirty Venetian blinds and points at a particularly rough spot on the table. Peter sees a glint of twisted metal and hears the angry snap of breaking glass. He flinches automatically.

His uncle notices but doesn't say anything.

'Come on, finish yer coffee and we'll put you to work, eh?'

For the first time, Peter raises his eyes off the table and looks at Ron who shudders involuntarily in response. He's momentarily lost for words, but Peter has seen that look before. The awkward way people stare when they know they shouldn't, but cannot stop themselves. They see something dark and disturbing in Peter's blue eyes. The scar which begins high on his right cheek and explodes across his eye socket into the expanses of his forehead is ugly, and his blue eyes are steely cold. Empty.

Ron is already outside by the time Peter rises to his feet. The stiffness in his knee is only a minor contributor to his reluctance though. He can see through the window of the office out into the yard where his uncle strides purposefully towards a white XY GT Falcon. It looks out of place among the bent and busted vehicles which are strewn around in some roughshod semblance of order. The bonnet of the old Ford is raised, and Peter sees that a cloth has been draped over the fender and into the engine bay which he knows contains a 5.8 litre V8. Standing at the window, Peter wistfully watches his uncle set to work and he feels torn. Yesterday's boy wants to bolt through the door and into the yard and get his hands dirty and ask a million questions, but today's broken man is rooted to the floor. He's afraid. His guts are churning.

Apparently unconcerned by Peter's no show, Ron works away methodically with only an occasional pause to utter an expletive and shake his hand from some injury or other. Peter feels dizzy, so he sits down. The room begins to darken as though someone has closed the blinds, and he can hear voices. Faint whispers which are too soft to be understood. Glass shatters then tinkles on the floor. Plastic snaps and pops. Metal grinds and screeches. The door opens suddenly and a familiar voice slices into Peter's waking nightmare.

'You comin' or what?' queries Ron. 'I could use a hand out here.'

Too stunned to speak, Peter sits there until the question is repeated and then finally, with considerable effort he tells his uncle that he is on his way. The screen door slams shut again and Peter jumps to his feet: a surprising show of agility.

Out in the yard, Peter shields his eyes with one hand and fumbles in his pocket for his sunglasses with the other. Lighting another cigarette, he surveys the yard which leaves him dazed as his thinks of all the crashes that resulted in these cars ending up here. He can't help but wonder about the drivers and the passengers, the lucky ones, the not so fortunate and…the dead. Running his hand over the scar on his face, Peter can't decide whether he is lucky or not. Everyone said so. Look at the car, they said, it's a miracle you survived. He snorts and spits on the ground.

Walking over towards the XY which is the subject of intense attention from his uncle, Peter tries desperately to change the tape playing in his mind; a highlights package of the night of his crash except that it's mostly lowlights. He remembers the thrill of approaching the car with his mate Miles telling him all about how the keys were in the ignition and no one was watching it. How they could roll it down the street for fifty metres or so and then kick her over. Miles had said he would drive to start off with then Peter could have a go. He recalls Miles exact words as he released the handbrake on the Datsun 120Y, and they began to push it down the street.

'We'll just drive her till she runs out of juice and then nick off and leave. Sweet, eh?'

It had been sweet at the start. They got away with no trouble, then jumped in and Miles fired the engine. Exhilaration blocked out everything Peter should have been feeling and thinking but it faded quickly like a delicate flower under the hot sun. Miles was driving like a maniac. Several times Peter told him to take it easy, but the other laughed it off by saying the car wasn't theirs so it didn't matter if they trashed it and that Peter should chill out and enjoy the ride. Peter was anything but chilled out, and after just five minutes in the car with Miles, he began to fear for his safety.

'This yours?' asks Peter of his uncle, as he leans on the opposite fender to the one where the cloth is laid out.

Ron stands and wipes his forehead with what he thinks is a clean cloth. A greasy streak replaces the lake of sweat. 'Yeah.'

Ron doesn't seem to say much, and Peter thinks he's changed since his run in with cancer eighteen months ago. That had knocked everyone around but most of all the man himself. Of course, he fought like the tough old tiger he is but the Big C strikes fear into the hearts of the bravest of men. From the first indicators that something was wrong through the full diagnosis and onto the treatment, he talked about beating it but he knew, as did the whole family that realistically he was only a fifty fifty chance. Even now, long past the operation to the remove the tumour from his stomach and with the nightmare of chemotherapy treatment beginning to fade in his memory, the shadow of death plagued him. That's what he jokingly called his remission: the shadow of death. Since then he had slowed down, slowed his speech, slowed his thinking and slowed the pace of life. Cancer had aged him. Peter remembers family get-togethers with his aunt and uncle, and their rapid fire verbal exchanges: combative yet somehow complementary and strangely sweet. Every now and then that sharp tongue of his would return to the fray and his family glimpsed the former Ron but suffering wounds the soul and rips the fabric of personality. It alters perception: changes everything, and Peter knew it.

'What's the problem?'

'No problem,' says Ron without removing his head from deep

in the engine bay. 'Just replacing the oil filter.'

Something catches Peter's eye; a sliver of reflected light or rapid movement beyond the row of wrecks behind the XY. He stares for a moment, but nothing moves. Curious still, he wanders over toward the area. Ron's voice follows him, but it fades so he ignores it. The remnants of a red HJ Monaro crouch on the dusty ground sandwiched between an early 80's Bluebird and a Nissan Urvan. With its passenger's side completely caved in from what must have been a high-speed impact, the Monaro looks sad. Peter feels for it. He used to own one. In the unbroken driver's headlight Peter sees a light: weak as though about to die from lack of power. Of course, it has no power. He lowers himself gently to the ground then lower still so his eye is level with the headlight. Weirdly, his heart races and he forces himself to swallow and revive his dry mouth. Shielding the headlight from the sun with his hand he continues to stare into it, fascinated by the dim light. Surely it is his imagination. It's impossible.

Raising his head from the headlight to the bonnet he sees a figure behind the wheel of the car and springs backward in alarm. When he looks again it is gone. Peter feels like he has seen a ghost. It looked like him. The cloud of dust he created lingers in the air around him momentarily before casually drifting down but Peter doesn't move. He can't. There is no trick of light here because the windscreen of the Monaro is non-existent. No optical illusion can be blamed for the apparition in the driver's seat. It grips the steering wheel with two bony hands and smiles the twisted smirk of a maniac. Is that the sound of an engine?

Finally, and with considerable effort, Peter shakes off the horrified torpor and carefully pushes himself to his feet. When he looks again into the cabin of the Monaro, the spectre is gone.

He squeezes his eyes shut then opens them slowly. Nothing.

As his uncle has not given him any work, he decides to wander around the yard to kill some time. Maybe he'll find a rare treasure among the bones of yesterday's automobiles. He comes to realize the wrecks are actually laid out in rows, albeit haphazardly, and despite the obstruction of an occasional crumpled bonnet or concertinered boot, he can see all the way down this row to the Colourbond steel fence at the bottom of the property.

He passes several compact Mazdas, a seventy's model Mercedes, two Falcons, and a Kingswood before he stops dead in his tracks: mid stride in front of a Datsun 120Y. Its headlights are on. That's what he notices first, seconds before the death driver from the Monaro appears behind the wheel. It laughs but Peter doesn't know at what. It turns the steering wheel to the left, then to the right and back again quickly, simulating the action of negotiating a tight corner, then snickers as though the action should mean something to Peter. He stares in terrified fascination. Sounds of violent destruction assault his ears: crunching, smashing, tearing, crying, screaming. Peter swallows hard, forces himself to take a breath. The sounds get louder.

Behind the wheel of the Camry next to the 120Y, another ghostly vision chuckles as its bony hands slap the dashboard. Music plays from somewhere: the sounds of AC/DC hard rocking in to join the cacophony. Peter doesn't move because he can't, but he turns his head slowly to see that the whole row of wrecks is now inhabited by ugly wraiths. They hoot and holler as though revving themselves, together with their imaginary engines, while crouching at a make believe starting grid waiting for the checkered flag to fall, and the race to begin. With a bizarre and unexpected sense of relief, Peter realizes they are not interested in him. They do not seem to even be aware of him except for the driver of the Datsun 120Y who has ceased laughing and is now staring at Peter. The evil fire of its eyes scorches Peter's relief and turns his legs to jelly. He collapses.

Falling only to his knees, Peter can still see the spectre which is now beckoning to him. He shakes his head and opens his mouth to speak, but his mouth is so dry the hot air stings his tongue. The ghost driver patiently continues to motion for Peter to come, and finally he moves, almost automatically, towards the car. He feels disconnected as though he has been removed from reality, as though his body has been severed from his mind. Dread feelings have lost the struggle to avoid danger. He inches forward despite his fear.

As Peter approaches the driver's door, the death driver gestures for him to enter via the front passenger door which springs open suddenly. Still moving, his head spinning, his heart hammering in his chest, Peter feels inexorably drawn to the car now. It's too late to change his mind. Too late to flee.

He eases himself down onto the passenger seat aware of the driver carefully observing his every movement. Once seated, the door slams shut and there is sudden dramatic silence as though all the noise had been coming from a single source and someone had yanked the power cord from the socket. In that cold suffocating silence Peter sits with his eyes fixed on a comforting point of blue sky through the distant gum trees.

'Whose fault was it?'

His brain muffled by inertia and shock, Peter does not realize that the question is for him, and that the speaker is the death driver.

'Whose fault was it?'

Peter's throat is tight, constricted with fear and his words nearly choke him.

'It was my fault. I-' He doesn't get to finish his sentence.

'Whose fault was it?'

Before he speaks again Peter slowly turns his head to look at the interviewer from Hell. It seems that only the correct answer, the one it is seeking, will stop it repeating the question or perhaps, he reasons, it has no ability to communicate, no life in fact outside of what animation is injected by Peter's rabid imagination.

'Whose fault was it?' Its voice is persistent: taunting Peter.

Inside the Datsun 120Y the air is cold as though air conditioned and it is dark. Straining his ears, Peter vaguely catches a distant melody and he recognizes it.

When my baby's walking down the street,

I see red, I see red, I see red...

He remembers the song, *I See Red* by Split Enz because it was playing on the radio of the stolen 120Y just before it jumped the curb and skipped across someone's front lawn and ploughed into the side of their house. Sweat breaks out on Peter's forehead and after he wipes it with the back of his hand, he notices that the liquid oozing from his skin is not sweat. A crooked talon of evil grips his heart and squeezes. He gasps, then begins to cough as his heart restarts.

'Whose fault was it?'

Peter feels the desperate need to escape but senses the debilitating powerlessness of raw fear. He thinks he is dying as *I See Red* continues to bounce around the inside of the old Datsun; in and out of his head as though weaving insanity into his mind. His head spins as darkness encroaches the borders of his peripheral vision. If only he could think clearly. If only he could answer the question and satisfy the maniacal curiousity of the death driver.

'It,' begins Peter hesitantly, 'was an accident. It was no one's fault.'

The music stops. Peter has never experienced a deeper more frightening silence but he knows he has answered correctly. Without really wanting to, he turns again to look at the driver and finds it staring at him. Its hollow eyes thrust into his like long knives. He feels pain in his head, intense throbbing which threatens to explode and splash his brains all over the inside of the 120Y, but he can't look away.

It speaks. 'What do all these wrecks have in common?'

'They've been written off.'

Peter feels an unexpected elation. The pain and the fear remain but something has changed or more accurately something is changing. The iceberg of his heart is thawing. The dust of his desolation is being blown away. What is it? Peter is mystified by the rampant swirl of emotion he is experiencing. An inexplicable calmness descends on him like soft rain.

'You have a choice, Peter,' it says. 'You can stay with me and we can roam the never ending highway to Hell forever, with all the other write offs. Lost and hopeless.'

Peter wishes he could break the gaze of the spectral orator because he doesn't think he can stand any more pain. Tears explode from his eyes and a weeping howl from deep in his heart fills the air. He gets it. Understanding has risen like the light of dawn.

The death driver nods and attempts a smile which looks hideous.

'Leave the junkyard. You don't belong here. Forgive yourself.'

As Peter continues to look at the driver, its face begins to transform, and he recognizes the final visage.

'Miles?' He knows it is not his dead friend, but he wants it to be. He craves the opportunity to see him and speak with him again. The image of his friend nods.

'Leave the wrecking yard. You don't belong. The only person who has written you off, is you.'

Peter can hardly see now through the blur of hot tears but in the blink of an eye there is no longer anything to see. He is alone. Heat and light invade the interior of the Datsun and Peter feels different. Clean. Alive. Born again.

When he attempts to leave the car, he finds his knee does not protest; no stiffness and no pain. Peter takes a deep breath and sprints back down between the lonely forgotten car wrecks back to where his uncle is still tinkering under the bonnet of the XY. He has no idea how long he has been gone but presumes from Ron's disinterested greeting that it has not been long.

'I have to go, Uncle Ron,' he says breathlessly as he reaches the side of Falcon. Then before the other man can respond, Peter races away into the office and out onto Llandilo Rd. Out into his second chance life.

Twenty-Three

Millers Forest

(*first published in WiFiles, 2017*)

A gusting westerly tossed and bustled the willows as they struggled to form a guard of honour along a two hundred metre stretch of Raymond Terrace Rd. The sun scorched the earth in anger, melting the bitumen road and causing recently filled potholes to become sticky black puddles. Heat waves danced above the road distorting as they obscured, while the needle rocketed into the red zone taking his temper along for the ride.

'Damn it. Fuck!'

If you are not inside an air-conditioned room, then I suggest you hurry up and get yourself there. Thirty nine degrees and rising, folks and its only ten thirty. The Bureau forecasting storms for this evening but that's a long way off so stay cool and stay tuned. You're on ninety nine seven RhemaFM, Newcastle and the Central Coast. Good morning.

The middle of nowhere. The end of the line. Millers Forest. Blake Steele and a clapped out nineteen eighty five Falcon on the verge of a fiery death. The first week in March; a very bad week and it was getting worse for Blake. Lost his job, lost his girl, and losing hope. All he could think to say was, 'Damn it' and 'Fuck!'

As there was nowhere for him to stop and cool off, Blake chose to keep going. The air-conditioning roared in frustration as it blew hot air hard into the cabin so Blake switched it off, thinking to himself bitterly that he wished he could switch his life off.

What a disaster it was. What a total shambles. He liked his job but his boss was a complete tool, and Blake could not tolerate the biting sarcasm which that self promoter used to cover his own stupidity and dump on his employees. Blake seemed to be a particularly fond target of his. Maybe it was because Blake refused to kowtow to such an asshole. Maybe it was because he was sick of being the butt of his boss' stinging barbs. Humour he called it, and those who slobbered at his feet laughed along like mindless hyenas. Whatever the reason, his sacking was inevitable. You don't humiliate a man like that by decking him in front of his employees, without suffering some pretty direct and severe consequences. Good-bye job.

Sam was the sweetest girl he had ever known, good natured and devoted, naturally beautiful and intelligent. How the hell he ever snagged her as his girlfriend he would probably never know, but there she was; patient, kind and even tempered. Blake had a tempestuous nature and a short fuse and without Sam to mollify his rage, he often ripped headlong into trouble. So many transgressions, followed by so many sincere apologies followed by more sins. She seemed like a god to him sometimes but finally proved she was not by leaving him. Her final words? "Why don't you grow up and be a man! You're killing yourself Blake."

Blake had thought at the time and still did that her words were a bit over the top, unless she wasn't talking about physical death. That was a favourite topic of hers; spiritual life and death. Blake didn't know what she meant, and he didn't care. All he knew was that he felt terribly sorry and he missed her, and he knew he was a better person when she was around. Who would control him now?

Bang! Ssssshhhhh! A long harsh hiss.

'Damn it! Fuck!'

The Falcon angrily breathed its last and rolled to a stop, as Blake steered it off the road and onto the shoulder. In the stillness of Millers Forest, the sound of steam rushing from underneath the bonnet was like a hurricane. Blake sat there and stared through the torrent of steam down the long straight road and pondered his immediate future. Rage, although volcanic at the moment, seemed futile, but he was powerless to stop it. He flung the door open and almost fell out in the rush, then began frenetically kicking the side of the car with the underside of his heel. Soon he was exhausted, so he lumped his body behind the steering wheel and waited for the last of the storm to subside.

Drenched in sweat and disturbed by the smell of himself, Blake climbed out of the car again and began to walk towards a house which sat quietly on the left three or four hundred metres down the road. It was the only island in a sea of flat grassy meadows and it should have had a huge banner flying over it, proclaiming 'Last Hope'. His car was stuffed, it was hotter than hell and he didn't have any water. At the very least he desperately needed a drink, so he dragged his feet through the almost liquid bitumen and dreamed of salvation in Millers Forest.

As he approached the house Blake noted the windows were all shut but there was no sign of an air conditioning unit outside. There were two cars in the driveway; a dirty 78 Toyota Landcruiser, and a little red Hyundai. There was also a motorbike and although Blake was not a huge fan of motorbikes, courtesy of the shocking injuries a friend of his had suffered after crashing one into a fence, he could see beauty in their styling and appreciated the passionate feelings they aroused in some. It was all white, even the leather seat and had no badges to identify the make or model. He had never seen one like it.

Gravel crunched under his heavy feet as he walked down the driveway, past the vehicles towards the front door. He waved his hand over the bonnet of both cars but could not tell if the engines had been running recently or not. It was too damn hot.

The front door was closed. Blake listened closely but could hear no sound at all and that bothered him, and the bother turned into concern, and the concern suddenly became anxiety. He heard whispers in the hot wind and smelled something strange, something off, a rancid stench. Dizziness almost overwhelmed him as he reached out his left fist to knock on the door.

'Hello,' he said, as he knocked, without knowing how loudly he spoke. 'Hello! Is anyone home?'

Blake fell towards the door and might have heard a voice as it swung open and he crashed in on to the floor. The voice might have been asking for help but that voice might have been his own.

When he opened his eyes, he saw a horizontal Christmas tree. A long tree with presents jam packed at one end and a pair of runners standing on their toes. Blake sat up slowly and the room righted itself. He looked again at the shoes; pink and small. A little girl's shoes. Christmas tree? Presents? March?

'Hello?' said Blake weakly. 'Hello? Is anyone home?'

A heavy silence filled the room and Blake was afraid to disturb it by moving but when he spotted the opening to the kitchen, he carefully rose from the floor and walked in to get some water. The kitchen was so clean it literally sparkled as fingers of sunlight poked through the Venetian blinds and stabbed the faux marble benchtops and stainless-steel sink. Not a single glass, plate or utensil could be seen and there was a faint odour of lemon in the air. Blake turned the tap on and cupped his hands underneath the cool flow, before greedily shoveling the precious liquid into his mouth. Slowly life returned to his parched body.

'Hello?' he called again, having recovered his voice, 'Is anyone home?'

Nothing.

Blake tried to leave the kitchen but jumped back in fright as a woman stood in his way with outstretched arms and no hands. 'Help me!' she shrieked. 'Help me!'

Losing his footing, Blake slid against a cupboard and stared in disbelief at the horror of this woman. Handless, bleeding from the stumps and from cuts to her face and chest and arms and legs, she came no closer and spoke no further. A young woman with a lithe figure and firm breasts, her long brown hair was tangled and lank. She wore a long pink nightdress with no sleeves. Her eyes opened wide were crystal blue islands floating in bloody oceans and her mouth twisted in terror.

The smell of death was overpowering, and Blake was frozen by an artic chill which ran down his spine. What could he do? What should he do?

'Phone? I'll call an ambulance,' he said and with each word came more confidence. 'Where's your phone?' He stood quickly and searched the kitchen in vain.

'It's too late,' she said.

He spun around to the sound of her voice, but she was gone. Darting out of the kitchen, he quickly scanned the living room but found everything was as it had been when he first came in. The woman was gone. Running for the stairs, Blake was again stopped dead in his tracks but this time by a physical blow to his chest. A punch or a shove, he could not decide but it knocked the wind from his lungs and he crumpled to the floor gasping and clutching his chest. When he looked up, a man was standing at the foot of the stairs. He wore a pair of navy blue shorts and no shirt. Blood flowed from a long deep gash ripped across his hairy chest and there were smaller cuts on his arms and face; scratches like fingernail marks. He looked enormous but when Blake scrambled to his feet he realized the man was actually shorter then himself although considerably wider. He resembled a wrestler.

'Who the fuck are you and what are you doing in my house?'

Blake noticed that, like the woman, the man did not seem able to move from the spot where he appeared. He also felt the stench invading his nostrils once more and it was cold.

'The woman,' said Blake. 'She was badly hurt and asking for help. What happened here?'

The woman's voice said, 'It's too late.'

Blake turned quickly but the room was empty. In the seconds it took for him to realize it, the wrestler also disappeared.

Two and three at a time, Blake bounded up the stairs and began rapidly turning handles and opening doors. Bedroom one. Nothing. Bedroom two. Nothing. Master bedroom. Nothing. All tidy and clean, beds made. Moving into the ensuite bathroom cautiously, Blake sniffed the air and was surprised to detect nothing but a slight mustiness that you would expect if the house was shut up for any length of time. The bathroom off the master bedroom was also clean although not as clean as the kitchen. Blake left that room and back on the landing he stared at the last remaining door.

As he approached a child appeared in front of it. A little girl. She looked sad but there were no obvious signs of injury until Blake noticed her feet.

The girl followed Blake's gaze down to the stumps at the ends of her legs, and said in a shaky whisper, 'Daddy's very angry. I've been a naughty girl.'

A whirlpool in Blake's stomach reached up his throat and pulled his tongue down making him gag. He turned away from the girl and vomited on the carpet. Dry retching mostly as he had not eaten for hours.

'How could a man be that angry? To cut off your feet? What could you have possibly done to deserve that punishment?" Blake was speaking to the carpet because his head felt too heavy to lift and he was afraid to look again at the child. When she failed to answer, he knew she had gone without even looking. Needing more water, Blake dragged himself up off the floor again and entered through the last remaining door. The bathroom. The wrestler was sitting on the toilet.

'Hey, don't you fucking knock first,' he boomed, standing and shaking his clenched fist at Blake. 'Where's my fucking axe?'

Had Blake been watching a horror movie he might have laughed at someone being threatened with an axe by a naked man simply for interrupting him on the toilet but given the circumstances he was mortified. Was that all it took to make this man blow his stack? Was a forgetting of manners enough to turn him into a mindless beast of violence?

Despite his heart trying to tear a hole of escape through his chest, Blake somehow calmed himself sufficiently to ignore the man, and casually wandered over to the sink with and washed his face and hands, before cupping some much needed water into his mouth. Glancing in the mirror, he noticed the man had disappeared. With refreshment came clarity so Blake returned downstairs to look for the telephone. On the sofa sat on man dressed in white who did not seem to notice Blake as he entered the room.

His plan was not to engage the newcomer but unfortunately the telephone was sitting on a small coffee table right beside the man in white who sat still and remained apparently uninterested in Blake's activities.

Blake reached down for the phone but as he did his arm was grabbed in a vice like grip by the man in white.

'What?' cried Blake. 'Let go!'

As hard as he shook his arm he could not break free and the pressure was excruciating.

'Aren't you going to say excuse me before you reach across?'

Suddenly the man released his hold of Blake's arm, at the exact time he had been pulling with all of his might to get free. This caused Blake to tumble backwards and he might have fallen on the floor yet gain had it not been for the three people standing behind him into whom he cannoned.

Sunlight caught the edge of the axe blade, momentarily blinding Blake as backed away to a neutral corner of the room. That corner was where the dusty Christmas tree stood guardian over unopened presents and a pair of runners which Blake could now see, as he stood directly over them, were not empty.

'Okay, man in white,' said Blake pointing at him. 'What the hell is going on here?'

'Anger management. Is this your future?'

'Are you real?' answered Blake, ignoring the question.

Screaming. Chaos. Frantic movement. The voices of the man, his wife and their child all mixed in a frightening cacophony of anger and fear. Blake covered his ears and closed his eyes, praying for the noise to stop but on it went. The sounds of footsteps followed by more screaming, then crying, then sobbing and all else faded away to leave just the little girl's quiet voice, barely above a whisper, saying, 'Sorry, Daddy, sorry.' Then silence.

Blake was alone.

The image of the little girl haunted him. Everywhere he looked, eyes open, eyes squeezed shut, still he could see her. Sitting on the floor emotionally exhausted he began to think about Sam. The only goodness in his life and even she was past tense for him now. Marriage and children. Of course, she had raised the topic, and naturally he, not wanting to have children but definitely wanting her, had rebuffed her by laughing the subject off as being premature; something they could talk about later. Blake had run out of laters. He wondered if the man with the axe had wanted children or had his once beautiful young wife pushed him into fatherhood. Was his temper a symptom of the frustration he felt at losing control of his life and having to share too much of himself, his time and energy with others? Was he a time bomb waiting for someone to press the right combination of buttons to detonate him? Was Blake such a bomb? Would he have been, or could he be, the same sort violently abusive father? These questions were painful and frightening.

The smell of death returned to the living room, sneakily like a thief trying not to disturb wake anyone, and the chill squeezed his bones like an anaconda. Blake shook his head to break free of the melancholy which smothered him like a hot blanket and searched the room for signs of the restless dead.

In the silence he heard whispers, echoes of voices, screaming and crying. Soft and faint like the pulse of one on the brink of eternity. There was pain and misery in these whispers, and it was written all over the faces of the woman and her daughter as they appeared in front of Blake seated on the couch.

Blake was wondering what to say or if he should say anything at all when the door burst open and in rushed the man in white. 'Where is he?'

He looked at Blake, then at the other two. 'Where is he? If you know tell me. It's very important. Tell me,' he said, slowly coming closer to the three of them, 'so I can help you. You are in danger.' He was staring at Blake.

'I'm in danger?' said Blake. 'From what? Losing my mind? These ghosts can't hurt me.'

The man noted the way in which Blake waved at the two ghosts dismissively and shook his head. "You do not know what you are dealing with," he said. 'They can hurt you, but they don't want to. He, on the other hand, does. He's been very patient with you but you're still in his house. Uninvited.'

Blake stood up and demanded, 'Who are you?'

His answer was swallowed by a crash as the door slammed shut and the wrestler swung his axe into the back of it. Splinters flew in all directions. Some hit Blake in the chest, others passed through the woman and child on the sofa who sat passively embracing one another. The girl looked frightened but what, Blake wondered, did the dead have to fear?

'Judgement!' bellowed the man with the axe as he swung it around his head and into the door once more. 'Judgement!'

Blake noticed he had still not moved and was relieved to see his theory about the limited mobility of these ghosts was holding.

The man in white was the next to speak. 'The dead are afraid of judgement,' he said. 'Even more than the living fear the judgement seat.'

Focused on the man who answered his unspoken question, Blake missed the first step the wrestler took towards them, and the second and third steps. He noticed the girl press in tighter to her mother's breast and in the split second it took him to figure out why, the axe found a home in the man in white's ribcage via a forced entry through his back. Blake could just see the tip of the axe poking through under the man's shirt before a river of blood engulfed it, and he dropped to the floor.

Blake was confused and terrified. The killer had vanished again and so had the other two. He ran for the door, but it was shattered too badly to open, so he turned and ran for the biggest window behind the Christmas tree. Knocking the tree over, he ripped the curtains apart and flung the venetian blinds up and over his head. The window was locked, and the wrestler was standing outside staring in. An exploding shower of glass rained over Blake as the axe came through the window, hooked around the blinds and reefed them back out with it. For a moment Blake was caught, tangled in the blinds as they were pulled out of the house. He struggled free and scrambled backwards. Shards of glass stabbed into his hands mercilessly as he battled to regain his standing.

The man in white was no longer on the floor. Blake pushed the tree aside and desperately searched for something with which to defend himself. Kitchen. He darted for it but his arrival was greeted with the whistle of a blade through the air and into the door frame where it wedged. He froze as the madman wrestled with the axe trying to wrench it free, and the instant he succeeded, Blake fled for the broken window in the living room. As he ran for it he saw the glass had been repaired but he had no time to stop and he knew he was going to die if he could not leave this cursed house. The rush of adrenalin through his system masked the pain long enough for Blake to crash through the window and stagger to the ground and up on his feet again. Running. Running. Around to the front of the house. To the cars in the driveway. Any keys? Could he be so lucky? Not with the Hyundai but the Landcruiser's keys were in the ignition.

Blake jumped up into the driver's seat and looked instinctively in the rearview mirror. The woman was there.

'Please don't leave. Help us.'

Blake yelled at her, 'I can't fucking help you. There's nothing I can do. Nothing. Do you understand? You're already dead. You're dead! You're dead!'

Blake raved on like a madman until she disappeared, then he turned the key. The battery was flat. He slammed his hands into the steering wheel and swore continuously as the blood from his cuts flicked all over the inside of the car. Stopping at the sound of a loud crack, he studied his hand closely and realized he had broken his finger. Physically spent, he sat there behind the wheel and stared at his finger, fascinated by the bone sticking out at a weird angle through his bloody skin.

In the midst of a fury of pain and anger and frustration, Blake tried to think, tried to latch on to some logic, some sanity. He could not drive away, and he was sure as hell not going back inside the house. He decided to walk. There was a flicker of an idea to run but his strength was gone and he didn't know where he was going anyway.

He trudged up the driveway and out onto the road. Walking very slowly down the centre of the fiery bitumen, Blake's mind flooded with turbulent chaotic thoughts, and he lost track of time and direction. His eyes half closed only saw blurred shapes which his mind could not decipher and finally he dived to the hot hard ground unconscious.

* * *

'He's coming to.'

'No, don't move him yet. Let's get some fluids into him.'

'Is he talking? Did he say anything?'

At the sound of strange voices, Blake slowly opened his eyes but could not see anything. Panicking he tried to sit up while clutching for his eyes.

'It's okay, lay back. You're all right, just lay back now. Take it easy. I'll take these patches off for a second.'

Suddenly he could see. He relaxed but only until his eyes began to focus and he saw who it was that was talking to him. A man in white. He freaked out again. Jumping up off the ground, he saw a solid man with an axe and he ran, ignoring the yelling from behind him, and tried to figure out where he was. When he realized, when he saw the house, burning like a rampant inferno, it was as though a massive vacuum had sucked all the breath from his lungs and he collapsed again.

No salvation. No answers. The middle of nowhere. The end of the line. Millers Forest.

Twenty-Four

That Which Preys on the Weak

(first published in Roar and Thunder, May 2012)

*I*n the night. They sleep unsuspectingly, peacefully. Man and wife with their two young children between them smothered under blankets of cool air. Also in the air-conditioned upstairs room of the woman's sister's house are five other family members. Bangkok nights are always hot. Sleep is impossible without a cooled bedroom, and this house has only one of them. In the night, when nothing stirs but the creatures of darkness, and the minions of Hell, the house spirit roams freely.

In the half light, in the desert between waking and slumber where whispers are inaudible screams, and clear thoughts drown in thick soup, one of the children stirs. The boy, aged three, twists his little body and moans. And so, it begins.

The man is alert: sensitive to the sound and movement of his young son. He feels radiant heat. He smells something he can't define. The boy's moan escalates through crying to wailing, and he thrashes around in bed. After less than a minute, the man supposes, of his son's terrible sound piercing the quiet, everyone is awake, and voices float in and out. The voices are soft, concerned, sympathetic. They all want to help but the man decides to remove his son from the room. He's worried, panicking. His heart is beating too fast. He doesn't know what to do, how to pacify his son. He doesn't even know what's wrong.

Pain warns of injury as he struggles to lift the boy and hold on to him. If he's dreaming, then it must be the worst nightmare he's ever had. Surely, he should have woken by now. The voices fade as he approaches the door and it opens magically. Squirming and flailing in his arms, his son feels weightless, and the man feels hopeless. The child won't wake up. What's wrong with him? He's completely unaware of his surroundings. Doesn't know he is safe in his father's arms. Does not even recognize, let alone respond to, his father's frightened pleading.

Every shadow embraces a dark secret. The stairs are partially illuminated so he travels quickly down, ignoring the crevices and the devilry they conceal. It's an attack, a spiritual attack. He thinks briefly of the smaller room across the hall for the bedroom in which they were sleeping. Faint luminescence leaked out from under the closed door. He saw that. He noticed. The room not only contains the temple of the house spirit, but bone fragments and ashes of family ancestors, and hundreds of tiny idols. He remembers being shown the room, and some advice about paying his respects. As a guest, he should have paid his respects to the House Spirit. It was offended. The man has never seen these dark forces, the spirits of the air, at work before. He's only heard about them. He reaches the ground floor and stands, his feet glued to the floor as he battles to prevent his son from falling from his arms onto the hard, polished floor. Humidity assaults him. Is that laughter he can hear? Snickering?

Possession. That which preys on the weak lacks courage, is devoid of real power. The man intuits the need for prayer. He's hesitant at first, speaking quietly but firmly. Repeating a mantra, the name of the most powerful spiritual being he knows, the Author of life. He speaks his name. Again and again, sweating, dizzy. Nothing happens. The moaning and wailing continue. He's frantic. It's not working. God, when will this end? Why is this happening? He holds his little boy tight to his chest and continues to evoke the name above all names. Searing pain steals his words. Pain from his arm. What happened?

He concentrates on what he knows. Evil spirits cannot directly harm a person, but they can cause a person to injure themselves or hurt others. A tiny hand flies free and swipes the man's chin, cutting flesh with a sharp nail. Blood flows. He's shaking now from the strain, and fearful. He's afraid for his son's safety and scared that there is, in fact, no power to defeat this evil, to rebuke this demon. What he's heard and believed is wrong. Nothing's happening but he doesn't know what else to do. Overwhelmed by hopelessness, he starts to cry, but he doesn't stop praying. He's blubbering now. The words sound like gibberish in his ears. His back aches and the strength in his legs is fading.

The words, *daddy wee wee*, escape from the boy's mouth at the same time as warm liquid escapes his bladder. Urine wets the boy's pants, then mingles with sweat on the chest of his father, before pooling on the floor. All at once, the boy stops thrashing, and wailing and moaning, and it's over. The attack is over, the demon has left the child's body. The man glances towards the stairs, into the shadows and he curses the house Spirit.

Without moving or releasing his grip on his son, the man waits for another breath to fill his lungs and he gives thanks. Later, he'll berate himself for being so timid in the face of evil and for

306

doubting the power of the risen Christ. Now he simply savors the intense relief he feels, as pain reminds him of the physical nature of his spiritual fight, and the boy begins to cry because of the discomfort of urine drenched clothes.

In the night, having washed and changed their clothes, the man and his son rejoin the family in the air-conditioned bedroom. They drift back to sleep, trustfully, peacefully. Even the boy, who has forgotten the incident already, dozes off. The man has one eye on his son, and the other on the door. He sees the supernatural light from the other room creeping in under it. He won't be sleeping.

Twenty-Five

also by D.A. Cairns:

Love Sick Love

A ngus has battled an obsession with sex throughout his adult life. Although outwardly a model husband and father with a respectable life and a well-paying job, he has a shameful secret life which he has become highly skilled at hiding. He has also come to excel at self-justification. Although at times he feels what he is doing is wrong and he should stop, the harder he fights against the addiction, the deeper it takes hold, until finally he takes the easy way and surrenders to it.

Cassy is married to Angus and has no idea about his secret life. In fact, with her own worries she has been pulling away from him, emotionally and physically which is making his behaviour worse. Although she does not know it, Cassy is fanning the flames of an inferno which threatens to destroy their marriage.

Lovesickness: the eternal bane of humanity, the inescapable affliction which we simultaneously crave and fear. For Angus and Cassy, already in the thirteenth year of their marriage, the painful journey to true happiness has only just began.

Lovesick is a brutally honest and confronting story of love, sexual obsession and hope.

A Muddy Red River

Shane Archer is solid, dependable and reliable while his younger brother, Rob, is reckless, selfish and unpredictable. Never close during their formative years, and further divided by distance in adulthood, they live disconnected lives until the corkscrew of life pits them on a collision course. They love, they laugh, they lose and with broken hearts and messed up lives they find strength in the women they love and in their family. Could each be the agent of salvation for the other, or will they be torn apart forever? *A Muddy Red River* traces the course of the lives of broken people who discover power to overcome adversity.

Ashmore Grief

The story of an illegal immigrant who arrives in Australia by boat and goes on to become the Prime Minister. The story of a woman at the end of hope who is rescued from a smuggler's boat only to become enslaved. The story of a man who has lost his way, and needs a cause for which to fight, and a reason to live. These three lives collide in Ashmore Grief: an epic tale of struggle. The struggle to survive, the struggle to belong, and the struggle for purpose.

Loathe Your Neigbor

David Lavender is a man with a talent for making bad decisions. In his fortieth year on planet earth, a dangerous restlessness overwhelms him, and, as his marriage crumbles, and a dispute with his neighbor escalates, he responds to theses crises in his life with characteristic folly. Frozen out by his mysteriously indifferent wife, Lilijana. Baited by his cantankerous stepson, Tomo, and alternatively supported and rebuked by his two best mates, Matt and Chalky, will David successfully negotiate the minefield which his own discontent constructed, or will he destroy himself and everyone around him?

Devolution

2112 AD. For the sixty years following the Intercontinental War, Asia has been ruled by a delicately balanced coalition representing three major tribes; Newtonians, Deists and Adonites. The murders of two senators in separate incidents in Asia's capitol, Mumbay, now threatens the fragile peace that exists among them. Three young friends hold the fate of the world in their hands but don't even know it. In Devolution, romance and friendship, fear and respect, faith and folly, truth and lies, all confuse in a future world which no one would dare imagine.